LESLIE CHARTERIS

THE SAINT
ON GUARD

The American Reprint Company
MATTITUCK

Republished 1976

Library of Congress Catalog Card Number 81-71966
International Standard Book Number 0-89190-386-0

AMERICAN REPRINT COMPANY
Box 1200
Mattituck, New York   11952

Printed in the United States of America

PART I

THE BLACK MARKET

I

THE headline in the New York *World Telegram* said:

SAINT TO SMASH
IRIDIUM BLACK MARKET

The story itself was relatively slight for so much black type but it was adequately padded with a fairly accurate résumé of the Saint's career and exploits, or as much of them as had ever become a matter of record; for while the Saint himself was not naturally a modest man, there are certain facts which the dull legislatures of this century do not allow a person to publicise without fear of landing behind iron bars, and Simon Templar preferred bars with bottles to the less convivial kind.

However, the mere fact that the Saint was involved made the item meaty enough from a journalistic standpoint to justify the expenditure of ink, and it is probable that hardly any of the readers felt that the space could have been more stimulatingly and entertainingly employed.

Inspector John Henry Fernack was one very solid exception. He may have been stimulated, in an adrenal way, but he was certainly not entertained. He was, in fact, a rather solemnly angry man. But he had been conditioned by too many previous encounters with Simon Templar's unique brand of modern buccaneering to view the threat of a fresh outbreak without feeling a premonitory ache somewhere in his sadly wise grey head.

He came all the way uptown from Centre Street to the Saint's suite at the Algonquin, and thrust the paper under Simon's nose, and said grimly: "Would you mind telling me just what this means?"

The Saint glanced over it with lazy and bantering blue eyes.

"You mean I should read it to you, or are you just stuck on the longer words?"

"What do you know about iridium?"

"Iridium," said the Saint encyclopædically, "is an element with an atomic weight of 193.1. It is found in platinum, and also in lesser quantities in some types of iron and copper ores. In metallurgical practice it is usually combined with platinum, producing an alloy of great hardness and durability, suitable for the manufacture of electrical contacts or for boring holes in policemen's heads."

Fernack breathed deeply and carefully.

"What do you know about this black market?"

Simon ran a hand through his dark hair.

"I know that there is one. There has to be. That isn't any great secret. Iridium is one of the essential metals for war production, and it's awful scarce—so scarce that after Pearl Harbour the price shot up to about four hundred dollars a Troy ounce. The present official price is about a hundred and seventy dollars, or about two thousand bucks a pound, which is still very expensive groceries. If you can get it. But you can't get it."

"You're supposed to get it if you have the proper priority."

"So the Government gives you a pretty licence to buy it. They could probably give you a licence to buy a web-footed unicorn, too. And then all you have to do is find it."

"What's wrong with the regular markets?"

"They just haven't got it. There never has been much to spare, and the armament boom has just been going through it like steak through a shipwrecked sailor. And that consignment that was hijacked in Tennessee about a month ago did as much damage as putting an aeroplane factory out of production for six months. It wasn't written up that way, but that's what it amounted to."

The incident he referred to had made enough headlines on its own merits, nevertheless. The sheer callous audacity of the job was obvious front-page material, and the value of the loot ranked it with the great robberies of all time.

Three glass-lined quart containers of iridium powder—the usual method of shipping the metal—were being flown from Brazil to the Fort Wayne laboratories of the Uttershaw Mining Company. They were transhipped from Pan American Airways at Miami; and there was another transfer to be made at Nashville, Tennessee. Since the consignment was insured for three hundred thousand dollars, its actual value, there were two armed guards provided by the insurance company to supervise the transhipment at Nashville, but it is certain that no trouble was expected. Perhaps it was because the value of the cargo was only dimly appreciated, in spite of the figures on the policy: iridium was just a word to most people, it wasn't like jewels or bullion or any of the well publicised forms of boodle that automatically bring exciting thoughts to mind. Perhaps the guards were negligent, or merely bored; perhaps the precautions were simply routine, and nobody took the idea of such an attack seriously. Anyway, the result was already history.

A car drove on to the airfield while the case containing the heavy flasks was being unloaded. The two armed guards were shot down before they even realised what was happening, the case was thrown into the car, and the raiders were gone again before any of the spectators had recovered enough to make a move. It had been as simple as that.

Fernack said: "What do you know about that job?"

"Only what I read in the papers."

"You think some of that stolen iridium is finding its way into the black market?"

"I wouldn't drop dead with shock if it was."

"Then it would really be a thieves' market."

"I wouldn't quibble. I imagine you ought to have a priority number even to buy stolen iridium. The point is that it's an illegal market."

"But how could a respectable manufacturer buy in a market like that?"

"Respectable manufacturers have contracts with the Government. They want to fill those contracts, patriotically or for profit or both. If the only way they can get vital materials is that way, any of them are still liable to buy. It's just about as safe as any form of criminal connivance. Only one or two men in the firm would need to know, and iridium is compact and easy to handle in the quantities they use, and it would be the hell of a thing to track down and hang on them individually. So they have some iridium, and none of the workers who are using it is going to ask questions or give a damn where it came from, and maybe they had it in stock all the time."

"How would they set out to buy it?"

The Saint stretched his long legs patiently, and regarded Fernack with kindly tolerance.

"Henry," he said, "this frightful finesse and subtlety of yours is producing the corniest dialogue. You make us remind me of the opening characters in a bad play, carefully telling each other what it's all about so that the audience can get the idea too."

"I didn't——"

"You did. You know just about as much about iridium and the black market and how and why it works as anybody else, but you're feeding me all the wide-eyed questions to see if I'll let something slip that you don't happen to know. Well, you're wasting a lot of time. I hate to tell you, comrade, but you are."

The detective's rugged forthright face reddened a little deep under the skin.

"I want to know who told you to stick your oar into this."

"Nobody. It was something I thought up in my bath."

"If there is anything in this black market story, it's being taken care of——"

"I know. By the proper authorities. How often have I heard that sweet old phrase before?"

"There are proper authorities to take care of anything like that," Fernack said religiously.

Simon nodded with speculative respect.

"Who?"

It was a little pathetic to see Fernack suffer. He ran a finger around under his collar and floundered in the awful pain of a frustrated mastodon.

"Well, the—the different agencies involved. We're all working with them——"

"That's fine," said the Saint approvingly. "So while we're all clumping around on our great flat feet, I thought I'd stick my little oar in and see what I could do to help."

"How do you think you're helping by trying to make a monkey out of everyone else?"

"Henry, I assure you I never presumed to improve on——"

The detective swallowed.

"In this interview," he blared, "you said that since the authorities apparently hadn't been able to do anything about it yet, you were going to take it in hand yourself."

Simon inclined his head.

"That," he admitted, "is the same thought in judicial language."

"Well, you can't do it!"

"Why not?"

"Because it's—it's——"

"Tell me," said the Saint innocently. "What is the particular law that forbids any public-spirited citizen to do his little bit towards purifying a sinful world?"

"In this interview," Fernack repeated like an overstrained litany, "you said you had a personal inside line that was going to get results very quickly."

"I did."

Fernack tied the newspaper up in his slow powerful fists.

"You realise," he said deliberately, "that if you have any special information, it's your duty to co-operate with the proper agencies?"

"Yes, Henry."

"Well?"

Fernack didn't really mean to blast the challenge at him like a bullet. It was just something that the Saint's impregnable sang-froid did to his blood pressure that lent a catapult quality to his vocal cords.

Simon Templar understood that, broadmindedly, and smiled with complete friendliness.

"If I had any special information," he said, "you might easily persuade me to do my duty."

The detective took a slight pause to answer.

It was as if he lost a little of his chest expansion, and had to find a new foothold for his voice.

When he found it, there was a trace of insecurity in his belligerence.

"Are you trying to tell me that that was just a bluff?"

"I'm trying to tell you."

"You really don't know anything yet?"

The Saint extinguished his cigarette, and shook another one out of the pack beside his hand.

"But," he said gently, "anyone who didn't know that might easily think it was time to get tough with me."

Fernack looked at him for a while from under intent but reluctant brows.

At last he said: "You're just using yourself for bait?"

"I love you, Henry. You're so clever."

"And if you get any nibbles?"

"That will be something else again," said the Saint dreamily; and Fernack began to come back to the boil.

"Why? It isn't any of your business——"

Simon stood up.

"It's my business. It's everybody's business. There are aeroplanes and tanks and jeeps and everything else being manufactured for this war. They need magnetos and distributors. Magnetos and distributors need iridium. There are millions of wretched people paying taxes and buying bonds and doing everything to pay for them. If they cost twice as much as they should on account of some lousy racket has a corner in the stuff, every penny of that is coming out of the sacrifice of somebody who believes he's giving it to his country. If the war production plan is being screwed up because materials are being shunted off where they aren't most urgently needed—if the aeroplanes and the tanks aren't getting there because some of the parts aren't finished—then there are a lot of poor damn helpless lads having their guts blown out and dying in the muck so that some crook can buy himself a bigger cigar and keep another bird in a gilded cage. I say that's my business and it's going to be my business."

He was suddenly very tall and strong and sure, and not lazy at all, and there was something in his reckless fighting face of a mocking conquistador that held Fernack silent for a moment, with nothing that seemed to have any point at all to say.

It was just for a moment; and then all the detective's suspicion and resentment welled up again in a defensive reaction that was doubly charged for having so nearly been beguiled.

"Now I'll tell you something! I've been getting along all right in this town without any Robin Hoods. You've done things for me before this, but everything you've done has been some kind of grief to me. I don't want any more of it. I'm not going to have any more!"

"And exactly how," Simon inquired interestedly, "are you going to stop me?"

"I'm going to have you watched for twenty-four hours a day. I'm going to have this place watched. And if anybody comes near this bait at all, I'm going to know all about them before they've even told you their name."

"What a busy life you are going to lead," said the Saint.

During the next twenty-four hours, exactly thirty-eight persons called at the Algonquin, and asked for Mr. Templar, were briefly interviewed, and went back to their diverse affairs, closely followed by a series of muscular and well-meaning gentlemen who replaced each other in the lobby of the hotel with the regularity of a row of balls trickling up to the plunger of a pin-table.

After that, the Police Commissioner personally called a halt.

"It may be a very promising lead, Fernack," he said in his bleached, acidulated way, "but I cannot place all the reserves of the Police Department at your disposal to follow everyone who happens to get in touch with Mr. Templar."

The Saint, who had hired every one of his visitors for that express purpose, enjoyed his own entertainment in his own way.

It was still going on when he had a much more succinct call from Washington.

"Hamilton," said the dry voice on the telephone, for enough introduction. "I saw the papers. I suppose you know what you're doing."

"I can only try," said the Saint. "I think something will happen."

He had visualised many possibilities, but it is doubtful whether he had ever foreseen anything exactly like Titania Ourley.

II

MRS. MILTON OURLEY was a great deal of woman. She was constructed according to a plan which is discreetly called statuesque. She wore brilliantly hennaed hair, a phenomenal amount of bright blue eye-shadow, and fingernails that would have done credit to a freshly blooded cheetah. Her given name, naturally, was not her fault; but it might have been prophetically inspired. If she was not actually the queen of the fairies, she certainly impressed one as being in the line of direct succession.

She plumped herself down on the smallest available chair, which she eclipsed so completely that she seemed to be miraculously suspended some eighteen inches from the floor, and speared the Saint on an eye like an ice-pick.

"If you want to know all about iridium," she said, "I came to tell you about my husband."

Simon Templar had taken more obscure sequiturs than that in his stride. He offered her a cigarette, which she declined with fearful cordiality, and sank one hip on the edge of a table.

"Tell me about him."

"He's been buying iridium in the black market. I heard him talking about it to Mr. Linnet."

Her voice became a little vague towards the end of the sentence, as if her mind had already begun to wander. Her eye had already been wandering, but only in a very limited way. Nevertheless, it had not taken long to lose a large part of its impaling vigour. It was, in fact, becoming almost wistful.

"Do you like dancing?" she asked.

"I can take it or leave it alone," said the Saint cautiously. "Who is Mr. Linnet?"

"He's in the same kind of business as my husband. He makes electrical things. My husband, of course, is president of the Ourley Magneto Company." Her rapidly melting eye travelled speculatively over the Saint's tall symmetrical frame. "You look as if you could do a wonderful rumba," she said.

Only the Saint's incomparable valour, which is already so well known to the entire reading public of the English-speaking world, enabled him to face the revolting tenderness of her smile without quailing.

"I hope I never disappoint you," he said ambiguously. "Now, about your husband——"

"Oh, yes. Of *course*." Her pronunciation of the last word was a caress. "Well, he used a lot of iridium. I don't know much about his business—I think business is so *dull*, don't you?—but I know he uses it. So does Mr. Linnet. Well, last night we had dinner with Mr. Linnet, and—well, I had to powder my nose."

"Not really? Even you?"

"Yes," said Mrs. Ourley vaguely. "Well, when I came back, I just couldn't help hearing what Milton—that's my husband, Milton—and Mr. Linnet were talking about."

"Of course not."

"Well, Mr. Linnet was saying: 'I don't know what to do. I've got to have iridium to fulfil my contracts, and the market's cornered. I don't like any part of it, but they've got me over a barrel.' Then Milton said: 'I'll say they have. But you'll buy it and pay through the nose, just like me. You can't afford to do anything else.' And Mr. Linnet said: 'I still don't like it.' Then I had to go into the room because the butler came out into the hall, so I couldn't just stand there, and of course they stopped talking about it. But I can tell you it was a terrible shock to me."

"Naturally," Simon agreed sympathetically.

"I mean, if Milton and Mr. Linnet are buying illegal iridium, that makes them almost criminals themselves, doesn't it?"

Simon studied her seriously for a moment.

"Do you really want your husband to go to gaol?" he asked bluntly.

"Good Heavens, no!" She was righteously pained. "That's why I came to you instead of telling the police or the F.B.I. If Milton went to gaol I just wouldn't know how to look my friends in the face. But as a patriotic citizen I have my duty to do. And it wouldn't do any harm if you frightened him a bit. I think he deserves it. He's been so mean to me lately. If you could only have heard what he said to the nicest boy that I met in Miami Beach——"

It seemed to the Saint, quite abstractly, that he might have enjoyed hearing that; but he was just tactful enough not to say so.

He said: "What you've told me isn't exactly enough to convict him. And for that matter, it doesn't lay the black market in my lap either. But I'd like to have a talk with your husband."

"Oh, if you only would, Mr. Templar; You're *sooo* clever, I'm sure you could persuade him to tell you."

"I could try," he said non-committally. "Where do you live?"

"We've got a little place out at Oyster Bay. Milton will be home by half-past six. If you could manage to get out there—you could say you just happened to be passing and you dropped in for a drink——"

"Tell him we met in Havana," said the Saint, "and put him in the right frame of mind."

He got her out of the door with some remarkably firm and adroit manœuvring and came back to pour himself a healthy dose of Peter Dawson and restore his nerves.

The fortunes of buccaneering had brought many women out of the wide world and thrown them into Simon Templar's life, and it is a happy fact that most of them had been what any man would agree that a woman out of the wide world ought to be, which was young and decorative and quite undomesticated. But he had to realise that sooner or later such good luck had to end; and he had no idea of ignoring Titania Ourley, in spite of her unprepossessing appearance and even more dreadful charm.

It was like that in the strange country of adventure where he had worn so many trails. When you had no idea where your quarry was, there was nothing to bring it within range like the right bait. When you had no idea what your quarry was like, you had to find the right bait, and sometimes that wasn't at all easy, but when you had the right bait you were bound to get a nibble. And when you had a nibble, the rest depended on how good you were. Mrs. Milton Ourley was definitely a nibble.

He reached Oyster Bay soon after six-thirty, and after the inevitable series of encounters with village idiots, characters with cleft palates, and strangers to the district, he was able to get himself directed to Mr. Ourley's little place.

This little place was no larger than a fairly flourishing hotel, occupying the centre of a small park. Simon watched the enormous iron-studded portal open as he approached it with the reasonable expectation of seeing the hallway flanked with a double line of peri-wigged footmen; but instead of that it was Mrs. Ourley herself who stood fabulously revealed on the threshold, gowned and corsetted in a strapless evening dress that made her upper section look slightly like an overfilled ice-cream cone.

"Simon! You darling boy! How *wonderful* of you to remember!"

She insisted on taking both his hands as she drew him in, and still holding on to them when he was inside—doubtless under the impression that this gave her some of the winsome appeal of Mary Martin in her last picture.

He found himself in an immense pseudo-baronial hall cluttered with ponderous drapes and gilt furniture, and atmospherically clogged with a concentration of perfume on which it might have been possible to float paper boats. As Mrs. Ourley dragged him closer to her bosom, it became stiflingly plain that she herself was the well-spring of this olfactory soup.

"I was just driving by," Simon began as arranged, "and——"

"And of *course* you had to stop! I just *knew* you couldn't forget——"

"What the dabbity dab is going on here?" boomed a sudden wrathful voice from the background.

Mrs. Ourley jumped away with a guilty squeal; and Simon turned to inspect Mr. Ourley with as much composure as Mrs. Ourley's over-zealous interpretation of her part could leave him.

"Good evening," he said politely.

He saw a very short man with enormous shoulders and an even more enormous stomach swelling below a stiff white shirtfront. He carried a raggedly chewed cigar in thick hirsute fingers, and his black beetling brows arched up and down in apoplectic exasperation.

"Tiny!" he roared at his wife, thereby causing even the Saint to blink. "I've told you before that I'll make no effort to control your comings and goings outside of this house, but I will not have you bringing your gigolos into my house!"

Mrs. Ourley bridled automatically.

"But he's not a . . . I asked him to drop in."

"So," said Milton Ourley thunderously, "you admit it. Well, this is just about the last——"

"But, Milton," she protested coldly, "this is Mr. Templar. Simon Templar. You know—the Saint."

"Jumping Jehosaphat!" roared Mr. Ourley. "The what?"

Simon turned back from the Beauvais tapestry which he had been surveying while he allowed the first ecstatic symptoms of marital bliss to level off.

"The Saint," he said pleasantly. "How do you do?"

"Dabbity dab dab dab," said Mr. Ourley. A new flood of adrenalin in his blood-stream caused him to inflate inwardly until he looked more than ever like a bellicose bullfrog. "Tiny, have you gone out of your mind? Asking this crook, this—this busybody——"

"Milton," said Mrs. Ourley glacially, "I heard you and Mr. Linnet talking about iridium last night. And since Simon is trying to break up that racket, I thought it would be a good idea to bring you two together."

Milton Ourley stared at the Saint, and his broad chest seemed to shrink one or two sizes. That might have been only an impression, for he stood as solid as a sawed-off colossus on his short stocky legs. Certainly he did not stagger and collapse. His glare lost none of its fundamental bellicosity. It was only quieter, and perhaps more calculating.

"Oh, did you?" he said.

The Saint fingertipped a cigarette out of the pack in his breast pocket. For his part, the approach was all ploughed up anyhow. He had given Titania Ourley little enough script to work with, and now that she had gone defensively back into simple facts it was no use worrying about what other lines might have been developed. Simon resigned himself to some hopeful adlibbing, and smiled at Mr. Ourley without the slightest indication of uncertainty in his genial nonchalance.

"You see?" he murmured. "Tiny has brains as well as beauty."

Ourley's red face deepened into purple again.

"You leave my wife out of this!" he bellowed. "And as for you, you can get out of here this minute, *Mister* Templar. When you've got any authority to come barging into other people's affairs——"

"You heard the name," Simon replied softly. "Did you ever hear of the Saint asking for any authority?"

" 'And seem a saint when most I play the devil,' " said another voice, a deep cultured voice from somewhere else in the hall.

Simon looked around for it.

He saw, in one of the doorways, a tall spare man whose dinner clothes seemed to have been poured over his figure, smiling and twirling a Martini glass in one manicured hand. Grey at the temples, his face was hard and almost unlined, cut in the aquiline fleshless pattern of a traditional Indian chief.

"I don't want to break anything up," he said, "but all the excitement seemed to be out here." Ignoring Ourley, he sauntered towards the Saint with his free hand outstretched. "I've heard a lot about you, Mr. Templar. My name's Allen Uttershaw. I'm supposed to run that Uttershaw Mining Company. I heard somebody talking about iridium. Are you going to get that stolen shipment back for us?"

"I don't know," said the Saint. "I'm afraid I only heard about you a few days ago."

"Full many a flower is born to blush unseen," Uttershaw said tolerantly, his smile widening.

Ourley made a gesture of frightful frustration with his cigar.

"What is all this?" he barked. "Who said that?"

"John Kieran," said Uttershaw gravely; and Simon looked at him with new interest. It began to seem as if Mr. Allen Uttershaw might be quite a fellow.

Mr. Ourley didn't have the same pure intellectual detachment. He repeated his outraged gesture with italics in smoke.

"Dabbity dab dab dab!" he roared. "Has everybody gone nuts? First I find my wife has brought this meddler into my home to spy on me, and then you keep on quoting poetry. Or maybe it's me that's crazy."

"Milton!" said Mrs. Ourley sternly.

Uttershaw took Simon by the arm and started to lead him easily into the living-room from which he had emerged.

"Milton, I'm ashamed of you," he said. "What will Mr. Templar think of your hospitality?"

"I don't give a dab dab what he thinks," fumed Ourley, pattering helplessly after them. "My hospitality doesn't include welcoming crooks and spies with open arms."

"Now, after all—surely Mr. Templar is at least entitled to the chance of saying something for himself." Uttershaw turned to a tray on which a shaker and a row of glasses were set out. "How about a drink, Mr. Templar?"

"Thanks," said the Saint, with equal urbanity.

He took the glass that Uttershaw handed him, gazed into it for a moment, and then swept his cool blue eyes again over the faces of the other two men.

"I didn't exactly come here to spy," he said frankly. "I didn't actually come here with any plans at all. But after what Mrs. Ourley told me, I was certainly anxious to talk to"—he inclined his head— "Mr. Ourley. I thought I might possibly get you to talk to me. You know that I'm interested in the iridium situation, and it seems that you've had some dealings with the black market. You might like to tell me about it."

"My wife is an irresponsible imbecile," Ourley said balefully. "I'm just a business man with a contract to fill, and I'm filling it."

"Anyone who buys in a black market, of course, is technically compounding some sort of misdemeanour," Simon went on imperturbably. "But in this case it goes a little further. Iridium isn't so common that a black market can just scratch it up out of a junk pile. And Mr. Uttershaw will certainly remember a recent robbery in which two men were killed. It seems rather obvious to me that at least some of this black market iridium is coming from that stolen shipment which started the shortage in the first place. In that case, anyone who buys it is not only receiving stolen goods, but in a sort of way he's an accessory to murder."

"Fiddlesticks!" exploded Ourley. "What do you propose to do when you get some information—turn it over to the Junior G-Men or cash in on it yourself?"

"Milton!" repeated Mrs. Ourley, aghast from her quivering bust to the crimson-tipped toes that protruded through the front of her evening sandals.

"Considering my reputation, the question is not out of order," Simon said equably. "And the answer is that I shall deal with any facts I can get hold of in whatever way I think they would do the most good."

"Well," rasped Ourley, "in that case I'd be seventy-seven kinds of a dab dabbed idiot if I told you anything—if I knew anything, that is," he added hastily.

Simon's gaze was dispassionately unwavering.

"Would you say the same thing to the police or the F.B.I.?"

"You're dabbity dab well right I would. My business is still my own business until these dabbity dab New Dealers take what's left of it away from me."

Uttershaw stepped up with a gold lighter for the cigarette which the Saint was still holding unlighted between his fingers.

"Do you know anything about this iridium black market, Milton?" he inquired curiously.

Ourley's mouth opened, and then closed again like a trap before it parted a second time to let out words.

"I have no information to give anyone," he said; "especially to interfering dab dabs like this. And that's final."

"I only wondered," Uttershaw said suavely, "because naturally I'm interested myself. Of course that iridium shipment of mine was insured, but I couldn't insure my legitimate profit, which would have been quite reasonable. And after all, we all have to make some kind of living. Besides, I can't help hating to think that some crooks are making a fantastic profit where I'm really entitled to a fair one. Personally, I wish Mr. Templar a lot of luck. And I'm sure the Government would be behind him."

"Don't talk to me about the Government!" Ourley blared, his face ripening again. "What I still want to know is what right a meddling son of a dab blab like this Templar has to go around sticking his nose into my business and making passes at my wife and crashing into my house to cross-examine me. And I want him the hell out of here!"

" 'The eagle suffers little birds to sing,' " Uttershaw remembered soothingly; and Ourley's eyes bulged with his blood pressure.

"I wish everybody would stop throwing quotations at me," he howled. "Who said that?"

"Clifton Fadiman—or was it F. P. A.?" said Uttershaw good-humouredly.

Simon Templar emptied his shallow glass and set it down. It seemed rather sadly clear that he was not going to make any substantial progress there and then, and his nibble still left him a secondary line that might be more profitable to play on. He had that in his mind as he bent over Mrs. Ourley's diamond-sprinkled hand with somewhat exaggerated formality.

"It's been nice to see you again—Tiny," he said, and added with a malice that saved him from shuddering: "Perhaps we shall dance that immortal rumba one of these days." He bowed to the spluttering Mr. Ourley. "I still hope you'll think this over, Milton. I do really. Prison life is so slimming," he said; and shook hands with Uttershaw. "If you hear anything in professional circles, I'm at the Algonquin. We might have lunch one day."

"I'd love to," Uttershaw said cordially. "I'd still like to know why you should take so much trouble."

Simon turned at the door. There were certain little touches and lovely curtains that he could never resist.

" 'I sing because I must,' " he said softly, and was gone.

They heard his car starting up and crunching away down the drive, and there was a longish silence in the room.

Then Milton Ourley found his voice again.

"Now what the dabbity dab goes on?" he yelped. "He sounded as if he was quoting poetry, too. You've got everybody doing it. What did he mean?"

Allen Uttershaw held up his glass and turned it meditatively.

" 'I sing because I must,' " he repeated. For a moment his handsome bony brow was burrowed with thought. Then, just for another moment, it cleared. He went on: " 'And pipe but as the linnet sings . . .' "

His voice died away, and left only his clear grey eyes drifting over Ourley's congested face.

III

Mr. Gabriel Linnet, according to the Manhattan directory, had a residential address just off Madison Avenue in the Sixties. It proved to be a three-storey whitestone house with an air of solid prosperity which was quite different in style from that of the Ourley palazzo, but which obviously indicated a similar familiarity with spending coupons.

No lights showed from the windows as Simon stopped his car outside, but it was impossible to tell at a glance whether that might only be the effect of blackout curtains. There was another kind of light, though, that the Saint saw as he stepped out—a spark like a durable firefly hovering over a vague greyish shape in the darkness of the entrance porch. As he came to the steps, the shape developed into an ermine wrap encasing a girl who was perched on the stone balustrade beside the front door, and the firefly was a cigarette in her hand. The faintest subtlest fragrance, a thing not to be mentioned in the same breath as the stupefying reek of Mrs. Ourley, crept into his nostrils as he came closer and touched his mind with a quite fanciful excitement.

He took a pencil flashlight from his pocket with a pretence of searching for the door-bell, but he was careful to turn it clumsily enough so that the beam passed over her face.

At least, it was meant to pass over; but when he saw her clearly his hand stopped, and he could no more have kept it moving for a moment than a conscientious bee could have kept flying past a freshly opened flower.

She had long-bobbed blue-black hair that shone like burnished metal, and long-lashed eyes that looked the same colour. Her face was a perfect oval of softly-modelled olive, ripening into moist lips that were in themselves a justification for at least half the poems that have been written on such subjects. She was the kind of thing that a castaway on a desert island would dream about just before the seagulls started talking back to him.

The Saint should have had his mind on nothing but the job in hand; but he was still a long way from such dizzy depths of asceticism. She was so much more what a woman out of the wide world should have been, so completely everything that Titania Ourley was not, that he didn't even realise how long he looked at her before she gave him a hint of it.

"Are you quite through?" she said icily; and yet even then her voice matched the picture of her so much better than the mood that the rebuke was warmer than most other women's welcomes.

The Saint turned his light downwards so that it wasn't directly in her eyes, and she could see him equally by the reflected glow; but he didn't turn away himself.

He said, in a low reckless breath:

> *"Barbara the Beautiful*
> *Had praise of lute and pen;*
> *Her hair was like a summer night,*
> *Dark and desired of men . . ."*

She sat utterly still for a few seconds.

Then she said: "How did you know my name was Barbara?"

"I didn't," he said. "I just came from a Quiz Kids re-union, and I've got a bad attack of the quotes. I'm sorry. Is your name Barbara?"

"Barbara Sinclair."

"It's a nice name."

"Now that that's settled," she said, "why don't you run along? Can't you see I'm busy?"

"So am I," said the Saint. "Don't go away now. I shan't be long."

He turned his light back on the front door, searching for the bell again.

"You're wasting your time," she said: "There's nobody in."

He took his fingers from the bell without touching it, and sat on the stone railing beside her.

"For some reason," he murmured, "that begins to seem strikingly unimportant."

"I've been here for half an hour," she said.

"I suppose life is like that. I wouldn't keep you waiting on my doorstep for half an hour."

"You don't really have to keep me waiting on anyone's doorstep for half an hour."

After an instant, he brought out a cigarette of his own and lighted it and took his time over the job.

"I suppose," he said carelessly, "you wouldn't be hinting that we might go and get a drink and maybe gnaw a bone somewhere."

"No," she said. "But a man with a car is an awful temptation these days. How's your gas ration?"

"Very healthy," he said. "How is your conscience?"

She stood up, and sent her firefly spinning on one last incandescent trajectory out into the street.

"Starving."

He turned the car south on Madison, considering places where this shining hour might be best improved, and she sat just close enough beside him so that he was always aware of her with his shoulder, and the faint insidious sweetness of her was always in the air he breathed.

Then they were in a rooftop restaurant, in a corner booth with the lights of Manhattan spread out below them, and there were shaded candles on the tables and soft music, and there were oysters and green turtle soup and much fascinatingly inconsequential chatter, and the ermine wrap was over the back of her chair and she was wearing a dress that left no questions about whether her figure would match her face; and then there was *coq au vin* and a bottle of burgundy, and more talk that went very quickly and meant nothing at all; and then the Saint lighted a cigarette and stretched his legs contentedly and said: "Of all the possible things that I might have run into this evening, you are the last thing I was expecting—and incidentally I'm afraid you're much more fun. Why were you waiting on Comrade Linnet's doorstep?"

"That," she said, "is my affair."

He sighed.

"I might have known it. You were obviously too beautiful to be lying around loose."

"Are you going to disappoint me now?" she said mockingly. "I thought the Saint was a buccaneer—a man who took what he wanted, and damn the torpedoes."

Simon had the last glass of wine in his hand, moving it under the candlestick to enjoy the rich purity of its colour. He put it down with the liquid in it as smooth and unrippled as if it had been frozen.

"How did you know my name?"

"After that picture of you in the paper yesterday," she said casually, "who wouldn't?"

"You've known all the time?"

"Of course." She gave him a quick smile with the slightest troublement in it. "Please—did I say anything wrong? I'm not a celebrity hunter. That isn't why I came with you. I just wanted to."

"I was just a little surprised," he said.

She looked out of the window at the sparsely scattered stars that the dim-out had left below; and then she said, without her eyes meeting his directly: "Couldn't we get out of here? Haven't you got an apartment somewhere? Or I have. And a radio. I'll buy you a drink and we can get some sweet music on WQXR and talk about Life."

He drew slowly at his cigarette.

"That could be swell," he said; and her eyes turned to his face again.

"I'll have to make a phone call and break another date," she said with a smile. "But it doesn't seem to matter a bit."

He stood up while she left the table, and then he sat down again and propped his cigarette arm on one elbow for about as long as it took to absorb three more long and contemplative drags.

Then he got up and strolled unhurriedly out of the restaurant.

He strolled past the bar, past the men's room, past the hat-check girl. There was an elevator engorging a flock of satisfied diners. Almost accidentally, it might have seemed, the Saint drifted in on the heels of the last passenger, and was dropped with ear-numbing swiftness to the street.

Ten minutes later he was on the steps of Gabriel Linnet's house again.

This time he rang the bell.

He rang it two or three times, but there was no response.

He felt so still inside that he could hear his own pulses drumming. There might be some perfectly ordinary explanation for the fact that the house seemed empty. Yet Linnet had dined with the Ourleys the night before; and if he had been planning to close up his house and go away somewhere, Mrs. Ourley would almost certainly have mentioned it. And unless Mr. Linnet was an eccentric who preferred to sweep his own floors and wash his own dishes, there should have been some servant on duty at that hour in a place that size.

And of course Barbara Sinclair had always been too good to be true. . . .

The Saint wondered if he deserved to be shot. But he was going to find out.

He took a pin from his coat lapel and used it to jam the doorbell on a steady ring, and stepped back. It could have been a major operation to force that entrance and a street front was not the ideal place for such operations at any time, but he had already noted a narrow alley that ran between the Château Linnet and its next-door neighbour, and if such an alley didn't lead to a side entrance he couldn't think of any other reason for it to be there.

There was a side entrance, and like most side entrances it looked much less of a problem than the front door.

The Saint cupped his pencil flashlight under his hands for a preliminary diagnosis of the lock.

And as he looked at it, it receded slowly before him.

The movement was so gradual and stealthy that it didn't register instantaneously. At first it could have been only an insignificant hallucination, an effect of the movement of the light in his hands. He had to become at first unthinkingly aware that the continuous pealing of the doorbell which could be heard somewhere inside the building was growing clearer and louder; and at the same time his brain had to consent to recognise the improbable report of his eyes; and then he had to put the two things together; and then the door had unquestionably opened more than an inch, and a gossamer commando of intangible cockroaches raced up from between his shoulder-blades into the roots of his hair.

Somebody was opening the door from within.

It was too late then to switch out the torch and duck—even if there had been anywhere to duck to. The glow of light must have already been distinctively perceptible from inside the opening door. And for final proof of that, the door started to close again.

Simon's shoulder hit it with all his weight in about the same split second as it reversed itself.

The door travelled some six inches back and thudded in a rather sharp crisp way against some obstacle which let out a sort of thin yipping cough. Then it went on with much less impetus, while a straggly tumbling effect peeled off behind it.

Simon went in and shut the door behind him, flashing his light around even while he did that.

He saw a short flight of steps with the temporary obstacle sprawled at the foot of them. The obstacle was a thin, hollow-cheeked man who looked as if he had probably shaved two days before. If he hadn't, he should have. The point, however, was not suitable for immediate discussion, since the only potential source of first-hand evidence was not a good prospect for interrogation at that time. He had a vertical cut in his forehead where the edge of the door had hit him, and he looked very uninterested indeed.

Simon made sure of his continued neutrality by using his necktie to bind his ankles together, and then using the man's shoelaces to tie his wrists behind his back and link them with the Charvet hobble.

Then he went on quickly into the house.

He moved through a huge kitchen, a series of pantries, and up a flight of stairs to the main floor. He found himself in a bare but richly carpeted hall, with the front door facing him and a single onyx bowl of light burning overhead, and turned off his torch.

He didn't need any extra light to see the crudely drawn skeleton figure crowned with a symbolic halo which was chalked on one of the doors on his right.

"What a quaint touch," said the Saint to himself; but he was not smiling to himself at the same time.

The door was ajar. He pushed it open with his foot, and took the one necessary step into the room. It was a slightly conventional library with built-in bookshelves and warm wood panels and deep comfortable chairs, but all of it unmistakably tinged with the vision of an interior decorator. It seemed regrettable that this was yet another subject that could not be discussed with the person who would normally have been the most likely source of information; but it was a little obvious that there was at least one linnet who would never pipe or sing any more.

Aside from the simple probabilities, there were the initials "G. L.," embroidered on the breast pocket of the dark brocade dressing gown which the man wore over his tuxedo shirt and trousers. He lay on the floor in the middle of the room in an attitude of curious relaxation. But the piece of blind cord which was knotted around his throat so tightly that it had almost sunk into the skin could never have done his voice any good.

Simon Templar lighted a cigarette very carefully, and stood looking down at the body for a space that must have run into minutes, while he grimly tried to think of himself as a second-hand murderer. And all the time the doorbell was buzzing on one ceaseless monotonous note.

And then, abruptly, it was silent. After which it gave three or four distinct irregular peremptory rasps which could only have been produced by individual action.

The Saint came back into movement as if he had never paused, as if all those moments of intense and ugly thought had been nothing but the gap between the stopping of a cinema projector and the starting up again. In an instant he had flipped off the light switch, and he was crossing to the window. He had only to move the drapes a hair's breadth to peep out on to the doorway porch, and what he saw there enabled him to intellectually discard the effort of doubling back to the side door. He was a great believer in the economy of effort, and he could always tell at a glance when it would be completely wasted.

He switched the library lights on again as he went out into the hall, and opened the front door with his most disarming bonhomie.

"Hullo, there, John Henry," he said. "Come on in and play. Somebody seems to have been trying to frame me for a murder."

IV

THERE was no answering geniality in Inspector Fernack's entrance. He stalked in rather heavily with two plain-clothes men following behind him like a pair of trained dogs, and his tough square-jawed face was as uncompromising as a cliff. His straight stolid eyes drove at the Saint like fists. Then, in a quick glance around, they fell on the childish sketch on the library door, and his mouth set like a ridge of granite.

"Hold him here," he said, and went into the room.

He was gone only a couple of minutes, and when he came back he looked several years older. He spoke to one of his satellites.

"Have you searched him?"

"Yes, sir. No weapons."

"Go out and phone for a homicide detail—better not use any of the phones in here. Al, you go upstairs and look over the other rooms, but don't touch anything."

The two men left, and Simon straightened his clothes to restore his natural elegance from the disorder which the rough search of his person had produced. He could never have looked more at ease and debonair, as if it had never occurred to him that the most diaphanous cloud of suspicion could ever cast a shadow on his unspotted probity.

- "Quite a neat little job, isn't it?" he remarked affably.

Fernack stared up at him, and his gaze was curiously sad.

"If I hadn't seen it myself, I wouldn't have believed it," he said. "Simon, what in God's name did you do it for?"

The Saint's brows rose in balanced arcs of shocked incredulity.

"Henry—you couldn't possibly have some doddering notion in your dear grey head that I really did blow Gabriel's horn?"

"Off the record," Fernack said, relentless, "I was hoping against hope that the tip was a phony. But I might have known it would be like this one of these days."

"You've known people to try to frame me before."

"I've never seen such a cold case as this against you before."

Simon flipped ashes from the shortening end of his cigarette.

"There was a tip off, of course," he said languidly. "How did you get it?"

"On the telephone."

"Man or woman?"

"A man."

"Name and address?"

Fernack took a breath.

"I don't know."

"Did you talk to him yourself?"

"Yes. He asked for me."

"Why?"

"People do sometimes. Besides, it's been published quite a bit that I'm the man who's supposed to do something about you."

"Fame is a wonderful thing," said the Saint admiringly. "And what did this anonymous fan of yours have to report?"

"He said: 'I was passing Mr. Linnet's house on East Sixty-third Street, and I saw a man who looked as if he was breaking in. He looked just like the pictures of that fellow the Saint. I didn't get it at first, and then when I did I walked back and there were noises in the house as if there was a fight going on.' "

Simon nodded a number of times with the gravest respect.

"I can see that I shouldn't have underestimated your public," he drawled. "They come from a very talented class. They know just whose house they're passing on any street in town. With their cat-like eyes, they can recognise characters like me in dark corners in a dim-out. They can tell at a glance whether I'm trying to break in, or whether I'm just looking for the bell or the right key. And of course they know that you're the only officer in New York to call out on a case like that. They wouldn't dream of losing face by just mentioning it to the first cop they met on his beat."

The detective eased his collar with one powerfully controlled forefinger.

"That's all very clever," he said stubbornly. "But I came here. And Linnet has been murdered. And you're still here."

"Naturally I'm here," said the Saint blandly. "I wanted to see him."

"What for?"

"Because he manufactures electrical gadgets, and he needs iridium, and I heard he'd been buying from the black market. I thought I might persuade him to tell me a thing or two."

"And he wouldn't talk, so you strangled him."

"Yes," said the Saint tiredly. "I tied a string around his larynx to ease his vocal cords."

"And you left your mark on his door."

Simon glanced critically across the hall at the ungainly pattern of chalk lines that Fernack referred to.

"Henry," he said reasonably, "I'm not a hell of an artist, but you've seen some of my early original work. Would you honestly say that that was a typical job of mine? It looks kind of shaky and spavined to me."

The detective glowered at the drawing, and almost wavered. You could see the doubt beginning to curdle and grow heavier inside him, like a complicated meal in a fragile stomach.

"Besides which," Simon mentioned diffidently, "wouldn't it be just a little bit silly of me to leave that trade mark around at all in these days, so that you wouldn't even waste a minute before you had the drag-net out for me?"

"I've heard you say something like that before, too," Fernack retorted. "But it isn't my job to throw out evidence just because it looks silly. You give me your story, and we'll start from there."

"Figure it for yourself," Simon persisted inexorably. "Somebody wanted to keep me from talking to Linnet in the worst way. They wanted it badly enough to make quite sure he wouldn't sing. And they thought they could tie it off with the corny slickness of putting me out of action at the same fell swoop. So they must be just a little bit worried about me. And it also suggests that our iridium merchants may have something quite ingenious to put over while I'm presumably languishing into the jug. Now would you like to play their game for them, or shall we try to make sense?"

Fernack studied his face with intractable doggedness. He might have been about to make any comeback, or none at all. It was one of those teetering moments that might have toppled on either side.

And it inevitably had to be that moment when the plain-clothes man called Al appeared at the top of the stairs with another individual who was a stranger to all of them, to whom he was probably trying to give sympathetic assistance, but who looked more as if he were being frog-marched into a back room for a friendly rubber of third degree. This specimen wore the black coat and striped trousers of a conventional butler, and his fleshy face was as distressed as the face of any conventional butler would have been at the humiliation of his production.

"I found 'im," Al announced cheerfully, helping his patient down the stairs with much the same tenderness as he would have helped any old drunk. "The guy slugged him when he opened the door, an' tied 'im up an' locked 'im in a closet."

There was a different and hardening detachment about the way that Fernack waited until the man had been shepherded down to his level, and said: "Would you know the man who slugged you if you saw him again?"

"I don't really know, sir. He had his coat collar turned up, and there wasn't much light on the porch, but he seemed to be fairly tall and slim. He had an air-raid warden's armlet on, and I was looking at that mostly, because he was saying we had some lights showing that shouldn't have been; and then he pointed to something behind me, and I turned to look, and that's when he must have hit me, because I don't remember anything more."

"Could it have been this man here?" Fernack asked flatly, stabbing his thumb back at the Saint.

The butler's puffy eyes hesitated over actuality and recollection.

"It could have been, sir. I wouldn't like to be too definite, but this man was built a bit similar."

You could feel the weakness ebbing out of Fernack like the fluidity of setting concrete. He turned on his heels to face the Saint again, and his jaw was tightening up again like a trap.

"Well," he said, "you were going to tell your story. Go on with it."

Simon found a rim of floor that was clear of the late Mr. Linnet's beautiful carpet, and studiously trod the stub of his cigarette out on it. In the same leisured tempo, he lighted another to replace it. He had a sense of incipient anti-climax just the same.

It was, admittedly, a little bit on the hammy side to have tried to talk himself through his contract without showing any trumps; but as a challenge to professional vanity the temptation had been irresistible. He only resigned himself to quit because he realised that time was marching on, and fun might be fun but it had to take second place to the ultimate exigencies of the clock. He could certainly have played a lot longer, but there were more urgent things to do.

"I'm sorry to disappoint you," he said, "but it's really dreadfully simple. Somebody else knew I was coming here to-night. Somebody didn't want Comrade Linnet to sing to me, and the same person wanted to stop me doing any arias of my own. It all went together into the pretty picture you see before you. As a matter of fact, I wasn't even supposed to be caught here at all. That was just a little too tight for practical timing. But I actually was waylaid on the doorstep by a very ornamental piece of grommet, and I took her to dinner, and then the stall was to lure me to her apartment for some soft music and hard practice; and then I was supposed to have no alibi at all for these vital moments."

"That's interesting," Fernack said unyieldingly. "Go on."

"Unfortunately for the ungodly," said the Saint, "I was much cleverer than they expected me to be, and I ditched my waylayer and came back here in a hurry. I got here in what the most original writers call the nick of time. As a matter of fact, the bright boy who actually garrotted Comrade Linnet was on his way out at the moment. Then he sort of collided with a door, and got tired and went to sleep, so I tied him up and kept him for you. You'll probably even find some fresh remains of chalk on his fingertips to clinch it for you."

Fernack's face underwent a series of gradual and well-rounded reconstructions that was fascinating to watch. Each phase was a complete and satisfying production in its own right, so rich and full-bodied that only the most niggling critic would have complained that their climax was something very like a simple incredulous gape.

"Then why the hell couldn't you say so before?" he squawked. "Where is he?"

"You were having such a lovely time sending me to the chair, it seemed a shame to break it up," said the Saint. "But he ought to be where I left him, in the basement. Would you like to say hullo?"

He turned and led the way back as he had come in; and Fernack followed him without a word.

They went down the stairs, past the series of pantries, and through the huge kitchen to the place where Simon had left his captive. And that was when the incipient anti-climax suddenly ceased to be incipient at all, and in fact turned a complete somersault and made the Saint's stomach turn one with it.

For the cadaverous gent with the cracked forehead wasn't there any more.

There was just nothing to argue about in it. He wasn't there. The entire area of stone flooring at the foot of the back steps was burdened with nothing more substantial than a probable film of New York grime.

Simon Templar stood and gazed down at it with the utmost restraint for several seconds; until Fernack said impatiently: "Well, where is this man?"

"This is going to make you very unhappy, Henry," said the Saint, raising his eyes, "but he doesn't seem to be here any more. I'm afraid he must have had a boy friend who came back for him. The way I had him tied, he couldn't possibly have gotten loose by himself. But he's certainly gone away."

The gastric ulcers of innumerable haggard authors bear witness to the awful responsibility of attempting an adequate description of such scenes as this. The present chronicler, however, having much more respect and affection for his mucosa, intends to court no such disaster. He proposes to leave most of the detailed etching to the imagination of the reader, for whose lambent perspicacity he has the very highest regard.

He will nevertheless go so far as to give a slight lead by mentioning that the calorific swelling of a moderately understandable indignation caused Inspector Fernack's face to give a startling imitation of an over-ripe plum which is receiving an unexpected hypodermic from a jet of high-pressure steam.

"All right," Fernack said, and his voice had the slow burn of molten lava. "I can't blame you for trying, but this is the last time you're going to treat me like a moron."

"But Henry, I give you my word——"

"You can give your word to a judge, and see what he thinks of it," snarled the detective. "I'm through. I'm going to take you down to Headquarters and lock you up right now, and you can save the rest of it for your lawyer!"

"And I thought you were a real professional, Henry. If you'd only stationed a man at the back door, as I was sure you would have, instead of getting so excited——"

"Are you coming along?" Fernack asked glowingly. "Or am I going to have to use this?"

Simon glanced down regretfully at the revolver which had appeared in the other's fist.

He might conceivably have been able to take it away. And apparently there was no one to stop him outside the back door. But he was reluctant to hurt Fernack seriously; and he knew that even if he succeeded the call would be out for him within a space of minutes, and that would be a handicap which might easily be crippling.

And just the same, nothing could have been much more manifest than that the last chance of talking the situation away had departed for the night. There is such a thing as an immutably petrified audience, and Simon Templar was realistic enough to recognise one when he saw it.

He shrugged.

"Okay," he said resignedly. "If you can't help being a moron, I'll pretend I don't notice. But if you'll take any advice from me at all, please don't be in too much of a hurry to call in the reporters and boast about your performance. I don't want you to make a public spectacle of yourself. Because I'll bet you fifty dollars to a nickel you won't even hold me until midnight."

He lost his bet by a comfortable margin, for Hamilton was away from Washington that night; and the far-reaching results of that delay were interesting to contemplate long afterwards.

A little after ten the next morning, a rather rotund and unobtrusive gentleman with the equally unobtrusive name of Harry Eldon presented Fernack with his credentials from the Department of Justice and said: "I'm sorry, but we've got to exercise our priority and take Templar out of your hands. We want him rather badly ourselves."

Somewhat to his own mystification, the detective found that he didn't know whether to feel frustrated or relieved or worried.

He took refuge in an air of gruff unconcern.

"If you can keep him where he belongs, it'll be a load off my mind," he said.

"You haven't made any statement about his arrest yet?"

"Not yet."

Fernack could never have admitted that he had been sufficiently impressed by the Saint's warning, combined with the saddening recollection of previous tragic disappointments, to have forced himself to take a cautious breathing spell before issuing the defiant proclamation that was simmering in his insides.

"That's a good thing. You'd better just forget this as well," Eldon said enigmatically, "Those are my orders."

He took Simon Templar out with him, holding him firmly by the arm; and they rode uptown in a taxi.

The Saint filled his cigarette-case from a fresh pack, and lighted the last one left over, and said: "Thanks."

"I had a message to give you," Eldon said laconically. "It says that this had better be good. Or somebody else's neck will be under the axe."

"It will be good," said the Saint.

"Where do you want to be let off?"

"Any drug store will do. I want to look in a phone book."

It was just a chance that Barbara Sinclair's apartment would be listed under her name; but it was. It lay just off Fifth Avenue, across from the park.

When Simon arrived there, he found that it was one of those highly convenient buildings with a self-service elevator and no complications in the way of inquisitive doormen, which are such a helpful accessory to the *vie bohème*.

He rode up to the floor where he had found her name listed in the hall, and rang the bell. After a reasonable pause, he rang it again. There was still no answer; and he proceeded to inspect the lock with professional penetration. It was the usual Yale type, but the way it was set in the door promised very little opposition to a man whom the master cracksmen of two continents had been heard to mention with respect. He took a thin strip of flexible metal from a special compartment in the back of his wallet, and went to work with unhurried confidence.

It took him less than a minute, and he went into a living-room which could have served as a model of relaxing and fussless cosiness to any lady who wanted her gentlemen friends to feel much better than at home.

He took three steps into the room, and a syrupy voice said: "The hands up and clasped behind the back of the neck, please, Mr. Templar."

V

Simon did as he was told, while he turned to locate the welcoming committee. He realised that he had been quite conspicuously careless: because there had been no answer to the bell, he had assumed that there was nobody home. Which seemed to have been an egregiously rash assumption.

He found himself considering two separately unreliable trigger fingers.

One of them, which had appeared from behind the door, belonged to the thin blue-chinned specimen who had had such an unfortunate collision with a slab of functional timber the night before. He wore a broad patch of adhesive tape across his brow as a souvenir of the occasion, and if there was any spirit of Christian forgiveness and loving-kindness in his secret soul it had not yet had time to dig its way out into his sunken eyes.

The other man, who must have been the owner of the grenadine voice, stood in the doorway of the bedroom. A glimpse of the room behind him formed a sudden sensuous woodcut of black painted floor and white snow leopard rugs, black marble fireplace and white leather panelled walls, ebony and white corduroy furniture—the sort of room from which a man like that would most naturally seem to emerge. For aside from the plated automatic in his hand, he was outwardly a very boudoir type. In contrast with the hapless butler of doors, whose clothes hung on his skinny frame like washing on a line, this exhibit was tailored to the point of being almost zoot-suited. He had glossy black hair with three beautiful regular waves in it, and the adenoidal type of Latin countenance which belongs with the male half of a ballroom dance team. He smiled steadily, showing teeth that were very white and slightly buck.

"So you walked into the parlour, Mr. Templar," he said.

"You have the advantage of me," Simon said genially. "Would you like to introduce yourself, or are you the man of mystery?"

The wavy head bowed.

"Ricco Varetti—at your service. And on your left is Cokey Walsh, who will now proceed to search you."

Simon nodded.

"We nearly met last night, only something came between us. I suppose you were the guy who rescued him?"

"I had that pleasure. By the way, it's a little surprising to see you.

We really expected that the police would detain you much longer than this. How were you able to get away so soon?"

"I told them I had an appointment with the hairdresser for a new permanent, so of course they had to let me go. You'd understand."

The scrawny warrior stepped back from his search with malevolence in the thin gash of his mouth.

"So this is the guy, is it?" he said.

"This is the guy, Cokey," Varetti agreed.

"The guy who gave me this crack on the head."

"Yes, Cokey."

"Lemme have him, Ricco. All to myself."

"Not yet, Cokey."

"The sonofagun bust my head open," Cokey argued. "Lemme get a piece of rope and put him out of my misery."

"Not yet, Cokey."

The Saint's expression was interested and sympathetic.

"After all, we do have to make up our minds about me," he murmured helpfully. "Cokey is just trying to be practical. Now, what are the possibilities? We could all just stand around here for ever, but one day we might get bored with our own conversation. Of course, you could always shoot me; but then one of the other apartments might hear and get curious about the noise. You might take me for an old-fashioned ride; but that's kind of a luxury these days, what with the tyre situation and gasoline rationing and everything."

"Or," said Varetti, in the same vein, "we might call the police again and give you back to them for breaking in here."

"That's quite an idea," Simon admitted. "But I was under the impression that this apartment belonged to Miss Barbara Sinclair. Are you sure that you mightn't have to do a little awkward explaining about why you're here yourselves and how you got in?"

As bait, it was worth the casual try; but Varetti's greasy smile was toothily unchanged.

"I think you forget your position, Mr. Templar. Yes, I am sure you do. I ask the questions. You answer them . . . I hope. If not, I shall have to ask Cokey to help you. And that wouldn't be nice. I'm afraid Cokey doesn't like you."

"I like him," Cokey said glitteringly. "I'll show you, Ricco. Just lemme tie a piece of rope around his neck and show you. He bust my head open, didn't he?"

"You see?" said Varetti. "He does like you. And there are plenty of things you ought to be telling us. Yes. Perhaps he has the right idea."

"He must have one sometimes," Simon conceded. "Anyone with his looks has to have some compensation."

"You shut your trap," said Cokey with cold savagery; and the Saint raised one mildly mocking brow at him.

"Well, well, well! What coarse idioms you do use, Cokey, old chum. I didn't think you'd really be sore about our little game of hide-and-seek last night. I thought that would all be under the heading of business as usual."

Varetti flashed him another dental broadside.

"Cokey has his feelings," he said. "You hurt his pride last night. So he's entitled to a little revenge. . . . Go and find your piece of rope, Cokey. We'll try to make Mr. Templar take us into his confidence."

Everything had been diverting enough up to that point; but there is always a stage in such situations where the fun can go too far, and Simon Templar was very sensitive to those subtle barometric changes. He could feel this one all the way from his fingertips to his toes.

He said coolly: "While we're all getting so friendly, would you mind very much if I took my hands down from this uncomfortable position and had a cigarette?"

"Go ahead," said Varetti. "But don't try anything clever, because I'd hate to have to deprive Cokey of his entertainment."

The Saint let his hands down and eased his shoulders as he took out his cigarette-case, watching Varetti with thoughtful blue eyes like flakes of sapphire.

He was not, he told himself, a slave to snap judgments. He tried to be broadminded and forbearing; he tried to find in even the most repulsive creatures some redeeming spark that would allow his heart to warm towards them. But even with the most noble effort, it was becoming cumulatively plain to him that he and Mr. Varetti could never be as brothers. He did not like any part of Mr. Varetti, from his marcelled hair to his pointed shoes. And he particularly disliked Mr. Varetti's idea of suave dialogue—no doubt partly because it was too much like a hammy imitation of his own. He was going to enjoy doing something about Comrade Varetti.

He selected his cigarette with care from one end of the case—it was the single cigarette that had been left there when he refilled it, as it was always left there when he refilled, for the Saint was never totally unprepared for any emergency. He lighted it, and strolled across the room to deposit the match in an ashtray as Cokey came back from the kitchen.

He was figuring and manœuvring for position with the oblique innocence of a cat encircling a pair of sparrows.

"Before this gets too unpleasant," he said, "couldn't we talk it over?"

"You talk," said Varetti, with his teeth glaring. "I'll listen."

Simon hesitated a moment; and then with the most natural gesture of decision he put his cigarette down in the ashtray and moved around towards Varetti, while Cokey came around to follow him.

Varetti said: "Not too close, Mr. Templar. You can talk from there."

Simon stopped a step farther on. Varetti's gun, trained steadily on his mid-section, was about four feet away. Cokey was to his right and a little farther off, but he had put his gun away to have both hands free for the length of cord he had found.

"Look," said the Saint. "All this business——"

It was at that point that the cigarette he had left in the ashtray went *bam!* like a small fire-cracker, which in fact it was.

Varetti would probably have been too smart to fall for any ordinary stall, but he would have been less than animate if he could have heard that noise with no reaction. His head and eyes switched away together; and that was all Simon really needed. The fact that this involuntary movement also happened to angle one side of Varetti's jaw into an ideal position for receiving a left hook was actually only a bonus.

The Saint took one long step forward, and the impetus of his stride added itself to the impact of a fist that must have made Mr. Varetti think for one split second that he had received a direct hit from a block-buster bomb. After that immeasurable instant he did no more thinking at all; he slid down the door frame like sloppy plaster down a wall, and Simon picked the shiny automatic out of his unresisting fingers as he dropped.

Cokey Walsh backed away with a wild attempt to get his own automatic out again, but he was too tangled up with the garrotting cord which he had been twisting around his hands for a good purchase. Without even bothering to reverse the gun that he had taken from Varetti, Simon bonged him firmly on his already tender brow, and once again Mr. Walsh passed into slumberland. . . .

The Saint lighted himself another and less stimulating cigarette, and paused for a bare moment's thought. His mind was still gyrating with questions that he had still had no chance to ask, and which now seemed condemned to further postponement on account of the magnificent lethargy of the potential respondents. On the other hand, after such a promising introduction, Miss Sinclair's interesting and unusual apartment should be at least worth a little more detailed survey. But there was no telling how soon some other interruption might crop up in such an unconventional ménage; and whatever form it might take, it seemed fair to assume that the presence of a pair of unconscious bodies on the living-room floor would do nothing to facilitate coping with it.

In order to dispose of that difficulty first, he took the two bodies by the collar, one in each hand, and dragged them into the bedroom, in which process he nearly tripped headlong over a rawhide suitcase which someone had thoughtfully left out in the middle of the floor. He was still rubbing an anguished shin when he heard the rattle of a key in the front door lock and went back hopefully into the living-room.

"Hullo, Barbara," he said blandly. "I was afraid I'd missed you."

VI

In her street clothes, she looked just as exotic and exciting as she had the night before. Her tailored suit had obviously been conceived by a Scottish sheep, born on a hand loom north of the Tweed, and lovingly reared by a couturier with a proper admiration for the seductive curves of her figure. The inevitable hat-box which is the badge and banner of the New York model dangled from one gloved hand; but you would still have seen her as a model without it, if only because such a sheer physical perfection as hers simply demanded to be pictured. Simon observed, with dispassionate expertness, that even broad daylight could find no flaw in the clear olive smoothness of her skin.

Another and less simple observation was that she seemed at first too surprised and angry to be afraid.

"Well, I'm damned," she said, "how did you get in here?"

"I burgled the joint," said the Saint candidly.

"You've got a nerve," she said. "On top of what you did to me last night."

The act looked quite terrific. But the lift of the Saint's right eyebrow was only mildly impudent.

"Did they make you wash a lot of dishes?" he inquired interestedly.

The flare in her eyes was like lightning reflected in pools of jet. She was certainly wonderful. And it was no help to her at all that anger only cleared her beauty of the magazine-cover sugariness and gave it a more vivid reality.

"So you're damned smart," she said in a frozen voice that came like icicles out of a blast furnace. "You make a fool out of me in front of half the waiters in New York. You stick me with a dinner check for about thirty dollars——"

"But you must admit it was a good dinner."

"And then you have the gall to break into my apartment and try to be funny about it." Her voice thawed out on the phrase, as if she was coming out of a momentary trance into the full spoken realisation of what he had actually done; and then it sizzled like oil on hot coals. "Well, we can soon settle that——"

"Not so fast, darling."

His arm shot out almost lazily, and he hardly seemed to have moved towards her at all, but her wrist was caught in fingers of steel before she had taken more than one full step towards the telephone.

He stopped her without any apparent effort at all, and calmly disengaged the hatbox and tossed it into the nearest armchair.

"Before you add half the cops in New York to half the waiters, in this audience of yours," he said, "I think we should talk some more."

"Let me go!" she blazed.

"After all," he continued imperturbably, "it is a pretty nice apartment. And you did invite me here originally, if you remember. There must be some handy dough in this modelling racket for you to be able to keep up a *pied-à-terre* like this. Or, if it isn't a rude question, who else is contributing at the moment?"

Her ineffectual struggle almost ceased for a moment; and then, when it sprang up again, for the first time it had the wild flurry of something close to the delayed panic that should have been there long before.

"You must be crazy! You're hurting me——"

"And that," said the Saint, nodding towards a veneered cabinet against the wall, without any change either in the steel of his grip or the engaging velvet of his voice, "is presumably the radio whose dulcet tones were to beguile me last night—while I was being cosily framed into the neatest murder rap that I've had to answer for a long time."

"You crazy lunatic ..."

Her voice faded out just like that. And the fight faded out of her in exactly the same way, abruptly and completely, so that she was like a puppet with the strings suddenly cut.

"What do you mean," she whispered, "murder?"

Simon let go her wrist and put his cigarette to his mouth again, gazing down at her with eyes of inexorable blue ice. His mind was clear and passionless like the mind of a surgeon in an operating room. In the back of his mind he could hear the whirr of wheels in a production line, and again he could remember the candlelight and soft music and rich food and wine in a penthouse hideaway, and still behind that in his mind was the rumble of tanks and the drone of aeroplanes and the numbing thunder of shells and bombs, and men sweating and cursing in the smoke of hell; and the war was there in that room, he could feel it as fierce and vital as the hush in a front-line trench before an attack at dawn, and he knew that even in those incongruous and improbable settings he was fighting not one battle but many battles.

He repeated passionately: "I said murder."

"Who?"

"It's in the papers. But you wouldn't need to read about it."

Her eyes were pleading.

"I don't understand. Honestly. Who are you talking about?"

"The linnet will sing no more," Simon said. "And if I hadn't been a calloused sceptic and walked out on you last night, I'd be doing my own singing in a very minor key and a most undecorative cage."

She stared at him in utter stupefaction.

"Mr. Linnet? You mean he's been murdered?"

"Very thoroughly."

"I can't believe it."

"Nobody seems to believe anything these days," Simon remarked sadly. "But it's still no thanks to you that a lot of large and unfriendly policemen aren't showing me their incredulity right now with a piece of rubber hose."

Half of her mind still seemed to be unreached by his meaning.

"Who did it?"

"I think one of the gentlemen in your bedroom might be able to tell you."

"The what?"

"One of the men in your bedroom. I ran into him at the scene of the crime last night, but he got away. However, it's all right now. It was quite a jolly reunion."

"Are you still raving?"

"Come and see for yourself."

He took her arm and pushed her into the bedroom, kicking the door open with his foot. She stopped with a faint gasp on the threshold, her mouth open and one hand going to her throat.

"Who are they?" she begged.

"Friends of yours, I take it. Anyway, they were here when I arrived, and they seemed to feel very much at home."

"You're joking!"

"I'm not joking, darling. Neither were they. In fact, they were proposing to do some very serious and unpleasant things to me. It's rather lucky I was able to discourage them. But I must say I take a poor view of your choice of playmates."

She fought his cynical remoteness with wild and desperate black eyes.

"I've never seen them before in my life. I swear I haven't. You must believe me!"

"Then how did they get in here?"

"I don't know."

"I suppose they just broke in," Simon suggested, ignoring the fact that that was exactly what he had done himself.

"They might have."

"Or did they have a key?"

"I tell you, I don't know them."

"Who else has your key?"

It was as if he had hit her under the ribs. All the blood drained out of her face and turned the warm golden glow to a sick yellow. The strength seemed to go out of her with it, so that he felt her weight grow on the arm he was holding. He released her again, and she sank on to the bed as if her knees had turned to water.

"Well?" he said ruthlessly.

"I can't tell you."

"Meaning you won't."

She shook her head so that her long hair swirled like a dancer's skirt.

"No . . ." Her gaze was imploring, frantic, yet trying ineffectually to draw back and harden. "What are you trying to do anyhow, and what right have you got——"

"You know about me. I'm trying to break the iridium black market. And there was robbery and murder tied up with it even before I started. You may have heard that there's a small war in progress. Iridium happens to be a ridiculously vital material. Gabriel Linnet had had dealings with the black market, and I was going to talk to him last night. You were planted there to keep me away while he was having his voice amputated—and incidentally to make sure I wouldn't have an alibi so I could be hung for it."

"No," she said.

"If you aren't anything worse, you're just another butterfly trying to throw curves God didn't give her to toss around. Maybe you thought it was all good clean fun—great sport for a pretty girl to play Mata Hari and dip her little fingers into international intrigue ——"

"No," she said. "It wasn't like that."

"Then how was it?"

She twisted her hands together between her knees.

"I was planted there last night. That's true." Her voice was tight and strained. "But that isn't what I was told. I was told it was just business. That Mr. Linnet had hired you to try and spoil a business deal that—that this person I was doing it for was interested in. He said I just had to keep you away from Mr. Linnet for a certain time and everything would be all right. I never dreamed it meant any more than that. I still can't believe it."

"Who is this person?" he asked again.

"How can I tell you? I'd be betraying a trust."

"I suppose betraying your country and helping to hide a murderer seems much more noble."

Her clenched hands beat at her temples.

"Please don't—please! I've got to think. . . ."

"That might be a great beginning."

He was as pitiless and implacable as he could be. There was nothing in this that he could afford to be sentimental about. He was deliberately using his voice and personality like a whip.

She turned her face up to him with the mascara making dark smudges under her eyes, and the same pleading held in her voice.

"I'm so mixed up. This is somebody who's been very good to me . . . But everything I've told you is the truth. I swear it is. You must believe me. You must."

He knew that at that time he was as unemotional as a lie detector; and yet unsureness tightened the muscles of his jaw. He took a long inhalation from his cigarette while he assessed the feeling.

He had his own extra sense of truth that was like the ear of a musician with perfect pitch. He knew also that even that intuition could be deceived, because he himself had more than once deceived some of the most unco-operative critics. But if Barbara Sinclair was doing that, she had to be the most sensational actress that ever walked, on or off, a stage. It simply became easier and more rational to believe that he had met at least some of the truth than that he had met the supreme acting of all time.

His main objectives were unchanged. He had to convict a murderer, track down the stolen iridium that had been diverted into the black market, and uncover, erase, liquidate, or otherwise dispose of the upper case brain that controlled the whole traitorous racket. He had to do that no matter who got hurt, including himself.

But there was the slightest change in his tone of voice as he said: "All right. What about these two creeps?"

"I don't know who they are. Honestly. I can't even think how they got in here."

"Let's find out."

He made a rapid search of the two sleepers, and found no burglarious implements. But separate from the bunch of keys on Varetti's gold trouser chain, he found a single key in one waistcoat pocket. He took it to the front door and tried it. It worked.

He came back, showed it to the girl, and put it in his own pocket.

"They had a key," he said. "So by your own count, they must be pals of your boy friend. Does that help?"

She didn't answer.

"I might ask them some questions," he said. "How would you like that?"

"I'd like that," she said almost intensely.

He looked at Varetti and Walsh again; but they showed no signs of life whatever, and he regretted a little that he had dealt with them quite so vigorously. But the real motive of his question had been to get her reaction. The two men themselves were obviously dyed-in-the-wool mobsters of an older school, who would endure great persuasion before they opened up their souls and became confidential. And that would take time—quite probably too much time.

Simon located a closet full of feminine fripperies, and gave it a quick inspection. A suit of masculine pyjamas hanging just inside interested him quite a little—even if Barbara Sinclair had a weakness for masculine modes, they would obviously have been too big for her. But he made no remarks about them. He heaved the two mobsters in, one after the other, and locked the door.

"They'll keep for a bit," he said; and then his eye fell again on the rawhide bag which had damaged his shin.

He pointed to it.

"Were you thinking of going somewhere, or were they moving in?"

She hesitated, fighting another battle with herself before she replied.

"It isn't mine."

"Who does it belong to—your new boarders?"

"No. It belongs to—the same person. He left it with me some time ago. He said it was a lot of old books that he'd brought in from the country to give to the U.S.O., but he kept forgetting to do anything about it." Her eyes went back to him with a weak spark of hope. "Perhaps he just sent those men to fetch it."

"Perhaps he did," Simon agreed courteously. "Do you mind if I have a look at these old books?"

She shook her head.

"I suppose I can't stop you. But the bag's locked."

He looked at her humorously.

"I should have known that a bookworm like you would have tried to take a peek before this."

Her face flamed but she made no retort.

Simon started to pick up the suitcase, and was momentarily taken aback by his own lack of strength. It was a little distressing to discover that old age had caught up with him so quickly—in the space of a mere few minutes, to be exact. For he had handled the two limp gangsters without much difficulty.

He took a fresh grip, and heaved the bag on to the bed. Even for a load of books, it was astonishingly heavy for its size.

It was closed with a three-letter combination lock that surrendered its feeble little secret to the Saint's sensitive fingers in a few seconds; and he raised the lid and gazed down at two glass jars, about the size of quart milk bottles, solidly embedded in a nest of crumpled newspapers. Each of them was filled to the top with a greenish powder.

The girl was leaning over to look with him.

"I don't know whether you know it, darling," said the Saint gently, "but you have been taking care of about two hundred thousand dollars' worth of iridium."

VII

IF she had had any reactions left he might have suspected her again. It would have been too much like an effort to show the right response—however right it was. But now she seemed to have been stunned into a purely mechanical acceptance.

"This is what you were looking for," she said.

It was a simple statement, almost naïve in its tonelessness.

"I imagine it is," he said. "The shipment that was hijacked in Nashville. Or about two-thirds of it. That would be about right—a third of the shipment must be in black market circulation by this time."

He squinted down at the suitcase again as he reached for a cigarette, and his eyes settled on the combination of letters at which the lock had opened.

"Do the initials O. S. M. mean anything to you?" he asked.

Her face was completely empty. He was watching her. And so much depended on whether he was right, and whether he could see through the beauty of her face and not let it colour what he was looking for.

"Skip it," he said. "It was just an idea."

He lighted his cigarette, while she sat down heavily on the bed and stared at him in that numb kind of bewilderment. Her hands trembled slightly in her lap.

He said: "Your boy friend parked this stuff here with you—safely enough, because this is one of the last places where anybody would look for it. Probably even his best friends don't know anything about his connection with this place. And even if anybody who knew too much already did know, they'd never expect him to be so dumb as to leave a couple of hundred grand's worth of boodle lying around in a love-nest. Which is what we call the technique of deception by the obvious. . . . Yes, it was a good place to cache the swag. But now, apparently, your mysterious meal ticket is getting nervous. Maybe he's a little afraid of you and what you know. So he sent Humpty and Dumpty here to fetch it away." The Saint had slipped out of cold cruelty again as impersonally as he had slid into it. He said quietly: "Now what?"

She nodded like a mechanical doll.

"Just give me a chance," she begged. "If I can only make it right with myself . . . Can't you give me just a little time?"

He was sure now, and his decision was made. It was no part of him to look back.

"Not here," he said decisively. "We don't know who the next caller may be, and in any case we don't want Humpty and Dumpty waking up and hearing you. If any of the ungodly got the idea that you were talking to me at all, they might find a whole new interest in your health. And I'd rather not have to hold my next interview with you in the morgue."

Her eyes widened as she looked at him.

"You mean you think somebody might try to harm me?"

"There have been instances," said the Saint, with considerable patience, "where persons who knew too much, in this life of sin, have been harmed—some of them quite permanently."

"But he—I mean, this man wouldn't hurt me. You see, he's in love with me."

"I don't altogether blame him," said the Saint agreeably. "And I'm sure he would weep bitterly while he cut your throat."

He closed the valise quickly, hefted it again, and took her arm with his other hand.

"Let's go," he said.

She raised herself slowly from the bed.

"Where?"

"Some place with room service, where you don't have to be seen and where it would take weeks to locate you."

He herded her briskly out of the apartment, and stabbed at the button of the self-service elevator. The car was still on that floor, and he followed her in as the door rolled back.

"And there, my love," he continued, as the antique apparatus began its glubbering descent, "you will sit in your ivory tower with the night chain on the door, refusing all phone calls and unbarring the portals only to admit slaves bearing food which you are damn sure you ordered, or when you hear my rich and resonant voice announcing that I have a C.O.D. package for you from Saks Fifth Avenue. All characters who demand entrance with telegrams, special deliveries, flowers, plumbing tools, or dancing bears will be ignored. In that way I hope I shall save the expense of having to pay for cleaning a lot of your red corpuscles off the carpet."

Then he kissed her, because she was still very beautiful looking at him, and other things that were rooted in neither of them as people had forced him into a part that he would never have chosen, and he knew it even while it would never shake the lucid distances of his mind.

It was like kissing an orchid; and the seismic grounding of the elevator was only just in time to save him from the disturbance of discovering what it might mean to kiss an orchid that became alive.

He glanced up and down the street as he followed her to the cab which was fortunately waiting at the stand outside. There was nobody he recognised among the few people within range, but nowhere in Simon Templar's professional habits was there an acceptance of even temporary immunity without precautions.

"Penn Station," he told the driver. The girl looked at him questioningly, but before she could speak he said quickly: "We'll just catch the twelve-thirty, and that'll get us to Washington in plenty of time."

He chattered blithely on about non-existent matters, giving her no chance to make any mistakes, and glancing back from time to time through the rear window. But the traffic was thick enough all the way to make it almost impossible to be certain of identifying any following vehicle. He could only be secure by taking no chances.

He had the fare and tip ready in his hand as the taxi swooped down the ramp and wedged itself into the jam at the unloading platform. Without waiting for the cab to creep any closer, he hauled the heavy bag, shook his head at a hopeful redcap, grasped Barbara Sinclair by the elbow, and propelled her dextrously and without a pause through the crowded rotunda of the station to the escalators with a nimbleness of dodging and threading that would have brought tears to the eyes of a football coach. In a mere matter of seconds they were out on Seventh Avenue opposite the Pennsylvania Hotel.

"Not that one," said the Saint. "It's too obvious. I've got another place in mind. Let's joy-ride some more."

"But why——"

"Darling, that is a one-hack stand in front of your building. Anyone who was trailing us wouldn't have much trouble finding our last driver."

"Do you think he'd remember? He must have so many passengers——"

The Saint sighed.

"Didn't you ever wonder why taxi drivers always haul out a pad at the first red light and start scribbling in it? Did you think they were putting in a quick paragraph on the Great American Novel? Well, they weren't. That's a record that the Law makes them keep. Where from and to. So our driver doesn't need such a memory. With that note to goose him, he'll probably even remember that we were talking about going to Washington. Now if your glamour boy has any respect for my genius, which he may or may not have, he probably won't believe we went to Washington. But he won't be sure. If he's very bright, he will immediately begin to think of what I was talking about just now—the technique of deception by the obvious. And he will begin to feel quite ill. Uncertainty will breed in his mind. And uncertainty breeds fear; and fear often leads clever men to do quite unclever things. Anyway, this will all help to make him miserable, and since he never set me up in a fancy apartment I don't owe him anything. Taxi!"

He signed her into a small residential hotel off Lexington Avenue as the wife of an entirely fictitious Mr. Tombs whose sarcophagal personality had given him much private entertainment for many years, and left her there after he had made sure that she remembered his password seriously.

"You can do your thinking here, in pleasant surroundings," he said. "Search your soul to the core and make your decision. I'm sorry I can't stay to help you, but I have things to do while you wrestle with your private confusions."

Her eyes wandered around the apartment, and then back to him, in a lost sort of way.

"Do you really have to go now?"

She didn't have to ask that, and he wished that he didn't have to make an answer.

"I'm sorry," he repeated with a smile. "But this little war is still going on, and maybe the enemy isn't waiting."

The same bellboy who had just carried the rawhide suitcase in and out of the elevator met him in the small lobby with a somewhat unresolved blend of eagerness and suspicion. The contents of the bag alone weighed a full hundred pounds, and the Saint swung it in one hand as if it had been empty.

"The lining in this damn thing is all coming unstuck," he said casually. "Is there any place near here where I could get it fixed?"

The boy's dilemma resolved itself visibly in his slightly bovine eyes.

"There's a luggage store a couple of blocks down on Lexington," he said; and the Saint gave him another quarter and sauntered out, still airily swinging the bag.

Not being Superman, he was wielding it a little less jauntily when he turned into the store; but apart from a mild feeling of dislocation in his left shoulder he was able to amuse himself a little with the business of making the purchases which he had in mind—one of which was somewhat eccentric, to say the least, and fairly baffling to the proprietor of the adjoining sporting goods emporium.

His next stop was at the Fifty-first Street police station, where he

had a weighty message to leave for Inspector Fernack. Then he took
another cab to the Algonquin, and walked into the lobby just as the
grey handsome figure of Allen Uttershaw turned away from the
desk and caught sight of him.

"'The ass will carry his load,'" Uttershaw observed cheerily,
raising his eyebrows at the Saint's burden. "I was just asking for
you."

Simon surrendered his bag to a bellboy to be taken to his room,
and shook hands.

"With all the doormen in the Army, the ass has to," he said. "Do
you carry a pocket edition of *Familiar Quotations*?"

"A weakness of mine, I'm afraid," Uttershaw admitted. "But at
least it's a little more distinctive than the usual conversational
clichés." He sighed deprecatingly. "I was thinking of taking you up
on that invitation to lunch."

Simon realised that he was hungry himself, for the prisoner's
breakfast with which he had been regaled at some unholy hour had
not been planned to induce the vigorous vibrations to which his con-
stitution was accustomed.

"Why don't you?" he said.

They went into the bright panelled dining-room and ordered
Little Necks and sole veronique, with sherry for a preface. Simon
sipped his glass of pale gold Cedro and remarked: "This is a little
more restful than the love-nest we met in."

"'Domestic happiness, thou only bliss of Paradise that has sur-
vived the Fall,'" said Uttershaw ironically. "I seldom let my business connections lure me into their private lives, but sometimes one
just can't avoid it. I was sorry for you. If you'll forgive my saying it,
your method of getting to see him was clever enough in theory, but
if you'd known more about Milton Ourley you'd never have tried it
that way."

The Saint passed over the assumption that he had engineered his
introduction from the start, and appreciated Uttershaw's tacit and
friendly elimination of a number of unnecessary pretences.

"Do you think he could have talked if he'd wanted to?"

"If he'd wanted to. Yes. I don't doubt it. He seems to be getting
the iridium he needs, and he certainly isn't getting it from me. And
I'm not trying to sound like a great king of commerce, but the fact
remains that there just isn't any other legitimate way of getting it
that I wouldn't know about."

Simon considered the statement for a few moments while he
watched a waiter threading his way through the tables towards
them, brandishing platters of clams with the legerdemain of some

phenomenal cymbalist. He gazed down at them appreciatively as they settled in front of him seven beautiful bivalves, glistening with their own juicy freshness. The Saint felt very pleased about clams, in a generous and cosmic way. He was glad he had invented them.

He did careful things with horse-radish, tabasco, and lemon.

"By the way," he inquired casually, "has your insurance company offered any reward for the recovery of your iridium?"

"Ten per cent of the value of the amount recovered, I believe." Uttershaw's glance was mildly interrogative in turn. "Is that the motive of your interest?"

"Partly," said the Saint with a slight smile. "But only partly."

He speared a fat young clam from its shell, dunked it in cocktail sauce, and savoured its delicate succulence with unmitigated relish.

Uttershaw went through the same motions, but he went on looking at the Saint with a directness that contrived to be quite undisconcerting.

"I didn't miss your exit line last night," he said. "How much did the Linnet sing?"

"A little less than enough," Simon said warily. "You heard about him?"

"I read a morning paper."

"What did you think?"

Uttershaw hunched his shoulders faintly as he went for another clam.

"As a mere amateur at this sort of thing, I wondered whether he was punished for singing too much, or whether he was choked off before he really hit a tune. What's your opinion?"

Simon let the question go unanswered while he tasted his sherry again, and when he put his glass down he seemed to have a convenient impression that he had already answered and could start again on another tack.

"He made quite a lot of headlines," he observed idly.

"He was quite a figure in his business, you know," Uttershaw said. "You must have known him, of course."

"Fairly well. He brought his iridium from my firm—in the good old days when we had some."

"And then?"

"Then, I suppose, the poor devil dipped into the black market, with the results already noted. You probably know much more about that than I do. How deeply was he mixed up in it?"

Simon waited until the sole was in front of them and he had enjoyed his first taste; and then he said directly, but with the same amiable presupposition of a common intelligence: "How would it be if you told me why I should tell you anything, before you ask too many questions?"

"That's fair enough," Uttershaw agreed easily. "As I explained last night, I've got a financial interest. 'The loss of wealth is loss of dirt,' if you believe John Heywood—or should I have said Christopher Morley?—but it happens to be my dirt, and I think that's a responsibility as well as a privilege. The other interest is—well, I've got to be trite and call it patriotic. Then, I like you as a person; and I'd like you to bring this off. I'd like to help you, if I could; but I don't want to sound foolish by making great revelations which might be all old and stale to you."

"For instance," said the Saint, just as pleasantly, "what was the great revelation you had in mind?"

"I was wondering if you'd formed any definite conclusions about Ourley."

Simon enjoyed more mouthfuls. He was hungry. But he didn't miss any of the lines of sober anxiety in the other's thinly sculptured face.

"He appears to be a little man with a large wife," he said trivially.

" 'And though his favourite seat he feeble woman's breast,' " quoted Uttershaw mournfully. "Milton really does prefer them feeble, and with all that—shall we say?—giddiness of hers, Tiny Titania is as tough as her own stays. And while she likes her own dancing partners, she watches him like a hawk. He isn't even allowed to have a typist under forty in his office."

The Saint had a sudden strange creeping feeling in his spine.

"Does Milton take it and like it," he asked, "or does he still manage to get his fun?"

Uttershaw shook his head deprecatingly.

"I wouldn't know about that," he said. "I told you we were never very close."

"Didn't he ever talk?"

Uttershaw pursed his lips as he brought a hand up to his lean jaw and stroked his face meditatively.

"There was one time . . ." he said slowly, and stopped.

"Yes?"

"Oh, hell, it doesn't amount to anything. There was a stag affair at some escapist club for down-trodden business men that he belongs to, and he insisted on dragging me along. For some reason or other I couldn't get out of it, or perhaps I didn't think of an excuse quickly enough. Ourley . . . but it was all so alcoholic that it really doesn't mean a thing."

To the Saint, it felt as if the air about the table was charged with the static electricity of an approaching storm, but he knew that it was only a mystic prescience within himself which was generating that sense of overloaded tension.

"Suppose you give me a chance to decide that for myself," he suggested genially.

"Well, Ourley was pretty tight—most of them were—and he cornered me and babbled a lot of damn foolishness. I guess getting out from under Tiny's iron fist for even that one night had unsettled him, and given him delusions of grandeur. 'In vino veritas,' I suppose. Anyway, he was in quite a Casanova mood. Told me he had a key that Tiny didn't know about, and how he was really much too smart for her, and all that sort of thing. I didn't pay much attention, and I got away as soon as I could. Next morning he called me up and explained that he'd had too much to drink, which was obvious, and said he'd been talking a lot of nonsense, and would I forget it. I never gave it another thought, and of course I wouldn't . . ." Uttershaw broke off, and smiled rather sheepishly. "But that's just what I am doing, isn't it?"

VIII

THE Saint ate a little more, and scarcely noticed what he was doing. The creepy sensation in his backbone had spread out over his whole body, so that every bone in him felt faintly tingling and detached, and his brain was sitting up in a corner of the ceiling moving them with strings.

It was at that moment, for the first time, that a whole chain of the crazy pieces in his jigsaw fell together and began to make a section of a recognisable picture which did curious things to his breathing.

But all that was within himself again, and his face was a study in untroubled bronze.

"I wouldn't worry about it's going any farther," he said carelessly; and the other nodded, but went on looking at him with a lightly interrogative frown.

"Naturally. But I can't help wondering what made you ask."

"It just came into my head," said the Saint. "On the other hand, I'm wondering why you were thinking about Ourley."

"That isn't easy to say," Uttershaw replied hesitantly. "But I do know from my business dealings with him—and you may have gathered the same impression yourself—that Milton is a bit 'too grasping to care for mere delight.' And it seems to me that any man would need some very good reason for taking Titania to his bosom and keeping her there. . . . I know that some of Milton's financial manipulations have been—well, what you might call complicated. At least, complicated enough for him to keep most of his holdings in his wife's name."

"You're sure of that?"

"Quite sure. As a matter of fact, there are those who would believe that Tiny herself has had a lot to do with the planning and staging of some of those manipulations. There are sceptics who maintain that Tiny's giddiness is more or less of a pose. Although if that's true, the stakes must be very high for a woman to make such an awful caricature of herself."

"If Tiny is Milton's partner behind the scenes, and the duenna of the do-re-mi," Simon remarked thoughtfully, "it must make his home life even more interesting."

" 'Dire was the noise of conflict.' " Uttershaw laughed shortly. "You know, I'm still embarrassed about going on with this."

Simon moved his plate a little away from him with an unconscious gesture of finality, and reached for his Pall Malls. He extended the pack towards his guest, and said: "Let me try to help you. How far do you think Milton would go to create a new business life of his own?"

Uttershaw blinked before he bent to accept the Saint's proffered light. He straightened up and exhaled his first puff of smoke a little gustily.

"I hadn't even thought that far," he said, and suddenly he looked shocked and strained. "Do you really mean what I think you're getting at?"

"I was just asking."

"But that's unbelievable. No man could build up anything like this black market alone. He'd have to have at least some associates. And I mean plain criminal associates. A man like Ourley just wouldn't have any connections like that."

"Men like Ourley have had them before. It isn't a hell of a long time ago that speak-easy proprietors and bootleggers were quite social characters. You get to know a lot of queer people, when there are labour troubles or the competition gets rough. The impresarios who put on stag shows at escapist clubs for down-trodden business men move in and out of a world of queer people. Any man can make any connections he wants, if he wants them seriously enough."

Uttershaw made a helpless sort of movement with his hands.

"It seems so fantastic—to think of Milton Ourley as a criminal master mind. Why, he's—he's——"

"He's what?" Simon prompted quietly.

"He's such a dull, irascible, unimaginative, uninventive sort of windbag!" Uttershaw protested. "All he thinks about is how much money he's got, or how much he might make if it wasn't for Roosevelt; and what Tiny is doing with her latest gigolo or how he could be kept late at the office and go out on the town with the boys."

"A master mind," said the Saint didactically, "doesn't always go around with an illuminated forehead. That's the first thing to remember in this detective racket—if you read any stories. Besides which, he can really be just as stupid and boring as anyone else outside of his own field of brilliance. Why shouldn't he be? The greatest bacteriologist in the world could look like a half-wit in a gathering of structural engineers. And he could even be a pain in the neck at a soirée of other bacteriologists. He could be addicted to thunderous belching, or insisting on describing every stroke of his last golf game without——"

He broke off abruptly, and put a quick hand on the other's arm.

THE BLACK MARKET 55

The warning shift of his eyes was quite a pamphlet of explanation.

Uttershaw looked where the Saint's glance led him. And then his groan was so polite that it was almost inaudible.

He said, without moving his lips: "Talk of the devil."

Simon nodded, keeping a smile of recognition on his face. He had seen her come in while he was talking, and with the grim certainty of impending doom he had watched her methodically sifting the room with her eyes like a veterinarian working over a shaggy dog with a steel comb.

Now, like a pirate galleon under full sail sweeping down upon a freshly sighted victim, Titania Ourley came cleaving through the tables, her plump and expensively painted face set in the overpowering smile of a woman who remains steadfastly convinced in spite of all discouragements that her charm and beauty will carry her serenely past all the reefs and snags in the sea of life.

" 'Milton, thou shouldst be with us at this hour,' " Simon paraphrased under his breath, with a certain resignation.

" 'Templar hath need of thee,' " Uttershaw continued for him sympathetically.

" 'She is a wen,' " said the Saint, concluding the slaughter, and stood up to bow over the nearer of the two hands which she extended towards them with a prodigality that would have done credit to Mrs. Siddons at her Westphalian best.

Perched on the forward top of her head she wore a confection of fur, feathers, and what appeared to be a bunch of slightly mildewed prunes. It nearly fell into the Saint's coffee as she sat down, but she caught it in time and restored it to its point of balance with what looked like the insouciance of much practice.

"I felt I just *had* to see you and explain, Simon dear," she said. "Milton's behaviour was so downright disgraceful last night—wasn't it, Allen?"

Uttershaw tried to achieve some sort of pleasant and neutral vagueness; but the effort was hardly necessary, for Mrs. Ourley had only paused for a swift breath.

"I'd thought that perhaps later we might get in a rumba or two with the Capehart—I've got simply stacks and stacks of records—but as it was you couldn't even stay for dinner. And after I'd told Frankfurter—he's our butler, and a perfect jewel of a butler if I ever saw one, and of course I've seen so many. But the way Milton acted. Well, really, it was a complete surprise to me. And after you'd taken the time and trouble to come all the way out to Oyster Bay and use up your gas and tyres and everything to try and help him out of that terrible iridium mess. We had a dreadful spat about it last night, and I told him he was either too rude to live or as good as a traitor; and he said—well, you heard how he talks when he's angry, and I can't bring myself to repeat it. But I was *so* hoping I'd find you here so that I could tell you it wasn't my fault."

"I never thought it was," said the Saint reassuringly, and was fortunately rescued from further contortions by the intrusion of a bellboy in search of Uttershaw for a telephone call.

"Excuse me," Uttershaw said, with a tinge of humorous malice, and went gracefully away.

Mrs. Ourley watched him go with a kind of middle-aged lasciviousness, dislocated her hat again as she turned back to the table, balanced it once more with the same nonchalant agility, and said: "Isn't he the most *charming* man?"

"A nice character," said the Saint.

"And he's a *divine* dancer. And always so wonderfully tactful. I don't know what I'd have done if he hadn't been there last night. Milton is simply impossible when he gets into one of his moods. It's a good thing they never last more than a few weeks. But really, Simon—I hope you don't mind me calling you Simon, but I'm beginning to feel as if I'd known you for years—really you *must* come out to dinner with us one night, I've got a simply wonderful cook —she makes pies that literally melt in your mouth, I mean literally melt."

" 'Simple Simon met a pieman, going to the fair,' " murmured the Saint, and immediately decided that this quotation mechanism was something that had to be taken firmly in hand.

"What? . . . Oh, you silly boy! Of course I didn't mean anything like that. But my cook really is a treasure."

"You look like a living tribute to her genius," said the Saint with a straight face; and Mrs. Ourley beamed.

"You say the *sweetest* things. But I was telling you about Milton. I know I shouldn't talk about my own husband, but he's ridiculously jealous. He . . ."

Simon listened with the utmost interest to her description of some of the unreasonableness of Mr. Milton Ourley, and while he listened he was studying the face of the woman across the table.

He had to admit that the ideas which Uttershaw had planted were astonishingly fertile. There was a rapacious ruthlessness below the surface of gabbling imbecility which Titania Ourley displayed to the public which could make a lot of surprising pictures of her plausible. Without knowing anything else about her, he knew that she would make a dangerous enemy; and he knew that the effusive gush which enveloped her like her appalling perfume could provide a lot of study for a post-graduate student of camouflage.

The tale of Milton Ourley's derelictions went on and on while the Saint thought about it. He nodded regularly and made encouraging noises in the right places, and managed to look quite disappointed when the recital was interrupted by the return of Allen Uttershaw.

"Do sit down," said Mrs. Ourley hospitably. "I was just telling Simon—I mean Mr. Templar—I mean Simon——"

"I'm sorry," Uttershaw said suavely. "I am still a working man, you know. That call was from my office, and I'm afraid some other working men are getting impatient."

"You're a meanie!"

Mrs. Ourley made a *moue*. This was undoubtedly something she had read about in a magazine. In her interpretation, it looked a little as if she had just detected the presence of a dead rat in the room.

"Forgive me," Uttershaw said. "It isn't because I want to 'scorn delights and live laborious days.'" He turned to Simon, and held out his hand with a smile that contained a hint of wicked amusement which had nothing to do with the ordinary urbanities. "I'm glad to leave you in such good company," He glanced at Mrs. Ourley again. "By the way, where is Milton?"

"He's down the street at the Harvard Club, having lunch with some dreary man from Washington—at least, that's what he *said* he was doing," she added darkly. "Lately, I've had my suspicions as to what Milton is doing when he tells me he's doing something else, if you know what I mean. Why?"

"I might want to get in touch with him this afternoon," Uttershaw said casually, but his eyes returned rather conspiratorially to the Saint as he was finishing the sentence. "Well—I enjoyed our talk. Let's meet again soon."

"Very soon," Simon promised.

He sat down again as Uttershaw sauntered out, and saw that Mrs. Ourley was following this departure with a tinge of speculation that had not been in her oestrous gaze before.

"Now, why do you suppose he might want to find Milton?" she asked.

She was talking more to herself than to him, but the eyes that she swung back towards him were no longer vacant.

"And he was having lunch with you. . . . Is it something about the iridium?" she asked sharply.

Anyone could have noticed the change in her tone, the steel showing through the whipped cream, the spikes under the feathers.

Simon reached for his coffee and took a sip.

"That's rather obvious, isn't it?" he said calmly. "You know that I'm gunning for the black market. You know that Allen Uttershaw was about the biggest dealer in iridium before the shortage. So I guess the subject may have been just accidentally mentioned."

Her pale and slightly protruding eyes became almost metallic. The thickly rouged lips thinned out, and the puffy features had congealed under the lacquered skin.

"What did he tell you?" she demanded.

The Saint didn't answer. He merely slanted his eyebrows into a line of bland and blunt inquiry that was exactly as eloquent as a speech. Without articulating a syllable, it wanted to know just what the hell business of Titania Ourley's it was what Allen Uttershaw had told him; and she caught the precise meaning of it like a fighter walking into a straight left. You could almost see the impact of its connecting with one of the receding tiers of chins that sagged from beneath that suddenly hard mouth.

She recovered with a celerity that earned his reluctant admiration. When he gave her that cynical challenge of the eyebrows she had been within a hair's breadth of menace and domineering; now, in a moment, she was leaning back again and delving into an enormous handbag to excavate a cigarette holder that looked like a jewelled pipe from a cathedral organ, and she was just as vapid as she had ever been.

"I'm afraid I'm much too inquisitive," she prattled. "I keep forgetting that you're the Saint, and anything people tell you is sacred. After all, I did make you my own father confessor, didn't I? . . . But I admit I *am* curious." She bent forward again so that a comber of hothouse odours practically splashed into the Saint's nostrils. "Not that I ever gossip about anybody—Heaven knows that my worst enemies can't say *that* about me! But to tell you the truth, I've often wondered about Mr. Uttershaw."

IX

Simon Templar replenished his cup with the last dribble from his rationed coffee-pot, and reflected that life could certainly open up a wondrous variety of perspectives when sundry citizens began to look sideways at one another. It was a sizeable item in the mental overhead which he would have preferred to leave out of his budget, but he compromised by showing no visible reaction at all and letting his mind remain passive and receptive.

Titania Ourley, who was apparently waiting for shocked amazement to spread over his features, seemed moderately disappointed when his face remained unmoved but expectant. Neverthless, she surged closer over the table, buffeting him with another tidal wave of exotic stenches which he decided must have been concocted in a cocktail shaker.

"I wouldn't be at all surprised," she said portentously, "if somebody investigated Allen Uttershaw one of these days and found out a lot of funny things. Oh, I know he's a marvellous dancer, and he's always so perfectly *perfect*, if you know what I mean, but haven't you noticed that there's something *secret* about him? I hate to say it when he isn't here to defend himself, but do you know, sometimes I think he isn't quite *normal*!"

"Really?" drawled the Saint. "You mean he——"

"Oh, no—nothing like *that*!"

Simon was prepared to give something to know what "that" was that Allen Uttershaw was nothing like. He suspected the worst, in Mrs. Ourley's peculiar mind.

He applied an expression of fascinated suspense to his mask, and waited.

"When I say that," she elucidated, "I mean that he's—he's— well, I can only say that he must be anti-social." Her voice became positively vibrant. "Do you know, out of all the times we've invited him to dinner, last night was the first time he's been to see us in *months*!"

She relaxed triumphantly, with the air of having furnished incontrovertible evidence that the subject under discussion was a dangerous case who should be lured into a padded cell at the earliest opportunity.

Simon clicked his tongue gloomily, shaking his head at the dreadful realisation that his recent companion was indisputably an incurable schizophrene. His manifest distress spurred Mrs. Ourley to further expansions.

"Not only that," she said, in confidential accents that could not possibly have been heard more than three tables away, "but I think he has a grudge against Milton. Of course, he's just as friendly and charming as he can be when he's with us, but he does things behind Milton's back."

"How horrible," muttered the Saint solemnly, with no qualms at all that either innuendo or sarcasm would register on that target.

He was absolutely right, for whatever satisfaction the experiment was worth.

"Yes, indeed," she trilled. "For instance, when Milton was put up for one of Allen's clubs, only a while ago, he was voted down. And I have it on *very* good authority that it was Allen who black-balled him. And after he'd been a guest in our home, too!"

Simon searched for words to express his revulsion at such perfidy, but before he had formulated the fitting phrase he was saved by the bell again. The same heaven-sent bellboy stood by the table again.

"Telephone, Mr. Templar."

"Thank you," said the Saint, and really meant it.

He went out to the booth in the lobby and said: "Hullo."

"What the hell," roared the voice of Inspector Fernack, like a bursting dam, "are you doing there?"

The Saint smiled, and picked a cigarette out of the pack in his pocket.

"Hullo, John Henry," he said cordially. "I'm just finishing lunch and making love to a retired Ziegfeld girl. What are you doing?"

"How did you get loose?"

"I didn't. The F.B.I. turned me loose. I promised to be a good boy, and they took one look at my cherubic countenance and knew they could trust me."

"If you think——"

"I do, Henry. And don't you send half a dozen squad cars scream-ing up here to grab me again, because if you do the F.B.I. will hear about it at once, and then they'll think I've violated my parole by getting into bad company and associating with policemen again, and of course they'd have to come right over and ask to have me back."

"I don't believe——"

"But you must, Comrade. If you don't you're liable to look awful foolish. And that would never do. Think of your dignity. Think of the prestige of the Force. And if that's too much work for you, call Brother Eldon's office and verify it."

There was an interval of silence, during which Simon could almost see the detective's aorta labouring like a stimulated blowfish.

Finally Fernack said, in a painful parody of his ordinary voice: "Templar, what are you doing in this set-up?"

"You heard from Fifty-first Street?"

"Yes." It was a grudging admission. "But——"

"Then at least you've got something."

"But where did you find it?"

"I can't tell you yet. But at least I'm giving you a break. Don't you think I'm being good to you? I don't think you appreciate it. Think of the glory I'm helping you to grab for yourself. And now I'm going to give you some more. By to-morrow, you'll have half the morning paper headlines all to yourself."

Fernack said suspiciously: "What's this?"

"In just a few minutes, any bright bull who walks into my suite here will be able to pinch a couple of old-timers. Their names are Ricco Varetti and Cokey Walsh. They will be trying to steal a very handsome piece of luggage from me, and they might even be attempting some private unpleasantness on my person. You've got their records, no doubt."

"I know 'em both. But what've they got to do with——"

"You'll find out. Come on over and play some *flagrante delicto*."

"I can't," Fernack said tormentedly. "I've got to go into court on another case in just a few minutes."

"Then send someone else."

"Is this on the level?"

"Word of honour."

After a second or two Fernack said: "I'll send Kestry and Bonacci. I think you've met them."

The Saint had met them. The acquaintance dated back to the first episode in which he had met Inspector Fernack, and it had been enlightening. The recollection drew his mouth down in a tight line that still did not embitter his eyes.

"I guess they can take care of the situation," he admitted. "As a matter of fact, there must be very few situations in which these two goons couldn't take care of themselves."

"I expect they can keep out of trouble," Fernack agreed with ponderous deference. "But what are they supposed to hold Varetti and Walsh for?"

"I don't know what technical charge would be the worst they'd settle for," said the Saint, "but if they can't work out a good one on the spot, they must have slipped a lot since I met them. And anyhow, I'm sure they'll be able to do some great detecting in a back room with a rubber hose. Or has this priority business gotten so tough that you can't even buy your laboratory equipment any more?"

The receiver seemed to grow hot against his ear.

"You can be funny about that some other time," Fernack grunted. "But I'm telling you, if this turns out to be another of your——"

"Henry," said the Saint patiently, "I haven't got much more time to waste. And if you're just trying to keep me here until your flying squad arrives, don't say I didn't warn you."

"I haven't got any flying squad out after you."

"Then why did you call me?"

"I just wanted to find out if you'd been back; and when they put you on the wire——"

"Your little heart had kittens. Now cancel the prowl car and carry on. I've got a job to do."

"But where did you——"

"I'll call you back in a little while," said the Saint. "Keep in touch with your office, give my love to the judge, and I hope you win your case without perjuring yourself."

He hung up on a last imploring squawk from the other end of the wire, and went back to the dining-room to close out an interrupted chapter.

He still wanted to hear a little more from Mrs. Ourley, and yet he was conscious of time ticking away, and of the vital connections that he had to make. But there was nothing he could ignore, and no prejudice that he could permit to blind him to the reversals of new knowledge.

He sat down again as if no counterplot at all had intervened, and picked up the conversation as smoothly as if he had never been away at all.

"I don't think Milton needs to worry about a little thing like a club membership," he offered. "He must be doing pretty well these days."

"I can't complain," Mrs. Ourley said smugly. "Although of course the taxes are frightful and I don't know what we shall do next year if That Man keeps on trying to ruin everybody. But I make Milton save every penny he can; and then I take care of it for him. One of these days, when I've got enough put by, I'm going to buy some War Bonds. I think War Bonds are a wonderful investment. . . . But I know you don't want to be bored with things like that. I don't think any young man, I mean any *attractive* young man, should ever be bothered about money matters."

"Neither do I," Simon agreed. "But quaintly enough, there isn't any organisation giving away free meals and clothing and alcohol to attractive young men."

The old gleam was in Mrs. Ourley's eyes, but her voice burbled on with the same analgesic inanity.

"You just haven't met the right people," she insisted, and eyed the place next to him archly. "Or else you're just too shy with them, making them sit out in the middle of the gangway when there's plenty of room——"

Simon moved the table and made room for her on the banquette beside him. Her circumambient nimbus of perfume moved in with her and pushed away the lunchers on the other side.

"I wish you weren't so terribly busy," she said, and went on to develop her theme without waiting for him to confirm or deny. "You ought to find time to cultivate some people who might help you. I mean *really* help you. Of course, dashing about after criminals must be very exciting, but is it an altogether complete life?"

"I don't really know," said the Saint mildly. "You seemed to think it was fairly complete when you came to see me and asked me to dash after Milton."

She giggled in a thin falsetto.

"I *was* thoroughly mad with him," she confessed. "But then I didn't know you personally like I do now. Now I'm just thinking of you as a friend, and I do so want you to do well for yourself. So I was just wondering why you'd want to work so hard and run such frightening risks, when I imagine there'd be plenty of people who'd pay you, oh, *enormous* amounts of money just for being yourself."

Simon looked up at her, and his blue eyes were icily clear.

"You mean there might be somebody who'd bribe me quite lavishly to leave this iridium racket alone?" he asked, and his voice was completely lazy.

Mrs. Ourley laughed again, making a noise which probably sounded to her like the tinkling of fairy bells. It sounded exactly like broken glass going down a garbage chute.

"You *do* say the funniest things! I was only thinking how nice it would be if I could take you to see the new show at the Copacabana. And the music is just heavenly. It does the most exciting things to me. Milton told me he'd have to work late to-night, and I was hoping . . ."

She babbled on, and Simon made vaguely helpful responses. But behind it his mind was far away and running like a machine. The electrification that he had felt a few minutes before, that had spread

out and become pervading, was something as firmly with him now
as the meal he had just eaten.

He knew that he had almost everything in his hands now. At
least, he had as much as he was likely to get. The rest of it lay with
his own judgment and perception and choice. He had to read character and motive and physical possibility right. He had to take apart
the things people had said, and distinguish the sinister from the
stupid, and be a razor edge of separation between the stupid things
that looked sinister and the sinister things that looked stupid. He
had to eschew all red herrings and perceive only the one true fish.

And he couldn't sit there for ever while he made up his mind. He
had to move. He had to move swiftly and rightly, before there was
another murder to be solved, and another sacrifice to be accounted
to the dull golden gods who had declared themselves for the enemy.

And at that perfect point he raised his eyes and saw Milton Ourley
standing at the entrance of the dining-room.

X

It is a simple fact that the Saint was not even surprised. The appearance of Mr. Ourley was merely the natural and inevitable slipping of a link in a chain that had been forming for some time, a chain that must ultimately be so solid and inescapable that the failure of the link to make its appearance would have dissolved every other materialising loop. And this link was so ineluctable that it was uncannily like seeing a revival of some half-remembered play, rather than meeting a new and sudden complication.

He said: "Don't look now, but I think your husband is joining us."

Mrs. Ourley did look, of course; but she did not come out with the squeak of coy consternation which one might reasonably have expected from her past performance in her own hallway at Oyster Bay. Instead, her carmined nails dug into the tablecloth so hard that they left furrows in the linen, and her complexion paled under its crust of powder until she looked like a fat frost-bitten ghost. The sheer coagulation of her face was a distillate of all that unearthly majestic austerity that wins battles in the committee meetings of women's clubs.

"Let me take care of this," she said ominously, and stood up.

She moved with surprising swiftness for her bulk, and she met Milton Ourley halfway down the room. Once again she was like a stately galleon ploughing through a cluttered harbour. Milton might have been compared with a squat broad fussy tug, except that it was the galleon which took him in tow. Simon could hear something like a hoarse spluttering "dabbity dab dab," like a rumble of distant thunder, but it made just as little difference to the general flow of motion. Mr. Ourley might actually have made a great physical effort to struggle towards the Saint's table, but the achievements of his kampf were not readily discernible. Borne like a cockleshell upon his spouse's regal bow wave, he was washed back into the lobby, still booming like a frustrated foghorn, and disappeared from the scene.

Simon kept his head down while he examined and signed the check that was already on the table, and then he caught the eye of the *maître d'hôtel* and brought him over with a mere wisp of a gesture.

"Raúl," he said, "how could anyone get out of here without going through the lobby?"

If the *maître d'hôtel* had his own and incidentally erroneous theories about the Saint's motives, he was far too polished a diplomat to give them any expression. In addition to which, and for no professional reasons, he had long since taken the Saint under his generous wing.

"There is a back way out," he said. "Would you like to see it?"

"I might even fall in love with it," said the Saint.

They went down to the other end of the dining-room, through well-organised pantries and one end of the clean busy kitchen, and past a row of food lockers to a wire-mesh door where the timekeeper rose from his little table and a plate of roast beef to let them out. Beyond that there was a short narrow passage and another door that opened inconspicuously on to Forty-fourth Street.

Simon stopped and looked back the way they had come. He pointed.

"Is that the service elevator?"

"Yes, sir. Do you want to use it?"

"That would get me upstairs and back again without going through the lobby too, wouldn't it?"

"Yes, sir."

The Saint rubbed his chin.

"I'd like to do that first. But will George here let me out when I come down again?"

"Of course." Raúl turned to the timekeeper. "Please let Mr. Templar out whenever he's ready." He turned back to the Saint with a flourish. "Is there anything else I can do?"

Simon grinned as he strolled back towards the service lift.

"You've done plenty already, Raúl," he said. "As it is, I expect you've broken all the regulations in the joint, and Mr. Case will probably fire you."

The *maître d'hôtel* shrugged cheerfully.

"Regulations are for everybody else, but not for the Saint." He said to the elevator operator: "Take Mr. Templar upstairs and bring him down again any time he wants to come." He smiled at the Saint with the happy magnificence of a mayor who has just bestowed the keys of his city, and said with charming impersonality: "Do you wish to leave any message?"

Simon shook his head.

"Just stay out of trouble and pretend you didn't see me go."

"But I won't have seen you go, Mr. Templar," said Raúl. "I won't look."

He turned his back, and Simon stepped into the car and was wafted upwards at a suitable pace for a sedate hotel.

He glanced at his wrist-watch automatically as he stepped out on the third floor, but it was almost a reflex movement and the position of the hands scarcely impressed itself on him at all. The real timing was all in his head—it was a matter of how long it would have taken to discuss this and decide that and then to do something about it. He was working to almost psychically close tolerances, and an error of even a few minutes in his mental clocking might have catastrophic results. And even then he was trying to time-table something so nebulous that his own intuition was practically the only guarantee that it would work out that way at all.

He slid the key into his door with millimetric stealth, and went into his suite with weightless feet and one hand on the gun which he had borrowed from Mr. Varetti before lunch. He had been caught once that day, and he was not going to make the same mistake again.

But apparently he was still within his margin of time—if it had any real existence at all. There was no one in his living-room, or behind the portières that shut off the bedroom, or in the bathroom or the closet or under the bed. He took each hazard separately and methodically, making no sound to betray his presence until he had covered all of them.

Even then he was very quiet, and denied himself a cigarette that he would have enjoyed because he didn't want to leave fresh smoke in the air.

The suitcase which he had sent up stood beside the sofa in the living-room. He didn't touch it.

The iron structure of the fire escape ran outside the bedroom window. Simon had chosen his suite for that reason; but it could work two ways. The front door of the suite could be penetrated in one way or another, but it would present difficulties. Simon thought it would be the fire escape.

The hallway from the front door met the living-room at an angle so that there was a corner from which he could cover any entrance from equal concealment. He flattened himself into it and waited as patient and motionless as a statue in a niche.

Somebody in the adjoining suite turned on a radio at full volume, and it blared away for two or three minutes before it was turned down. Even then, it was too loud.

Of course, it might be the front door. Either Varetti or Walsh might be good with locks, or might be clever enough to con a master key out of somewhere. Or they might even be tough enough to try it with a frontal assault, on a simple smash-grab-and-run basis.

It was curious how he had always assumed that it would be Varetti and Walsh. Even when he spoke to Fernack on the telephone. He had left them locked up in Barbara Sinclair's closet intending to have been back there by that time and busy with the job of advancing their acquaintance on his own terms; but all that had been changed for quite a while. He wasn't quite sure how long ago he had been sure that they were no longer waiting where he had left them, but it seemed now that he had always been sure that they wouldn't be there. It was one of those fourth-dimensional elisions that saw an end before it could pin down all the steps and stages through which the end would come about.

He knew that Varetti and Walsh were out again, because only since they were out again could certain other things have happened. Or, conversely, because other things had happened, they must be out again.

And the rawhide suitcase was standing beside the sofa and someone would come to get it.

It wouldn't take much shopping around to settle on one of the suites directly above the one he was in. And from any such starting point a fire escape that ran down through a gloomy inside courtyard that nobody would ever want to look out at anyway would present virtually no problems at all. . . .

He could really have enjoyed that cigarette.

But how long could he afford to wait, backing his hunch, while he might always be wrong, and the fox might be away in another spinney?

The radio next door was blatting forth some emetic commercial about the perils of fungoid feet or some such attractive ailment. He could hear every word as if he were in the room with it. He wondered if it would be loud enough to drown one of the sounds he was listening for.

But it wasn't.

He heard it.

It was the slow cautious rasp of a window-sash being eased quietly upwards. And, after that, the subdued rattle of the slats of the venetian blind being lifted from below.

So it was the fire escape and the bedroom window; and he had not waited in vain.

There had been an instant of tingling stillness when he heard the sound, but now he was as smooth and cool as a hand-trued machine, and his pulses were as light as the ripples on a landlocked bay at sunset. Now he backed noiselessly out of his neutral corner and flattened himself easily along the wall, towards the front door and away from the rooms, so that the visitor would have to step clear into the living-room before he could see the Saint at all.

The Saint's ears followed the movements in the bedroom step by step. He heard the occasional scuff of exploring feet, and a hoarse "Hurry up! hurry up!" There was the clicking of the blind again, and more movement. It was surprising how you could hear sounds, after all, in spite of the radio: when it came to the point, these sounds had a totally different texture, so that there was no confusion, just as you could have heard a hiccup in the next seat in a movie in spite of the sound effects of a news-reel bombardment. He could even hear the thin strained sound of consciously controlled breathing.

In addition, he became ethereally aware of a new richness in the atmosphere which he could still identify in spite of his recent bludgeoning by the assorted smells of Mrs. Ourley, and he knew that he was perceiving the particularly obnoxious pomade of Mr. Varetti even before the sleek head that wore it slid into his sidelong field of vision.

Varetti stood looking down at the rawhide bag as Cokey Walsh followed him out of the bedroom.

"Here it is," he said, with superfluous but deep satisfaction.

"If only that sonofagun Templar was here too," said Mr. Walsh, "I'd like to . . ."

He enumerated a few things he would have liked to do which it would be useless to repeat here, since the elevated minds of the readers of this reportage would never believe that any person could have such depraved ambitions.

Varetti, a more practical man, cut him off in the middle of a fine phrase with the kind of question which from time immemorial has nipped the poet's prettier fancies in the bud.

"Why don't you shut your trap?"

He picked up the heavy bag with an effort.

"We'll walk down the stairs and walk straight out the front," he said.

"Suppose he's in the lobby," Cokey suggested.

"You go ahead and make sure he isn't."

"I wanna see that sonofagun again."

"You'll have plenty of time."

Varetti turned towards the door. And there the Saint faced him, elegant and graceful and smiling, with his gun level and tremorless at his waist and blue lights of devilish mockery dancing in his eyes.

It seemed quite unfortunate at that moment that the Algonquin Hotel had omitted to provide two vats of soft plaster of paris among the otherwise well-planned furnishing of the joint. If it had not been for that almost incredible lack of foresight, the cataleptic rigidity of the two men might easily have allowed the Saint to immerse them and withdraw them again without the slightest disturbance of their articulation, thereby creating a pair of moulds for which any wax museum would have been glad to bid. But such sad wastes are an inevitable symptom of our unplanned economy, and Simon Templar had learned to exercise his philosophy on them.

He said, without undue gloom: "The hands up and clasped behind the back of the head, gentlemen—if you don't mind my borrowing your own fancy formula, Ricco. Although to be quite candid it just struck me that your vocabulary had slipped a bit. Or is it because you save your party dialogue for the cash customers?"

Varetti put the bag down gradually and deliberately, and raised his hands in the same way, so that his movements were rather like those of a trained snake; and his eyes were a snake's eyes, bright and beady and unblinking.

"How the hell did you get here?" demanded Mr. Walsh, almost indignantly.

"I heard you wanted me," said the Saint, "so I came a-running. A little faster with the hands, if you don't mind, Cokey. . . . Thank you. . . . Now, if you'll both turn your backs I'll see whether you've picked up any new weapons since we last met, and if you are very polite I may refrain from goosing you."

Apparently they had been rushed out of either the time or the opportunity to replenish their armoury, or else they had anticipated no such disconcerting need for one, for the only trophy which rewarded his excavations was a six-inch jack-knife from the pocket of Comrade Varetti with a trick spring that whipped the blade open when you pressed a button.

The Saint was not too disappointed. He had discovered before then that it is only in the less conscientious crime stories that the ungodly are endowed with inexhaustible reserves of artillery from which they can rebound on a few minutes' notice from any setback, armed to the teeth again and spitting javelins; and moreover he realised that the armament programme must have placed additional handicaps even on the hoodlums who were accustomed to buy their gats by the carton. But he did not complain. He was not the complaining type. He was prepared to make his small contribution to the exigencies of global war.

He put the knife through its paces with the most detached and fascinated interest while he allowed the two men to turn around again.

"Very ingenious, Ricco, and quite a credit to the Mafia, or whatever your dear old alma mater was," he observed appreciatively. "I'm afraid you must have been a very bad little boy when you were young."

Varetti showed his white rabbit teeth in a smile that was half a snarl.

"You'll find out what kind of a bad boy I am before we're through," he said. "Your luck will run out one of these days, and I'm going to be there when it does. You and your exploding cigarettes! I certainly was a chump to be taken in by an old gag like that."

"You certainly were, brother," Simon agreed consolingly. "But you can cheer yourself with the thought that smarter men than you have fallen for it before. And now, if we have to keep up these oldworld courtesies, may I trouble you two creeps to back off and park your bottoms on that beautiful sofa behind you? Keeping the hands in the same position, if you don't mind. . . . That's the idea. . . . I want you to be comfortable, because I still think of you as my guests, and we are now going to have a brief chat about one thing and another."

With just a little more thoughtful reluctance than Walsh, Varetti sank obediently on to the couch; but there was no shift in the bland display of his incisors.

"Don't you know you're wasting your time?" he asked. "We aren't going to tell you anything. Why don't you just call the cops?"

"And then?" Simon inquired, smiling and silky.

"Then you'll have to prove that you didn't invite us in here. And you'll have to explain why you were so mad when we found that you had a bag of stolen iridium in your apartment."

The Saint's eyes danced with boreal lights.

"Mr. Walsh," he said, "would you be good enough to open the bag that Ricco is talking about? . . . Go on. . . . I won't shoot you."

In a state of partial hypnosis buffeted between the menace of the Saint's gun and the impudent spear-tips in the Saint's eyes, Mr. Walsh slid dubiously off the sofa to obey. He laid the suitcase on its side, and clicked the catch. He raised the lid. He looked.

So did Ricco Varetti.

They beheld what must have been one of the finest collections of assorted spheres that had even been hastily improvised. It ranged from the ripe solidity of bowls that should have been booming smoothly down polished alleys, down to ball-bearings designed to speed the wheels of roller skates, and down from there to buckshot and B.B. pills for airguns. It included baseballs, cricket balls, billiard balls, and one large sand-packed medicine ball. It was a truly amazing crop of balls.

"All right," said the Saint amiably. "Let's have a showdown on that basis. The cops are on their way already, whether you believe it or not, and they are a couple of tough babies. They'll be crashing in here in a matter of minutes—if they take that long. I'm giving you this one chance to scream everything you can remember about your boss man; and if you don't want to play with me I'm sure that Kestry and Bonacci will just love showing you the town."

XI

To any individual who, like the present chronicler, is acutely conscious of the need to conserve paper in order that there may never be any lack of raw materials on which the latest governmental artist can design new forms to be filled out in sesquicentuplicate, the mere thought of wasting one milligram of precious pulp which might be better devoted to the production of monogrammed kleenex is instinctively repugnant. Your correspondent therefore proposes to expend no words on describing the reactions of Messieurs Varetti and Walsh, beyond mentioning that they looked as if they had been kicked three inches above the navel by an exacerbated elephant.

Whereafter, as an equally simple matter of record, it was Cokey Walsh who digested the ultimate total into the single sizzling sentence without which all detective-story dialogue would have dried up long ago.

"I ain't talking."

"That remains to be seen," said the Saint, with proper patience, having been in stories before. "But you'll have to start with some sort of alibi when the cops arrive, and I thought you might like a rehearsal."

Varetti moistened his lips.

"That's still easy," he said. "You brought us in here and started all this. You say we were trying to steal something. Well, what was it and where did you get it?"

"You're doing fine," said the Saint encouragingly. "Go on."

Varetti shrugged.

"I don't have to go on for you. But I can tell you that if there's going to be any squealing at all, Cokey and I will squeal on you first. And if we have to take any rap, we'll share it out with you. We could even say that you were in with us all the time, until you started to double-cross us just now."

"That's right," Cokey chimed in brightly. "When we found out what you was up to, we didn't want any part of it. So we was just tryin' to do our duty and turn you in."

The Saint sighed.

"I can't stop you dreaming," he said, "but do you honestly believe that even the dumbest cop you ever hoped for is going to buy a yarn like that from a couple of characters like you?"

"What's wrong with our characters?" Cokey demanded aggrievedly. "Our word is as good as yours——"

"But is it?" Simon asked gently. "I imagine that your record must be rather involved. And I don't suppose you got your name because of your passion for drinking colas. I can see other stuff in your eyes now. Are you quite sure that a junkie's word is as good as mine? What do you think, Ricco?—and incidentally, how is your police record? Will the Y.M.C.A. vouch for you? Are you in line for an honorary commission in the Salvation Army?"

Varetti said nothing. He stared back at the Saint with adequate outward composure, and Simon gathered that he had all the misdirected courage of his profession. The Saint didn't underestimate Mr. Varetti, in spite of his revolting clothes and coiffure.

There was, meanwhile, the matter of a cigarette which was becoming increasingly overdue. . . . Simon dipped into his breast pocket and secured one with his left hand, without the most microscopic shift of the automatic in his right. He fished out a match booklet in the same way, and began shaping a match over without tearing it out, in order to strike it one-handed.

He said: "I don't have to make speeches to you, either. I just hope you don't think I'm kidding about Kestry and Bonacci. Because if you do, we're wasting a lot of time, and we haven't got much to spare."

Varetti's mouth curled derisively.

"Don't give us that stuff. You didn't know we were coming here until we walked into the room."

"That's true. I was only guessing that *you* were coming. But I knew that somebody was. I knew that somebody would be checking on me here, and I couldn't bring that bag in my pocket. Therefore somebody would know that something had gone wrong. And somebody would want to do something fast about getting the bag back. That's what I told Inspector Fernack; and that's why Kestry and Bonacci are on their way. I do hope you know Kestry and Bonacci. They don't have any of those Lord Peter Wimsey whimsies, but they get a lot more confessions in their own way. Are you looking forward to a romp with them in the massage parlour?"

The hoodlum glared at him with hot hateful eyes.

"I don't believe you," he said flatly. "It's a stall, that's what it is."

"Is that all you're betting on?"

Varetti's mouth was a tight line.

"If you mean I should spill, there isn't a chance."

Simon wiped his bent match over the striking strip on the booklet and put the flame to his cigarette.

He said: "How about you, Cokey? How are you looking forward to going without your inhaler for a while? Have you ever been through that experience before? I expect you have. On top of being slapped around a bit, it's quite a lot of fun—isn't it?"

Cokey Walsh's face was pallid and lined. With his hands clasped behind his head as he had been ordered, only his elbows could tremble. But they did. His eyes were jittering buttons in a yellow mask.

"Remember it, Cokey?" Simon asked gently. "Remember how all your nerves jump and twitch, and you're all empty inside except for your stomach being a tight knot in the middle, and there are hammers inside your head beating it apart from the middle, and you know that if it doesn't stop you're going to scream and go crazy?"

Cokey swallowed twice as if he were trying to get a tough dry mouthful down his throat.

"I——"

"You're not talking, either," Varetti cut in savagely. "Take hold of yourself, Cokey! This punk hasn't got a thing on us, except maybe a breaking and entering charge that won't stick. You make one peep, and you'll wind up in the hot squat—unless I croak you first. Which I will, so help me!"

Cokey struggled again with the bolus of dry hay in his gullet.

"I ain't talking," he rasped again. "You can't make me talk."

Simon Templar took a deep rib-lift of smoke down into his system and let it circulate leisurely around. But the pulse in the back of his brain that was ticking away seconds had nothing leisurely about it. Time marched on, inexorably and alarmingly, and he was getting nothing out of it. There was no doubt that Cokey would sing eventually, if he had any music to give out, but there was also no doubt that he would take quite a little loosening up. Any fears he had of the police or even of the Saint himself were still plainly dominated by his fear of Varetti. And Varetti was still dominated, for one reason or another, by someone else. And it was still an impasse, and time was slipping away like water out of a bath. . . .

And the Saint's idle smile still didn't change as he let the smoke out through it and held the two gonsels with easy and impossible blue eyes.

"Now let's face a few facts, kiddies," he said quietly. "You were sent here to collect a lot of very valuable green dust. You don't find any. You pick up a collection of spherical souvenirs which cost me quite a lot of dough, but which don't have such a terrific market value. Therefore you are not going home and collect a great big commission on the trip. In fact, your boss may not even be pleased with you at all. . . . . I'm trying to be honest with you, boys. I bought another bag and put the boodle you're looking for in it, and it's safe now where you'll never get your hands on it again. So you can't win. And Kestry and Bonacci will beat it out of you eventually, anyway. Why not tell me now and let me save you a lot of pain?"

"You're scaring me to death," sneered Varetti.

He should have been scared. For the Saint was most dangerous when his smile was gentle and detached like that. And it wasn't always a physical danger. Varetti was tough enough to brace himself against that, at least for a time. He was concentrating on that.

And so it was unfortunate for him, and for certain other people, that he was psychologically satisfied with that threat alone. It was clear enough to him so that it was twisting up his nerves and drawing on all his resistance, while his constructive imagination was fully occupied with a desperate groping for some trick of escape. And that left him nothing to spare with which to encompass the really frightening idea that all of that build-up might only be a feint in force for a much more complicated attack in depth. He watched the falling bludgeon and never saw the stealthy approach of the stiletto.

The Saint stepped closer, and he looked taller and harder, and the edges were sharpening in his voice.

"Sure, Ricco, you're tough," he said. "You can take plenty. But how much can your girl friend take? How long will she keep her mouth buttoned when we start working on her? And where are you and Cokey going to find the answers when she sings about you?"

"She can't sing about us," Varetti retorted. "She doesn't know anything."

There were tiny beads of moisture on his face. Simon could see them as he drew closer still.

"Oh, no?" he said in a voice of silken needles. "What makes you think the boss never talked to anyone except you? What makes you so sure he never told her anything? Are you quite ready to take your chance on what she'll spill when I talk to her?"

Varetti laughed, in a sort of nervous triumph.

"You won't ever talk to her! The boss is taking care of——"

He was exactly that far when Kestry and Bonacci arrived, turning a key in the door and entering with a rush, rather like a pair of stampeding hippopotami, which in other respects they slightly resembled.

They came in with their guns drawn, and Simon stepped back to give them room to take over, without even glancing at them or shifting his gun until they had the scene under control. There was the snick-snack of handcuffs, and the Saint didn't move at once.

"Thank you," he said; and his eyes were still on Varetti.

"That's okay, pal." The big bulk of Kestry shouldered across his view, heavy-jawed and unfriendly-eyed. "How did you get here?"

For the first time Simon looked at him, and put the gun away in his pocket.

"It's my room," he mentioned calmly. "I was here when they arrived. Now you can take them away. They bother me."

"They won't bother you any more. They're both three-timers, an' they'll get the book thrown at them."

"That's fine," said the Saint cynically. "Unless they get the right lawyer. They've probably done it before."

"They won't do it this time. Not after they've sung. And they'll sing." Kestry was certain and unemotional like a rock, and no more changed or changeable. He said, without any alteration of stance or stare: "I still want to know more about you."

"Why don't you read a newspaper?"

"You just put a gun in your pocket. That makes it a concealed weapon. Where did you get it, an' where's your permit?"

The Saint put his cigarette to his lips and drew at it with a light easy breath.

"Fernack told you what to do," he said. "If you want to write in a new scene for yourself, you're on your own. Otherwise, I wish you'd just drag the bodies out. I'm in a hurry."

Kestry's eyes were bitter and glistening, the Saint's cool and bright little chips of sapphire with indefinable gleams of insolence shifting over them. It was a clash from which tinder might have been ignited at close range. But the measure of Kestry's defeat, and the value of its future repercussions, were plain in the heavy viciousness with which he turned back to his captives.

"Let's get 'em out of here, Dan," he said.

He grasped Varetti's arm in a ham-like fist and yanked him off the couch, while his partner performed a similar service for Walsh. Cokey let out a yelp as the steel bracelets cut into his wrists.

"Shut up, you," growled Donacri. "That ain't nothing to what you're gonna get."

He shoved the two men roughly towards the door.

Kestry took a last pointless look around, and followed. However, he turned to favour the Saint with one lingering farewell glower.

"It still don't seem right to be goin' out of here without you," he said; and the Saint smiled at him sweetly.

"You must drop in again," he murmured, "and get used to it."

He waited until the door had slammed after the departing populace, and then he picked up the telephone and called Centre Street.

Inspector Fernack must have gabbled his evidence and rushed back to his office like a broker returning from lunch during a boom, for he was on the wire as soon as Simon asked for him.

"This is the Voice of Experience, Henry," he said. "Your beef trust has just oozed out, taking Cokey and Ricco with them. I think they'll make noises eventually, so you can take your boots off and get ready to hear them vocalise. Now while you and the boys are getting cosy with them, I've got one final little job to do. So if you'll excuse me . . ."

"Hey, wait a minute!" The anguish in Fernack's voice was almost frantic. "If you've got any further information, you ought to——"

"My dear Henry, if I waited around to do all the things I ought to, I'd be wasting as much energy as you spend on your setting-up exercises."

"I don't do any setting-up exercises!"

"Then you certainly ought to. That fine manly figure of yours must be preserved. Now I really must get busy, because you've got plenty on your hands as it is, and I don't want you to have another murder to worry about."

"You let me worry about my own worrying," Fernack said grimly. "All I want to know is what else you know now."

"You didn't get the significance of the lock?"

"What lock?"

"Never mind," said the Saint. "It will dawn on you one of these days. Now I really must be going."

"But *where?*" wailed the detective.

The Saint smiled, and blew a slender smoke-ring through a teasing pause.

"I'll leave a note for you at the desk here. You climb on to your little bicycle and come and pick it up."

"Why not give it to me now?"

"Because I want to be there first. Because I want a little time to set the stage. And because cops rush in where Saints are smart enough to wait. Be patient, Henry. Everything will be under control . . . I hope. I'm just trying to make it easy for you. And please, when you get there, do me the favour of listening for a minute before you thunder in. I don't want to be interrupted in the middle of a tender passage. . . . Good-bye, now."

He hung up in time to disconnect a jolt of verbal heat and explosion that might have threatened the New York Telephone Company with a general fusing of wires between the Murray Hill and

Spring exchanges, scribbled rapidly on a sheet of paper, and sealed it into an envelope and wrote Fernack's name on it while he waited for the service elevator.

"Get this to the desk, will you?" he said to the operator as they rode down. "To be called for."

The timekeeper let him out, and he emerged from the side door on to Forty-fourth Street, walking east. In a few strides he turned into the Seymour Hotel, and walked quickly up the corridor towards the lobby. There he stopped for a minute, waiting to see if anyone entered after him. It was always possible that Kestry might have brooded enough to wait for him, or even that the ungodly themselves might have another representative lurking around. But no one followed him in within a reasonable time; and that part of the chase was won. For the Seymour ran clear through the block, and he went out on to Forty-fifth Street and stepped into a passing taxi with reasonable assurance that he was alone.

The clock in his head ran with sidereal detachment and precision, and on that spidery tight-rope of timing his brain balanced as lightly as a shadow.

He had had to put everything together very quickly and coldly; and yet it seemed to him now that he had always known just where each person who mattered would be, from instant to instant, as though they had been linked to him by threads of extrasensory perception. But he had to be right. He had to be right now, or else he had thrown away all the completeness of what he had tried to do.

And with that sharp sting of awareness in his mind he walked into the lobby of the hotel where he had left Barbara Sinclair.

He nodded to the desk clerk who had signed them in, and rode up in the elevator to her floor. He knocked on the door, and waited a little while. He said: "Saks Fifth Avenue, ma'am. A C.O.D. package for Mrs. Tombs."

XII

HE waited a little longer, and then the door opened two or three inches, and he saw a narrow panel of her face—hair like a raven's wing, a dark eye, and carmine lips.

He went in.

"I wondered what had happened to you," she said.

"I had lunch. I met some friends."

His eyes strayed over the room with the most natural unconcern, but they missed nothing. Actually it was in an ash-tray that he saw the proof that at least half of his timing had been right, but his glance picked up the detail without pausing.

Barbara Sinclair moved to a deep low chair by the window and sat down, curling one shapely leg under her. Her other foot swung in a short off-beat rhythm, so that every interrupted movement of it gave him a measure of the effort of will-power that was maintaining her outward composure.

"Has anything else happened?" she asked.

"Just a few things."

"Have you found out anything?"

"A little. . . . You know, this isn't such a bad place, is it? I must remember it next time some visiting fireman is asking me where to stay with his concubine."

He was strolling about the room as if he were estimating the general comfort of it and incidentally taking his time over choosing a place to sit down.

"It's not one of the tourist taverns, so he'd be pretty safe from the risk of an awkward meeting with one of the home-town gossips. And it's very discreet and respectable, which ought to put the lady in the right mood. There must be nothing like a dingy bedroom and a leering bellhop to damp the fires of precarious passion."

He arrived in front of a bookcase on which stood a tall vase of chrysanthemums filled out with a mass of autumn oak leaves. He stood with his back to the room, approving them.

"Chrysanthemums," he murmured. "Football. Raccoon coats. The long crawl to New Haven. The cheers. The groans. The drinks." He shook his head sadly. "Those dear dead days," he said. "The chrysanthemums are here, but the gridiron scholars are boning up on the signals for squads right. And as for driving to New Haven without any bootleg gas coupons. . . . But they are pretty."

"The management sent them up," she said. "I'm afraid I didn't think I was spotted as a concubine. I wondered if they thought we were honeymooners."

He laughed sympathetically, and took the automatic out of his breast pocket and nested it in amongst the leaves, still covering the vase with his back, while he was pretending to make improvements in the arrangement of the bouquet.

Then he turned again to look at her, and said: "It's too bad, isn't it? We never had that honeymoon."

"We would have had it, you know, if you hadn't been quite so clever about getting rid of me."

"I have a feeling of irreparable loss."

Her lovely face seemed to grow dark and warm from within as her long lashes dipped for a moment. Then she raised them again in a slow stare that could have had many sources.

"You really hate me, don't you?"

He shook his head judicially, his brow wrinkled by a frown that was very vague and distant.

"Not so much."

"You don't like me."

He smiled easily, and started to open a fresh pack of cigarettes.

"Like you? Darling, I always thought you were terrific. I would have loved our honeymoon. But unfortunately I haven't any instincts of the male scorpion. I never could see consummation and immolation as interchangeable words. And I wasn't nearly so anxious to get rid of you as you were to get rid of me—permanently."

"I didn't——"

"Know?" Simon suggested. "Perhaps not. Perhaps. But your boy friend did. And you must admit that he's clever. Within his own class, anyway. Clever enough, for instance, to set you up in that fancy tenement because it might always be useful to have a pretty girl on call to entertain the tired business man—or decoy the simple sucker. That is, when he didn't want her himself. A very happy way of combining business with pleasure, if you ask me. . . . Or is it rude of me to insist on this masculine viewpoint? Should I have thought of a girl friend instead—some nice motherly creature who . . ."

He raised a hand as she started out of the chair with dark eyes blazing.

"Take it easy," he drawled. "Maybe I was just kidding. It's obvious that the bag I found in your apartment was a man's. But so were the pyjamas that were hanging in the closet where I heaved Humpty and Dumpty."

Her hand went to her mouth, and her exquisite features suddenly sagged into a kind of blank smear. It was absurd and pitiful, he thought, how a few words could transform a lovely and vital creature into a haggard woman with neck cords that streaked her throat and eyes that were hollow and lustreless with fear.

"I don't know what you mean," she said.

"I've heard more original remarks than that," he said. "But if it's any help to you, I don't know what you mean either. I didn't say the pyjamas had any name embroidered on them—or did I?" —

She sank back on to the edge of the chair, her hands clasped in her lap, not comfortably or relaxed, but as if she had only paused there in the expectation of having to move again.

He slid a cigarette forward in his pack and offered it to her. In the same solicitous way, he lighted it for her and then lighted one for himself. He drew slowly at it, not savouring the smoke, and looking at her, and wondering why in a world so sadly in need of beauty he should have to be talking to her in this way and know that this was the only way to talk, and that was how it was and there was nothing else to do.

He said, with a slight but sincere shrug: "This isn't a fight. It might have been a beautiful honeymoon. But maybe it just wasn't in the cards. Anyway, it'll have to wait now."

She said: "I suppose so."

He said: "It's no use stalling much more. You were supposed to have made up your mind about telling me something. Have you made up your mind?"

She winced and looked down at the tangling and untangling fingers in her lap. She looked up at him, and then down again at her hands. Her mouth barely moved.

She said: "Yes."

"Well?"

"I'll tell you."

He waited.

"I'll tell you," she said, "sometime this afternoon."

"Why not now?"

"Because . . ."

The Saint took a great interest in the tip of his cigarette.

"Barbara," he said, "it may not occur to you that I'm giving you a lot more breaks than the rules provide. I never was a nut on technicalities, but the fact remains that you're a technical accessory. You know this man I want to talk to, the man who holds the key to most of this dirty business. You know that everything you keep back is helping him to get away with—literally—murder. And you spend the hours you've been here alone struggling with your conscience to arrive at the tremendous decision that you'll tell me all about it— at your own convenience."

"No," she said.

"I don't want you to think I'm getting tough with you, but I've known police matrons who developed bulging muscles just from persuading wayward girls that they ought to unburden their hearts in the interest of right and justice. And I'm sure that wouldn't appeal to you at all."

She made a thin line of her mouth and gazed back at him defiantly.

"You sound as if you'd said all this before."

"Maybe I have," he admitted equably. "But it doesn't make it any less true. Believe it or not, I've only got to pick up that phone and call a certain gent by the name of Inspector John Henry Fernack to have you taken into what is so charmingly referred to as 'custody.' Custody is a place out of earshot of any unofficial person which might be too inquisitive; and it isn't a very pleasant place. In custody, almost anything can happen, and often does." He blew a thoughtful streak of smoke at the ceiling. "You can still make your own choice, but I wish you'd make the right one."

The moment's flare had died out of her as if it had never happened.

She said, as if she were repeating a lesson that she had worked out for herself until it became an obsession: "I've got to tell this person —first. I've got to tell him that I'm going to tell you. I've got to give him a chance. He —he's been the kindest person I ever met. I was nothing—I was practically starving—I'd have done anything—when I met him. He . . . he's been very good to me. Always. I want to do what's right, but I couldn't just give him to you—like that. I couldn't be a Judas. At least they give foxes a start, don't they?"

Simon considered the question gravely, as though he had all the time in the world. He felt as if he had. He felt as if she was important, in a way that was important only to him; and there was always a little time for important things.

"They do," he said. "But that's only because they want the fox to run longer and give the valiant sportsmen a better chase. If they were just being noble and humane, they'd simply shoot him as quickly and accurately as possible, thereby saving him all the agonies of fear, flight, hope, and final despair. Of course that wouldn't be quite so sporting as letting him run his heart out against a pack of hounds, but the eventual result would be the same."

"Sometimes the fox gets away," she said.

"The fox never gets away in the end," he said kindly. "He may get away a dozen times, but there'll always be a thirteenth time when he makes one little mistake, and then he's just a trophy for somebody to take home. It's almost dull, but that's how it is."

"They've never caught you."

"Yet."

He went to the window and peered out. The sky was already darkening with the limpid clarity of sunset, the hour when it seems to grow thinner and deeper so that you almost begin to see through it into the darkness of outer space.

Without turning, he said: "I gather that you've already told the fox."

He heard her stir in the chair behind him.

"Yes."

He said, without anger, without disappointment, without anything: "I rather thought you would. I expected that when I left you. Because you really have too much heart for too little sense. I don't blame you for the heart, but now I want you to try and develop some sense."

"I'm sorry," she said, and she could have been. "But I can't do anything about it."

He turned.

"For heaven's sake," he said, "don't you get anything into your head? I told you I was expecting you to tip off the fox. Do you think I'd have expected that, and left you alone to do it, if I hadn't figured that you'd be doing something for me? I wanted you to make the fox break cover. I wanted him rushed into doing something that would give us a view of him. I wanted to force him into making the mistakes that are going to qualify him for his seat on the griddle. He's already made one of them, and any minute now he's going to make another. You've done that much to help him, and now you're doing your damn best to help yourself right into the soup with him. If that isn't devotion, I don't know what is."

XIII

HE saw the stunned shock petrifying her face, but he didn't wait for it to complete or resolve itself. He didn't have time. And now before she collected herself might be the best chance he would ever have.

He moved quickly across towards her and sat on the next chair, and his voice was as swift and urgent as the movement.

"Listen," he said. "This man is a crook. He is a thief—and stealing iridium is no different from stealing jewels or coffee or anything else. And in just the same language, he's a murderer."

"He never killed anyone——"

"Of course not. Not personally. He didn't have to. A crumb in his class doesn't need to pull triggers himself, or knot ropes around an old fool's neck. He has other men to do that—or other women. But that doesn't make him any less a killer. There was murder done in the first stealing, at Nashville. Two guards by the name of Smith or Jones or Gobbovitch were shot down. Just a couple of names in a newspaper. Probably they had families and relatives and friends here and there, but you don't think about that when you're reading. You click your tongue and say isn't it awful and turn on to your favourite columnist or the funnies. But Mrs. Jones has lost a husband who was a hell of a lot more real to her than your boy friend is to you, and the Gobbovitch brats are going to have to quit school after their primary grades and do the best they can on their own—just because your big-hearted glamour boy hired a couple of cannons to go out and do his shooting for him."

"Please don't," she said.

"I want to be sure you know just what kind of a man you're shielding. A cold-blooded murderer. And a traitor on top of that. Maybe he hasn't even thought of it that way himself. Maybe he's been too busy thinking about the money that was helping to keep you in that splendid apartment. But it's still just as true as if you both had your eyes open."

"It isn't true."

His face had neither pity nor passion, but only a relentless and inescapable sincerity that was out of a different universe from the lazy flippancy which he usually wore with the same ease as he wore his clothes.

"Barbara, there are little guys from farms and filling stations who wouldn't even know how it all worked who're fighting more odds than just the enemy because of what he's doing. They're wading through steamy slime in South Pacific jungles, and chewing sand in Africa, and freezing to death in their tracks in the Ukraine. But that doesn't bother your private Santa Claus, so long as there are still a few good chefs in Manhattan and he has plenty of green paper to pay for all the little luxuries that help to alleviate the hardships of the home front. And if you take his side, all that is true about you too."

"I'm not taking his side," she said desperately. "He's been good to me, and I'm just giving him a chance."

"Of course he's been good to you. You wouldn't have done anything for him if he hadn't. No crook or traitor or any other kind of louse can afford to be any other way with anyone he needs for an enthusiastic accomplice."

She rocked back and forth in the chair, with a kind of unconscious automatism, as though she was somehow trying to lull back all the tormenting consciences that his steady remorseless voice awakened.

"I've told you," she repeated dully. "I've told you I'll talk to you later. It's only a little while. And then you and all your policemen and secret service and F.B.I. men can go after him like a pack of wolves."

"There's just a little more to it than that," said the Saint quietly. "Us wolves, as you call us, would like to go after him very respectably, and give him a fair trial with proper publicity—just to encourage anyone else who might have similar ideas."

"How nice of you," she said.

He didn't know why he went on trying.

"The evidence you could give," he said rather tiredly, "could be quite important. That's just half the reason why I'm talking to you now, and using up all this good breath. The other half is because I'm trying to give you a break. This is your chance to get out from under. I'm not trying to sell you now. It's too late for that. But I've still got to try and make you see that the jig is up, no matter what you do; but you can come out in quite a different light if you just make it possible for me to swear quite truthfully that you'd cooperated to the fullest extent with those fine creatures whom John Henry Fernack loves to refer to as 'the proper authorities.' "

She gazed at him with dark empty eyes.

He inhaled through his cigarette again, and said with a glacial evenness that was beginning to grow a little bitter like a winter sunset: "I'm telling you very quickly that this is the best chance you'll ever have. Maybe the last chance."

She hesitated, with her lips working in tiny unconscious patterns. He might have interpreted any of them into an effort to frame the name that he was expecting; but that would only have been his own imagination, and it was not enough.

He still waited, even when it seemed too long.

He was that sort of dope.

And then her lips were still, and tight and sullen and lost again. It was exactly as if a mould had set.

"You'll have to wait," she said stubbornly; and he stood up slowly. "I told you," she said.

Simon Templar drew his cigarette bright once more without tasting it, standing quite still and looking at her.

Everything went through his memory and understanding like a newsreel pouring through some far-off chamber of his brain.

She was so very beautiful, so physically desirable; and in a light way that might eventually have had more to it she had once briefly been fun. When he had first seen her swinging her long legs on the porch of the late Mr. Linnet's home, he had thought that she was everything that a girl out of a story should have been. It was a pity that in real life story-book introductions didn't always end up the way story-books ended. But this was not anything that could be changed by wishing.

She was in love with, or hopeful for, or in fear of, or hypnotised by, or standing strongly and stupidly by a man who would have looked like an ideal practice target to savage staggering men in any of the localised hells of the war. And still, whatever the reason might be, there was a pattern set, and it was more solid than any momentary work of his could break.

She only had to speak two words, two words that made one name, one name that was already tramping through his mind; but she would not do that.

And he could understand that, just as he could understand the craters on the moon, without being able to do anything about it. He could understand it just as he understood Milton Ourley's lust for money and a different life from the one he was forced to live at Oyster Bay, and just as he understood Titania Ourley's eroding hunger for young men and rumbas, and just as he understood Fernack and Varetti and even Cokey Walsh and Allen Uttershaw who played with quotations like a tired juggler toying with a cigar.

If it wasn't for the impenetrable blockages like that, they could all have been such nice normal people.

Like Inspector Fernack, who had lived all his life by the manual which had been given to him when he joined the Department as a rookie cop, was really a nice person. He was straight and square and he knew the Law and he believed in it. When his human nature and his critical sense of realities came out, as it did sometimes, it hurt him. He tried to fight against it but it wasn't often much good. The mould was set and case-hardened; the reflexes were conditioned for keeps.

Barbara Sinclair could have married the son of the druggist at the corner of Main and Tenth, in her home town, and she could have bulged and slimmed as she produced future druggists or presidents. She could have gone to Saturday night dances and flirted mildly with her next-door neighbour's husband while she worried about whether Junior or Freddie or Ike had thrown off the covers and whether the hired girl had fallen asleep or was out keeping a rendezvous on the corner with the top sergeant who had just come into her life.

Milton Ourley could have been the boss foreman of a crew of dock wallopers, harmlessly loosing off his choleric tongue on the job of lashing bigger and better men into setting new records in ship loading. Little bull-shaped men like that usually made good bosses because they inevitably went around with their shoulders hunched and a chip on both. If only Milton Ourley had never gotten into the money and the money had never gotten into him, he might have been quite a worthy and worthwhile individual who would never have become involved with anything more criminal than a pair of black-market nylons.

Titania Ourley could have had a husband who knew how to dominate her as she really needed to be dominated, instead of one who had convinced himself and ended by convincing her that the only way to hold her was by pouring more and more wealth and power into her hands. Then she would never have had the fundamental frustration that had reversed itself into her own exaggerated desire to dominate—to dominate the mate whom she despised for being dominated, to conquer and dominate everyone else with whom she came in contact by any kind of gushing effort, to buy or bully the sequacious young men who could flatter her that the charms she had wasted on her ineffectual spouse were still intact and devastating.

Varetti and Walsh could have climbed a little way up any humdrum but honest ladder, but at the time when their choice was made the Noble Experiment was in full swill, and it was becoming a simple axiom on the tough street corners where they dawdled that a pint of ersatz gin worth twenty cents could be marketed for a dollar. But to get that market some other merchant or salesman might have to be eradicated, and so the shooting came next and it came with enough impunity so that before long there were no more qualms about murder than there were about swallowing one of the illicit drinks that the murder was done for, not any more for them than for the righteous law-breaking public who didn't see the blood on the bottles and didn't give a damn anyway. Cokey Walsh had gone to the snow for the plain practical nerve and speed that he needed, but on any moral issues his soul was as shark-skinned as Varetti's. The only difference now was that the days of their splendour were gone and they would do their killing for much less money, because they were stragglers from an army that had passed into limbo and like any other stragglers they had to live off the land as best they could.

Allen Uttershaw was easy to understand. He was a business man who should have been a dilettante. He was a good business man but his only interest in business was the ultimate goal of being able to get out of it and live the vague and graceful life that his peculiar dramatisation of himself required. If he had inherited a million dollars twenty years ago he would have been a timeless and contented flâneur in a world of sleek penthouses, velvet smoking jackets, first editions, vintage wines, silk dressing-gowns, and the conversation of connoisseurs. He would have sauntered with faultless charm and savoir faire through his elegantly lepidopteral existence, quoting his snatches of poetry with that disarming half-smile up his sleeve that always made you wonder if it was worth laughing at him because he had probably just finished laughing at himself; and such contrastingly clamorous subjects as Ourleys and Saints would never have clattered through his peaceful and platonic ken. . . .

So the newsreel ran through the Saint's mind and finished, and the projection room was dark and silent again.

And he was still looking at Barbara Sinclair, lifting the cigarette to his mouth again, with his eyes very blue and quiet and unchanging.

He was very sorry, more sorry than it was easily endurable to be, and it was all so stupid and wasteful; but that was how things really happened, and sometimes you had to know it.

The clock in his head went on all the time.

And it was no damn good giving her a second thought, because you couldn't change anything.

Because life was like that, and sometimes you were stuck with it.

And stories just didn't end that way, because there was always a miracle at the last moment; but this wasn't a story.

And that was that.

He said: "It doesn't make very much difference, because I know already."

"What do you know?" she asked, looking at him with empty eyes.

He strolled across the room and sat down again in an arm-chair beside the bookcase that was crowned with the bouquet of chrysanthemums. He felt curiously tired; but it was a tiredness of the spirit and nothing to do with the mind or body.

"I know practically everything," he said. "Including the name of the master mind you're trying to protect. Suppose I tell you all about it."

XIV

"We begin," said the Saint, after a little pause, "with the stealing of a three hundred thousand dollar shipment of iridium at Nashville, Tennessee, not so long ago, and our first two murders—Comrades Smith and Gobbovitch, or whatever their names were, who got a load of lead in their lunch baskets."

"I know all that," she said, with a gesture of her slender hands that might have been an effort to brush away the vision that came behind his words.

"I expect you do," said the Saint. "But we ought to begin at the beginning. Because this robbery really opened the way for the black market. It actually created a sudden and very serious shortage. And then the manufacturers who use the stuff, who were suddenly caught short like that, were informed that they could still get supplies—at a price. Some of them were in a spot where they were glad enough to get it at almost any price."

He glanced again into the jet-black eyes that were fastened on him; and he was still sorry, but he was only more sure.

"The black market salesman, no doubt, had inside information about who was most badly in need of his merchandise. Two of these guys were the late Mr. Linnet, and Mr. Milton Ourley. There may have been others, but I don't happen to know about them. I know that Linnet had some misgivings about selling out his country for the benefit of your private angel, but the Ourley Magneto Company was not so fussy."

He looked at his watch and checked it by the other clock in his mind.

"Meanwhile, I had decided to stick my delicate nose in. I made a statement to the newspapers that I was going to clean up this black market, and I said I already knew plenty that would make it unhappy for the operators. It was a damn lie. I didn't know a thing. But I figured that it might scare the operators into trying to cool me off, which might give me a chance to get a line on them; or it might encourage somebody to come and sing to me a little for any one of various reasons. It isn't the newest trick in the world, but it often works. This worked. It brought me a little bird named Titania Ourley. Maybe you know her."

Barbara Sinclair licked her lips.

"I've met her."

"Titania sang me a little song about her husband, whom she said she had overheard talking to Gabriel Linnet about their dealing with the black market. She seemed to think I ought to investigate him. A most unwifely idea, but that wasn't my business. At her suggestion, I went out to Oyster Bay to meet and talk to Milton. Unfortunately, it became rapidly clear that Milton and I were not destined to form a great and beautiful friendship. And he didn't want to talk to me at all. In fact, he practically threw me out on my ear."

Simon leaned his head back and looked at the ceiling, as if he could see pictures there.

"I made one rather tragic mistake first, though, I dropped an unfinished quotation that somebody must have finished after I left. Because anyone who heard it finished would have known that I expected Linnet to sing—if he hadn't started singing already. And they would have had a good idea that I was on my way to see Linnet then. Which was very tragic indeed for Gabriel." He blew a carefully constructed smoke-ring. "I did go to Linnet's, of course; and there I met you. And in due course you gave me a very attractive invitation."

She bowed her head over her hands clenched together between her knees.

"Soon after this," he added, "Fernack was called by some mysterious amateur sleuth who reported that I'd been seen breaking into Linnet's place. There was also some mention of noises like a fight going on inside."

"I didn't phone anybody except the boy I had a date with. I told you I had to break a date."

"You couldn't have called anybody else by mistake, could you? You couldn't have called your treacherous friend to report that I was duly hooked and under control, so the rest of the plot could go into production as scheduled."

She made no reply except to look up at him again. Tears glistened under her long lashes.

"Anyway," he said, "I came to my senses almost in time, left you with the check for a souvenir, and beat it back to Linnet's nearly fast enough to be in at the death. Quite an unpleasant death. They tied a rope around his neck, and his eyeballs were popping and his tongue sticking out. You should have seen him. It would have made you proud of your team."

He stood up and stretched himself a little.

"Well, I was duly arrested by the doughty Inspector Fernack, and it took me until this morning to get out of his clutches. I went to your apartment, and there I met Humpty and Dumpty and a certain piece of luggage. And, of course, we had our reunion. I suppose I should have been able to solve the whole story then, but I guess you still had me slightly dazzled. Because there were two lovely clues, and they were completely contradictory. First, the pyjamas in your closet——"

"You told me——"

"I know. They didn't have initials on them. But I could tell things by just looking at them. . . . And then there was that precious portmanteau of iridium."

"I told you how that got there."

"But you didn't tell me about the initials. You saw how the combination lock worked out when I opened it, didn't you?"

"No."

"Three very important letters, and you didn't notice them," he said reprovingly.

"I wasn't looking."

"You were hanging over my shoulder and watching everything I did. You couldn't have missed seeing them."

"I wasn't looking at that."

"Besides which, I asked you if the initials O. S. M. meant anything to you."

"They don't."

The Saint took out another cigarette and lighted it from the butt of the last.

"M. S. O.," he said, "in reverse. A subtle touch. But nothing to make a reasonably bright guy rupture a brain cell. In other words, our dear mutual friend."

There was a silence.

The Saint wandered towards the window. It was getting darker, and the skyscraper silhouettes around them were losing their sharpness against the velvet off-blue of the sky. He stood there for a moment or two, looking out.

"M. S. O.," he repeated. "Milton S. Ourley. So nice and simple. . . . And I still had to put it together. You ought to have saved me all that trouble."

"I told you——"

"I know. You'd tell me when you felt like it. But it's too late for that now. Maybe it was always too late. . . . But there was a time when the suspects were very vague. I even wasted a few minutes suspecting you. Oh, not as an active killer—I couldn't really visualise you garrotting Gabriel with your own strong hands, and besides a police surgeon decided soon afterwards that Gabriel was getting the tourniquet on his tonsils at about the time when you would have been trying to persuade an unfriendly head waiter that it wasn't your fault if your host sneaked out without paying for dinner. And also I'd collided with Cokey in the meantime. But somebody sent Cokey; and somebody sent Varetti—at least, I'm guessing that it was that fugitive from a tango tournament who rescued Cokey after I'd tied him up. It could conceivably have been you who was the master mind; but after some profound meditation I decided you just didn't have that much brain."

Her eyes smouldered like tarpits as she glared at him, and he realised that things happened to her beauty under stress.

He had a fleeting instant of wondering whether it was right for him to destroy so much loveliness piece by piece as he was doing, even to achieve what he had to achieve.

Then he thought about nameless men dying in foxholes or plunging out of the sky in flaming fortresses, and knew that it was still all right.

He said: "Believe it or not, I thought about Titania too. She makes sillier noises than you do, but she's a lot shrewder and tougher. I could see Milton with a mistress as ornamental as you, and I could see him going to all these lengths to get back a little of his own life. But I could just as well see Titania taking the last colossal step to get rid of Milton, whom she hates and despises, and at the same time make herself even richer and stronger than before. But what was wrong with that was that if she'd had the real master-mind cunning she wouldn't have stuck her neck out so far. She wouldn't have been so specific, and she wouldn't have dragged Linnet in. She wouldn't have made it so easy for the suspicion to be transferred to herself. So that was something else that didn't connect. I could see her as a phenomenally vicious and nasty woman with a great hate and jealousy in her complicated brain; but she wasn't subtle enough. . . . All that's just a lot of wordage now, of course, because I know all the answers."

"You're just talking," she said.

His lean face was untouched and impassive.

"I know the answers, and I can practically prove them. The police will put the rest of it together. There's only one person who could have done all these things. Who stole Uttershaw's iridium, and created the shortage at the same time as he set up his own black market with inside information. Who had Gabriel Linnet killed, because I was too damn smart and couldn't keep my stupid mouth shut. Who fixed you up for me, to make sure I wouldn't have an alibi for that murder. Who left that suitcase at your apartment, and who sent Varetti and Walsh with a key to pick it up, and who let them out of your closet a little while ago and sent them off to the Algonquin to pick it up again."

He smiled pleasantly at her, sipping his cigarette again while he measured her for his penultimate thrust.

"And," he said, "I know who's been planning to kill you at any convenient moment now, besides killing me."

He would never have believed that a face like hers could have loooked so bleached and frozen.

"Now I know you must be insane," she breathed.

He shook his head sadly.

"No, dear. Not any more insane than your beloved, who is very sane indeed. Sane enough to know that this is too hot now to take any more chances on you, because you know too much anyhow and you might still change your mind." The Saint's voice was utterly passionless and level, and his mind felt as if it were standing alone in the middle of a great empty hall. "Your life is running out while you're stalling, darling. And it doesn't make a bit of difference, because I did see those pyjamas."

"I wore those pyjamas," she said, "and I think your insinuations——"

"Why not save it? I can see where you might need all those histrionics. You'll need plenty of them for the most dead-pan audience you ever saw—the jury who'll decide whether to give you the electric cure or burden the taxpayers with the cost of your grey uniforms and oatmeal for twenty years. Which will be quite a change from Saks Fifth Avenue and *coq au vin*."

"You——"

"I am no gentleman," said the Saint regretfully. "Because I know that even if you did wear those pyjamas you didn't buy them—at least not for yourself. They would have been too big for you. They might have fitted Titania, but she would never go for any tomboy styles—she would be strictly for lace and chiffon, and lots of it. But they were also very obviously too long for Milton. Which confused me more than somewhat for quite a little while; but eventually it made sense. So the show down is right now, and this is the very last time I can ask you which side you're on."

Her lips were wooden.

"Presently."

He nodded.

"Yes. That's what you said before."

"Then why don't you go away now?"

"Because I want to be finished with this. And I think this is a perfect time to finish."

He moved towards the centre table, to the ashtray which had been his first landmark of all with its litter of crumpled butts. He stirred the mess with his fingers, and picked out one stub to hold up.

His eyes picked her up again like blued points of steel.

"When I came in here," he said, "I happened to notice that there was one cigarette in this ashtray that didn't have any lipstick on it. So I was quite sure that your boy friend was here already, and I've been talking to him as much as to you. Now that you've made your choice, and he's listened so patiently to what I've got on him, we can stop playing hide-and-seek. I'm quite certain that he's just inside the bedroom door, and I think it would be much more sociable if he came out and joined us."

" 'Journeys end in lovers' meeting'," said Allen Uttershaw, in his mild and ingratiating way. "Or would you prefer the other one— 'Journeys end in death'?"

XV

He stepped into the room with a gun held almost diffidently in his hand; but his eyes were much too calm for carelessness, and it was noticeable that his aim appeared to be steady and accurate enough.

"For the moment, the choice seems to be yours," said the Saint placidly.

He stood with his hands raised, and made no movement while Uttershaw circled cautiously around him, came up behind him, and felt over his pockets with unflurried thoroughness.

"You might put down your cigarette," Uttershaw said as he stepped back and circled into view again. "And if it explodes, I assure you I shall not look around."

The Saint smiled as he dabbed at the ashtray.

"So Ricco told you about that one, did he? I imagine he must have been quite pained about being taken in by an old gag like that."

"He did seem to have a grudge against you."

"I'm sure he has a much worse one by now."

"I was wondering about that. How did it happen?"

"I was expecting him. And I'm afraid he loused up the job again. Really, Allen, he did let you down. I bullied and badgered him until he was too bothered to keep two worries bouncing in his head at the same time, and then he dropped a couple of words which were just enough to tell me for sure that you'd be here and what you were planning to do."

Uttershaw smiled and nodded. It was just as though somebody were telling him about a friend of his whose record trout had gotten away because the leader broke.

"I knew I'd been disappointed when you arrived here," he acknowledged. "And I suppose the iridium is still safe in your room."

"Oh, no."

"What did you do with it?"

"It never was in my room. So I hope you won't disturb the atmosphere of my elegant estaminet by sending any more of your messengers after it. You see, after I left Barbara here I went to another luggage store and bought another bag and put the iridium in it, and I filled your bag with an assortment of sporting goods, of suitable weight and, I think, of rather an appropriate shape. Then I left the really valuable bag at a police station on the way home, to be called for later."

"Which police station?" asked Uttershaw; and suddenly his casual mien had vanished.

Now he looked rather like a polished grey vulture, and the transformation was so slight that it was startling.

The Saint shrugged.

"I'm afraid it wouldn't do you much good to know," he said. "I told the local mandarin that they were to be delivered to our pal Inspector Fernack. I mean those two pretty green bottles in the bag. And I'm quite sure they've been moved by now. You might be good enough to take a precinct, but I don't think even you could raise the troops to storm the bastilles you'd have to break into to get that dust back now."

He paused, and asked: "Incidentally, do you think one would have to pay income tax on a reward like your insurance company was offering? Not that tax-paying isn't a pleasure these days, but I have to think of my budget."

"I imagine you would," Uttershaw said judicially, his composure flowing back into him like a returning tide. "Did you make any other arrangements for Varetti and Walsh?"

"Only a welcoming deputation of two of the ugliest cops I've seen in a long life of looking at ugly cops."

Uttershaw's finely modelled face was as soberly thoughtful as if it had been concentrating on an ordinary business problem.

"The first time I met you, I was afraid something like this might happen," he said. "You really have been very clever. . . . Of course, when you walked into the Algonquin with that suitcase I knew you were getting on too well."

"I hoped somebody would think that."

"But I did think I was doing a pretty good job myself."

Simon nodded.

"You were terrific," he said sincerely. "With all the things that must have been skittering about in your mind, it was the coolest job I ever saw. It was quite a bit later when you spoilt it."

"When was that?" asked the other interestedly.

"When you improvised such a wonderful build-up for the Ourleys. It was just a little too pat. It fitted in just a little too neatly. You might have gotten away with just setting the combination on the bag to open at Qurley's initials—did you pick those for final insurance, or just out of your own sense of humour, by the way? . . . It doesn't matter. But you were just a little too coy about telling me that Ourley might have had a cosy corner of his own with somebody like Barbara waiting for him. And you were just a little too circumstantial and detailed about giving me the inside dope on the intricacies of the Ourley ménage. You bore down too hard on being the impeccable I-don't-want-to-say-this-*but* guy. But it couldn't possibly have been quite as good as that unless you'd known just a little too much. . . . All those little things, but what a big difference they make."

Uttershaw grimaced ruefully, the gleaming barrel of his gun still drawing a solid and level line at Simon's middle.

"This is an invaluable education," he remarked. "Please don't stop."

"Even then," said the Saint agreeably, "I had one or two tiny little doubts. But they went away when you were so careful to find out where Milton was, and when he arrived so aptly a few minutes later. I know it was brilliant of you to stop off at the Harvard Club to tell him his wife was having lunch with me, so that you could be sure he'd come bellowing back to make a commotion that would tie me up for long enough for you to get a start on a whole lot of new adjustments. But what you hadn't thought of was that even brilliance can be overdone. You were awfully good, Allen; and if it's any consolation to you, the only mistake you ever made was that you were just too good."

They might have been discussing a routine matter of merchandising policy.

" 'O what a tangled web we weave,' " Uttershaw said philosophically. "I suppose I really shouldn't have gone to the Algonquin at all to-day, but there was nothing about you in the papers in connection with last night's affair, and I had to find out if you were still at large. I happened to be in the neighbourhood, so I stopped in instead of telephoning. It seemed safe enough at the time. But if I'd been in another part of town, I'd have spent a nickel, and I wouldn't have run into you, and mightn't have had half this trouble. As you say, the little things make such a big difference."

"Exactly." In his own strange and equally fantastic way, the Saint was just as interested. He would always be interested, even with death waiting on an unpredictable trigger finger. "You had a beautiful racket, even though it could have looked slightly soiled if you'd considered the people who got hurt in the end. You stole your own property, collected the insurance, and still had the same goods to sell at even more than the legitimate market price. Of course, a few insignificant soldiers might have been blown apart as a derivative result of your business acumen, but soldiers are only hired to get blown apart, aren't they?"

Uttershaw rubbed his chin with a familiar gesture.

"I never really thought about that," he said, rather sublimely.

The Saint's eyes were not even regretful any more.

"But you threw it all away, Allen. And now you're going to have to die just like any other soldier, because you couldn't be satisfied with the dollars you already had in your bank account."

The lean grey man shook his head.

"I don't know about dying," he said. "Perhaps you've made a few miscalculations yourself. I think you're banking rather a lot on the testimony of Varetti and Walsh."

"I think they'll talk."

"I think you're forgetting what a good attorney could do to them on the stand. But I don't even think they will talk. All those things have been tried on them before. And they can't talk, if they want to get off without anything less than life. But they can plead guilty to just trying to rob your room, and get away with that, and wait for me to buy them a parole. Milton doesn't know much, and he wouldn't even dare to say that."

"But you're admitting everything to me."

"Why not? The only people who could make it hard for me are Barbara and yourself. And as you so rightly prophesied, I don't intend to allow either of you to go that far. I hate to do it, but you put me in this position."

"Allen!"

Barbara Sinclair moved towards Uttershaw in a wild kind of rush. She held out her arms as though she expected other arms to receive her; and the Saint's eyes narrowed as he snapshot his distances. But even before he could have stirred, Uttershaw's left hand reached flatly to meet her oncoming face, and sent her spinning back. She landed on the floor, with one hand clinging to an overturned chair.

"Allen," she said again, with a sort of incredulous tonelessness.

"Shut up," Uttershaw said coldly, and the snout of his gun was back on the Saint in the same instant, if it had ever wavered. "Keep still, please," he said; but the Saint had not moved. Uttershaw glanced at the girl again. "Mr. Templar told you all about it," he said. "You should have believed him. But as he seems to have discovered, you don't have enough brains."

The Saint memorised her blanched face with an expression that was too late for sympathy.

"I did tell you," he said.

"Allen—no!"

"Yes, my dear," Uttershaw said. "I'm afraid he was perfectly right."

Simon Templar took a deep breath.

"Speaking of being put in positions," he said clearly, "how will you like your position on the broiler at Sing Sing if you do this?"

"I'm not very worried about that," Uttershaw said with the same unreal removal from emotion. "You see, I was careful enough to take the elevator to two floors above this, and I walked down here. I also found a fine little back stairway, with an openable window that leads out on to a fire escape. Apparently the management of this hotel trusts its guests. So I'll have plenty of time for any other arrangements I may think of to account for what I've been doing during this time. And I shall certainly take your lecture to heart, and try not to be too brilliant. . . . I'm sorry, but it wouldn't be fair to leave you any false hopes."

The Saint looked at him with a face of stone.

Out of the corner of his eye he could see Barbara Sinclair also, still crouched on the floor, speechless and rigid and chalky in a trance of the real horror that she had so immutably refused to see.

But those choices were over now, for her as they were for Uttershaw.

And as they might be over for him, too, if he had been so preoccupied with other excessive cleverness that he had overdone his own, after all.

He said: "This makes quite a curtain."

He turned abruptly on his heel, and walked in an aimless way towards the bookcase.

And thought what an immortal laugh it would be if after so much staging the clock in his mind had never been really right.

And what a picturesque finale it was. . . .

" 'Our death is but a sleep and a forgetting,' " Uttershaw said gently; and the Saint stood still.

"I hope that will make you very happy," he said.

He thought that Inspector Fernack had delayed his entrance to the last possible filament of suspense, doubtless with all conceivable malice aforethought, and then chosen a peculiarly dangerous moment for it. But he admitted to himself that he had helped to ask for that.

And the temptation to repay the performance was almost more than he could resist, but he knew at the same time that that filament was too fragile to risk even with a breath.

He seemed to have no emotional feeling at all; but he had his own quality of mercy that was apart from all the other things.

As the door burst open, and Fernack lumbered in, and Uttershaw whirled at the sound, Simon Templar took his gun out of the vase of chrysanthemums and fired as carefully as if he had been on a target range.

XVI

THE Saint said: "No."

"Why?" wheedled Titania Ourley.

"Because you don't have to try to pump me for information like you did at the Algonquin, because I'm not investigating your personal nastiness or your husband's sub-rosa activities. That's been taken over by the—oh, Lord—proper authorities. Because you can read the newspaper for anything it's good for you to know. Because I hate to rumba. And," said the Saint, with dispassionate deliberation, "because you not only look like a cow, but you smell like tuberoses on a fresh grave."

He put the telephone back on its rest and lighted a cigarette, but he had barely brought it alive when the bell rang again.

The operator said: "I have a call from Washington."

"Hamilton," said the telephone, with pleasant precision. "Nice work, Simon."

"Thank you," said the Saint.

"I just wish that one of these days you'd bring 'em back alive. There is such a thing as good propaganda, if you don't know it."

The Saint hitched himself more comfortably on to his bed, and adjusted his bathrobe over his long legs. His mind was clouded with many memories, and yet the core of it was clear and sure and without remorse.

"Uttershaw wasn't such a bad fellow, in his own way," he said. "I guess my hand must have slipped. But if he had any time to think, I think he would have liked that."

The telephone played with its own static.

"What happens with Ourley?" it asked after a while.

"I just did a little more for him," said the Saint. "You could never hang anything on him in a court of law so far as this case is concerned; but he still has Titania, and I've come to the conclusion that as a life sentence she's even worse than Alcatraz. And with the encouragement I gave her a few minutes ago, she should be even better company than she was before."

"That Sinclair girl ought to get about ten years, with Fernack's testimony of what he heard from outside the door before he broke in," said the telephone callously. "She's a good-looking number, though, isn't she? What happened to you? Are you slipping?"

"Maybe I am."

"Well . . . Whenever you're ready, there is something else I'd like to talk to you about."

The Saint laughed a little, and it was silent and all the way inside himself, and deep and unimportant and nothing that could be talked about ever.

"I'll catch a plane this afternoon and meet you at the Carlton for dinner. I was just wondering what I could find to do."

He lay on the bed for a little while longer after he had hung up, smoking his cigarettes and thinking about several things or perhaps not anything much. But he kept remembering a girl with hair that had been stroked by midnight, and eyes that were all darkness, and lips that were like orchid petals. And that was no damn good at all.

He got up and began to pack.

PART II

THE SIZZLING SABOTEUR

I

SIMON TEMPLAR had met a lot of unusual obstructions on the highway in the course of a long and varied career of eccentric travelling. They had ranged from migrant sheep to diamond necklaces, from circus parades to damsels in distress; and he had acquired a tolerant feeling towards most of them—particularly the damsels in distress. But a partly incinerated tree, he felt, was carrying originality a little far. He thought that the Texas Highway Department should at least have been able to eliminate such exotic hazards as that.

Especially since there were no local trees in sight to account for it, so that somebody must have taken considerable trouble to import it. The surrounding country was flat, marshy, and reedy; and the sourish salty smell of the sea was a slight stench in the nostrils. The road was a gravelled affair with a high crown, possibly for drainage, and not any too wide although comparatively smooth. It wound and snaked along through alternating patches of sand and reeds like an attenuated sea serpent which had crawled out of Galveston Bay to sun itself on that desolate stretch of beach, so that Simon had seen the log a longish while before he was obliged to brake his car on account of it.

The car was a nice shiny black sedan of the 1942 or B.F. (Before Freezing) vintage; but it was no more incongruous on this ribbon of road than its driver. However, Simon Templar was noted for doing incongruous things. En route to Galveston via Texas City on Highway 146, he hadn't even reached Texas City. Somehow, back where the highway forked left from the Southern Pacific right-of-way, Simon had taken an even lefter turn which now had him heading southward along a most erratic observation tour of the Gulf coastline. A long way from the metropolitan crowding of New York, where he had recently wound up a job—or even of St. Louis, where he had been even more recently. Now his only company was the purring motor and an occasional raucous gull that flapped or soared above the marshland on predatory business of its own. Which didn't necessarily mean that that business was any less predatory than that of Simon Templar, who under his more publicised nickname of The Saint had once left sundry police departments and local underworlds

equally flatfooted in the face of new and unchallenged records of
predatoriality—if this chronicler may inflict such a word on the
long-suffering Messieurs Funk, Wagnalls, and Webster. The most
immediately noticeable difference between the Saint and the seagull
was the seagull's protective parosmia, or perversion of the sense of
smell. . . .

Yet the sun was still three hours high, and it was still twenty miles
to Galveston unless the cartographer who had concocted the Saint's
road map was trying in his small way to cheer the discouraged
pilgrim.

And there was the smouldering blackened log laid almost squarely
across the middle of the road, as if some diehard vigilante had made
it his business to see that no case-hardened voyager rushed through
the scenery without a pause in which its deeper fascinations might
have a chance to make their due impression on the soul.

Simon considered his own problem with clear blue eyes as the
sedan came to a stop.

The road was too narrow for him to drive around the log; and in
view of the tyre rationing situation it was out of the question to try
and drive over it. Which meant that somebody had to get out and
move it. Which meant that the Saint had to move it himself.

Simon Templar said a few casual things about greenhorns who
mislaid such sizeable chunks of their camp fires; but at the same
time his eyes were glancing left and right with the endless alertness
hardening in their sapphire calm, and his tanned face setting into
the bronze fighting mask to which little things like that could in-
stantly reduce it.

He knew from all the pitiless years behind him how easily this
could be an effective ambush. When he got out to move the
smouldering log, it would be a simple job for a couple of hirelings
of the ungodly to attack him. A certain Mr. Matson, for instance,
might have been capable of setting such a trap—if Mr. Matson had
known that Simon Templar was the Saint, and was on his way to
interview Mr. Matson in Galveston, and if Mr. Matson had had the
prophetic ability to foretell that Simon Templar was going to take
this coastal road. But since Simon himself hadn't known it until
about half an hour ago, it appeared that this hypothesis would have
credited Mr. Matson with a slightly fantastic grade of clairvoyance.

The Saint stared at the log with all these things in his mind; and
while he was doing it he discovered for the first time in his life the
real validity of a much handled popular phrase.

Because he sat there and literally felt his blood run cold.

Because the log moved.

Not in the way that any ordinary log would have moved, in a sort of solid rolling way. This log was flexible, and the branches stirred independently like limbs.

Simon Templar had an instant of incredulous horror and sheer disbelief. But even while he groped back into the past for any commonplace explanation of such a defection of his senses, he knew thta he was wasting his time. Because he had positively seen what he had seen, and that was the end of it.

Or the beginning.

Very quietly, when there was no reason to be quiet, he snapped open the door of the car and slid his seventy-four inches of whipcord muscles out on to the road. Four of his quick light strides took him to the side of the huge ember in the highway. And then he had no more doubt.

He said, involuntarily: "My God . . ."

For the ember was not a tree. It was human.

It had been a man.

Instead of a six-foot log of driftwood, the smouldering obstacle had been a man.

And the crowning horror was yet to come. For at the sound of the Saint's voice, the blackened log moved again feebly and emitted a faint groan.

Simon turned back to his car, and was back again in another moment with his light top-coat and a whisky flask. He wrapped the coat around the piece of human charcoal to smother any remaining fire, and gently raised the singed black head to hold his flask to the cracked lips.

A spasm of pain contorted the man, and his face worked through a horrible crispness.

"Blue . . . Goose . . ." The voice came in a parched whisper. "Mavis . . . contact . . . Olga—Ivan—Ivanovitch . . ."

Simon glanced around the deserted landscape, and had never felt so helpless. It was obviously impossible for him to move that sickening relic of a human being, or to render any useful first aid.

Even if any aid, first or last, would have made any difference.

"Can you hold it until I get some help—an ambulance?" he said. "I'll hurry. Can you hear me?"

The burned man rallied slightly.

"No use," he breathed. "I'm goner . . . Poured—gasoline—on me . . . Set fire . . ."

"Who did?" Simon insisted. "What happened?"

"Three men . . . Met last night—in bar . . . Blatt . . . Weinbach . . . And Maris . . . going to party—at Olga's . . ."

"Where?"

"Don't know . . ."

"What's your name? Who are you?"

"Henry—Stephens," croaked the dying man. "Ostrich skin leather case—in gladstone lining . . . Get case—and send . . . send . . ."

His voice trailed off into an almost inaudible rasp that was whisked away along with his spirit on the wings of the wind that swept across the flats. Henry Stephens was dead, mercifully for him, leaving Simon Templar with a handful of unexplained names and words and a decided mess.

"And damn it," said the Saint unreasonably, to no better audience than the circling gulls, "why do people like you have to read that kind of mystery story? Couldn't one of you wait to die, just one, until after you'd finished saying what you were trying to get out?"

He knew what was the matter with him, but he said it just the same. It helped him to get back into the shell which too many episodes like that had helped to build around him.

And then he lighted a cigarette and wondered sanely what he should do.

Any further identification of Henry Stephens was impossible. His hair was all burned off, his hands were barbecued from trying to beat out the flames of his own pyre, and the few remnants of his clothes were charred to him in a hideous smelting. Simon debated whether to take the body with him or leave it where it was. He glanced at his watch and surveyed the lonely country about him. There was still no living person in sight, although in the distance he could see a couple of summer shacks and the indications of a town beyond.

Simon moved the body gently to one side of the road, re-entered his car, and drove carefully around it. Then his foot grew heavy on the accelerator until the side road eventually merged with the main highway and took him on to Virginia Point.

It was inevitable that the Saint's irregular past should have given him some fundamental hesitations about going out of his way to make contact with the Law, and on top of that he had projects for his equally unpredictable future which argued almost as strongly against inviting complications and delays; but he heaved a deep sigh of resignation and found his way to the local police station.

The sergeant in charge, who was sticking his tongue out over a crossword puzzle in a prehistoric and dog-eared magazine, listened bug-eyed to the report of his find, and promptly telephoned the police across the Causeway in Galveston proper.

"I'll have to ask you to stay here until the Homicide Squad and the ambulance comes over to pick up the corpse," he said as he hung up.

"Why?" Simon asked wearily. "Don't you think they'll bring enough men to lift him? I've got business in Galveston."

The sergeant looked apologetic.

"It's—it's a matter of law, Mr.—er——"

"Templar," supplied the Saint. "Simon Templar."

This apparently meant no more to the local authority than John Smith or Leslie Charteris. He excavated a sheet of paper and began to construct a report along the lines which he had probably memorised in his youth, which had been a long time ago.

"You're from where, Mr. Temple?" he asked, lifting his head.

"Tem-*plar*," Simon corrected him, with his hopes beginning to rise again. "I just came from St. Louis, Missouri."

The sergeant wrote this down, spelling everything carefully.

"You got any identification papers on you?"

"What for?" Simon inquired. "It's the corpse you're going to have to identify, not me. I know who I am."

"I reckon so; but we don't," the other rejoined stolidly. "Now if you'll just oblige me by answering my questions— "

Simon sighed again, and reached for his wallet.

"I'm afraid you're going to be difficult, so help yourself, Lieutenant."

"Sergeant," maintained the other, calmly squinting at the Saint's draft-cards and driving licences and noting that the general descriptions fitted the man in front of him.

He was about to hand the wallet back without more than glancing into the compartment comfortably filled with green frogskins of the realm quaintly known as folding money when his eye was caught by the design stamped on the outside of the leather where a monogram might ordinarily have been. It was nothing but a line drawing of a skeletal figure with a cipher for a head and an elliptical halo floating above it. The pose of the figure was jaunty, with a subtle impudence that amounted almost to arrogance.

The sergeant examined it puzzledly.

"What's this?"

"I'm a doodler," Simon explained gravely. "That is my pet design for telephone booths, linen tablecloths, and ladies' underwear."

"I see," said the sergeant quite blankly, returning the wallet. "Now if you'll just sit down over there, Mr. Templar, the Galveston police will be here directly. It's only a couple of miles across the Causeway, and you can lead the way to the spot."

"Aren't you going to call out the posse to chase the murderers?" Simon suggested. "If they brought a horse for me, I could save some of my gas ration."

"You got something there," said the sergeant woodenly. "I'll call the sheriff's office while we're waitin'."

Simon Templar groaned inwardly, and saw it all closing around him again, the fantastic destiny which seemed to have ordained that nothing lawless should ever happen anywhere and let him pass by like any other peaceful citizen.

He fished out another cigarette while the second call was being made, and finally said: "I'm beginning to hope that by the time you get out there the seagulls will have beaten you to it and there won't be any body."

"There'll be one if you saw one," opined the sergeant confidently. "Nobody'll likely come along that beach road again to-day. Too early in the season for picnics, and a bad day for fishin'."

"I trust your deductive genius is on the beam, Captain, but at least two other parties have been on that road to-day already—the victim and the murderers."

"Sergeant," grunted the other. "And I don't know how you come to be on that road yet."

Simon shrugged, and spread his hands slightly to indicate that under the laws of mathematical probability the point was unanswerable. Silence fell as the conversation languished.

Presently there was a noise of cars arriving, and instalments of the Law filtered into the house. The sergeant put down his crossword puzzle and stood up to do the honours.

"Hi, Bill. . . . Howdy, Lieutenant Kinglake. . . . 'Lo, Yard. . . . Hiyah, Dr. Quantry. . . . This is the man who reported that burned corpse. His name is Templar and he's a doodler."

Simon kept his face perfectly solemn as he weighed the men who were taking charge of the case.

Lieutenant Kinglake was a husky teak-skinned individual with gimlet grey eyes and a mouth like a thin slash above a battleship prow of jaw. He looked as if he worked hard and fast and would want to hit things that tried to slow him up. Yard, his assistant, was a lumbering impression from a familiar mould, in plain clothes that could have done nicely with a little dusting and pressing. Dr. Quantry, the coroner, looked like Dr. Quantry, the coroner. Bill, who wore a leather wind-breaker with a dusty sheriff's badge pinned on it, was middle-aged and heavy, with a brick-red face and a moustache like an untrimmed hedge. He had faintly popped light-blue eyes with a vague lack of focus, as if he was unused to seeing anything nearer than the horizon: he moved slowly and spoke even slower when he spoke at all.

It didn't take Kinglake more than a minute to assimilate all the information that the sergeant had gathered, and to examine Simon's identification papers. He stopped over the line drawing which reminded him of the figures of boxers which he used to draw in the margins of successive pages of his Fiske's history and riffle to simulate a sparring match.

"Doodler?" he said in a sharp voice. "I——" He broke off as his eyes widened and then narrowed. "I've seen this picture before. Simon Templar, eh? Are you the Saint?"

"I bow to your fund of miscellaneous information," Simon responded courteously.

"Meaning?"

"That I am known in certain strata of society, and to a goodly number of the carriage trade, by that cognomen."

"Ah." Detective Yard spoke with an air of discovery. "A funny man."

"The Saint, eh?" rumbled the sheriff's deputy, with a certain deliberate awe. "Gee, he's the Saint."

"He said he was a doodler," persisted the sergeant.

Dr. Quantry consulted a gold watch in exactly the way that Dr. Quantry would have consulted a gold watch, and said: "Gentlemen, how about getting on?"

Lieutenant Kinglake held the Saint's eyes for another moment with his hard stare, and gave back the wallet.

"Right," he snapped. "Cut out the eight-cylinder words, Mr. Templar, and lead us to the body. You can leave your car here and ride with us. Yard, tell the ambulance driver to follow us. Come on."

Simon turned back to the sergeant as the party trooped out.

"By the way," he said, "the word for 'hole in the ground' is w-e-l-l, not what you have. Good-bye, Inspector."

He climbed into the seat beside Kinglake, reflecting that there was nothing much you could do when Fate was running a private feud against you, and that he must be a congenital idiot to have ever expected that his business in Galveston would be allowed to proceed as smoothly as it should have for anyone else. He got a very meagre satisfaction out of rehearsing some of the things he would have to say to a certain Mr. Hamilton in Washington about that.

II

THE mortal remains, as our school of journalism taught us not to call them, of Mr. Henry Stephens lay precisely where Simon had left them, proving that the sergeant at Virginia Point had been right in one contention and no one had come along that road in the meantime.

Lieutenant Kinglake and the coroner squatted beside the body and made a superficial examination. Detective Yard took his cue to demonstrate that he was something more than window-dressing. He began searching the area close to the body, and then thoroughly quartered the surrounding acre in ever-widening circles like a dutiful mastiff. Slow and apparently awkward, perhaps a little on the dull side, he was meticulous and painstaking. Bill the deputy sheriff found a convenient horizon and gazed at it in profound meditation.

Simon Templar stood patiently by while it went on. He didn't want to interfere any more than he had already; and for all his irrespressible devilment he never made the mistake of underestimating the Law, or of baiting its minions without provocation or good purpose.

Dr. Quantry eventually straightened up and wiped his hands on his handkerchief.

"Death by carbonisation," he announced. "Gasoline apparently. It's a miracle that he was able to speak at all, if this is how Mr. Templar found him. . . . Autopsy as a matter of course. Give you a full report later."

The hard-eyed Lieutenant nodded and got to his feet, holding out the Saint's top-coat.

"This is yours, Templar?"

"Thanks."

Dr. Quantry beckoned to the ambulance crew.

"Remove," he ordered briskly. "Morgue."

Kinglake made his own inspection of the crown of the road where Simon showed him he had first seen the body.

"He didn't do all that burning here—the surface is hardly scorched," he concluded, and turned to wait for the approach of his assistant.

Detective Yard carried some souvenirs carefully in his handkerchief. They consisted of a partly burned crumple of newspaper, and an ordinary match folder bearing the name of the 606 Club in Chicago. Kinglake looked at the exhibits without touching them.

"Galveston paper," he said; and then: "When were you last in Chicago, Templar?"

"A few days ago."

"Ever been to the 606 Club?"

"As a matter of fact, I have," said the Saint coolly. "I'm making a survey of the United States on the subject of stage and floor-show nudity in the principal cities in relation to the per capita circulation of the *Atlantic Monthly*. It's a fascinating study."

Lieutenant Kinglake was unruffled.

"What's the story, Yard?"

"There's a spot about twenty yards in off the Gulf side of the road where the reeds are all trampled down and burned. Can't tell how many men made the tracks, and they're all scuffed up by the deceased having crawled back over them. Looks as if a couple of men might have taken the deceased in there, and one of them could have poured gas or oil over him while the other lit the paper to set fire to him so as not to have to get so close like he would've had to with a match. Then they scrammed; but there ain't any distinguishable tyre marks. Victim must have staggered around, trying to beat out the flames with his hands, and found his way back to the road where he collapsed."

It was a pretty shrewd reconstruction, as Simon recognised with respect; and it only left out one small thing.

"What about the bottle or container which held the gasoline?" he inquired.

"Maybe we'll find that in your car," Yard retorted with heavy hostility. "You were at this club in Chicago where the matches came from——"

"The dear old match folder clue," said the Saint sadly. "Detective Manual, chapter two, paragraph three."

The deputy sheriff removed his eyes wistfully from the horizon, cleared his throat, and said weightily: "It ain't so funny, pardner. You're tied up closer'n anybody with this business."

"We'll check the newspaper and the match book for fingerprints," Kinglake said shortly. "But don't let's go off at half cock. Look."

He reached into his own pocket and brought out three match folders. One carried the advertisement of a Galveston pool hall, one spoke glowingly of the virtues of Tums, and the other carried the imprint of the Florentine Gardens in Hollywood.

"See?" he commented. "Where did I get this Florentine Gardens thing? I've never been to Hollywood. Advertising matches are shipped all around the country nowadays. This is as good a clue as saying that the other book proves I must have a bad stomach. Let's go back and get Templar's statement."

"Just so I get to Galveston before I'm too old to care," said the Saint agreeably.

But inwardly he took a new measure of the Lieutenant. Kinglake might be a rough man in a hurry, but he didn't jump to conclusions. He would be tough to change once he had reached a conclusion, but he would have done plenty of work on that conclusion before he reached it.

So the Saint kept a tight rein on his more wicked impulses, and submitted patiently and politely to the tedious routine of making his statement while it was taken down in laboured long-hand by Detective Yard and Bill the deputy simultaneously. Then there were a few ordinary questions and answers on it to be added, and after a long time it was over.

"Okay, Bill," Kinglake said at last, getting up as if he was no less glad than the Saint to be through with the ordeal. "We'll keep in touch. Templar, I'll ride back to Galveston in your car, if you don't mind."

"Fine," said the Saint equably. "You can show me the way."

But he knew very well that there would be more to it than that; and his premonition was vindicated a few seconds after they got under way.

"Now," Kinglake said, slouching down in the seat beside him and biting off the end of a villainous-looking stogie, "we can have a private little chat on the way in."

"Good," said the Saint. "Tell me about your museums and local monuments."

"And I don't mean that," Kinglake said.

Simon put a cigarette in his mouth and pressed the lighter on the dashboard and surrendered to the continuation of Fate.

"But I'm damned if I know," he said, "why the hell you should be so concerned. Brother Stephens wasn't cremated within the city limits."

"There's bound to be a hook-up with something inside the city, and we work with the Sheriff and he works with us. I'm trying to save myself some time."

"On the job of checking up on me?"

"Maybe."

"Then why not let Yard worry about it? I'm sure he'd love to pin something on me."

"Yeah," Kinglake assented between puffs of smoke. "He could

get on your nerves at times, but don't let him fool you. He's a first-rate detective. Good enough for the work we do here."

"I haven't the slightest doubt of it," Simon assured him. "But I've told you everything I know, and every word of it happens to be true. However, I don't expect that to stop you trying to prove I did it. So get started. This is your inspiration."

Kinglake still didn't start fighting.

"I know that your story checks as far as it goes," he said. "I smelt the liquor on that dead guy's mouth, and I saw your coat. I'm not believing that you'd waste good whisky and ruin a good coat just to build up a story—yet. But I do want to know what your business is in Galveston."

The Saint had expected this.

"I told you," he replied blandly. "I'm making this survey of American night life. Would you like to give me the low-down on the standards of undress in your parish?"

"Want to play hard to handle, eh?"

"Not particularly. I just want to keep a few remnants of my private life."

Kinglake bit down on his cigar and stared impartially at the Saint's tranquil profile.

After a little while he said: "From what I remember reading, your private life is always turning into a public problem. So that's why I'm talking to you. As far as I know, you aren't wanted anywhere right now, and there aren't any charges out against you. I've also heard a lot of officers here and there leading with their chins by thinking too fast as soon as they saw you. I'm not figuring on making myself another of 'em. Your story sounds straight so far, or it would if anybody else told it. It's too bad your reputation would make anybody look twice when you tell it. But okay. Until there's evidence against you, you're in the clear. So I'm just telling you. While you're in Galveston, you stay in line. I don't want your kind of trouble in my town."

"And I hope you won't have it," said the Saint soberly. "And I can tell you for my part that there won't be any trouble that someone else doesn't ask for."

There was a prolonged and unproductive reticence, during which Simon devoted himself wholeheartedly to digesting the scenic features of the approach over the channel of water known as West Bay which separates the island of Galveston from the mainland.

"The Oleander City," he murmured dreamily, to relieve the awkward silence. "The old stamping grounds of Jean Lafitte. A shrine that every conscientious freebooter ought to visit. . . . Would you like me to give you a brief and somewhat garbled résumé of the history of Galveston, Lieutenant?"

"No," Kinglake said candidly. "The current history of the town is enough to keep me busy. Turn at the next light."

Simon drove him to Headquarters, and lighted another cigarette while the Lieutenant gathered his rather ungainly legs together and disembarked.

"The inquest will probably be to-morrow," he said practically. "Where are you staying?"

"The Alamo House."

Kinglake gave him directions.

"Don't leave town till I'm through with you," he said. "And don't forget what I told you. That's all."

He turned dourly away; and Simon Templar drove on to register faithfully and with no deception at the Alamo House.

The coloured bell-hop who showed him to his room was no more than naturally amazed at being tipped with a five-dollar bill for the toil of carrying one light suitcase. But the Saint had not finished with him then.

"George," he said, "I presume you are an expert crap shooter?"

"Yassah," answered the startled negro, grinning. "My name is Po't Arthur Jones, sah."

"Congratulations. I'm sure that Port Arthur is proud of you. But the point is, you should be more or less familiar with the Galveston police force—know most of them by sight, I mean."

"Well, sah, I—er—yassah."

"Then I must tell you a secret. Lieutenant Kinglake and some of his pals are investigating me for membership in a private club that they have. I expect some of them to be nosing around to find out if I'm respectable enough to associate with them. Don't misunderstand me. If they ask you any questions, you must always tell them the truth. Never lie to detectives, Po't Arthur, because it makes them so bad tempered. But just point them out to me quietly and tell me who they are, so I can say hullo to them when we meet. And every time you do that, I'll be good for another fin."

The negro scratched his head, and then grinned again.

"Don't reckon they's no harm in that, Mistah Templah. That Mistah Kinglake sho' is a hard man. They ain't a single killin' he don't solve here in Galveston. He . . . Say!" The big brown eyes rolled. "How come you know 'bout Mistah Kinglake?"

"We had a mutual interest in what is known as a *corpus delicti*," said the Saint solemnly, "but I sold him my share. He's now checking the bill of sale. Do you follow me?"

"Nawsah," said Port Arthur Jones.

"Then don't let it worry you. Read the morning paper for details. By the way, what is the leading newspaper here?"

"The *Times-Tribune*, sah. They put out a mawnin' an' evenin' paper both."

"They must be as busy as bees," said the Saint. "Now don't forget our agreement. Five bucks per cop, delivered on the hoof."

"Yassah, an' thank yuh, sah."

The Saint grinned in his turn, and went to the bathroom to wash and change his shirt.

It was much later than he had meant to begin his real errand in Galveston; but he had nothing else to do there, and he didn't know enough about the entertainment potentialities of the town to be tempted by other attractions. It was most inconsiderate of Lieutenant Kinglake, he thought, to have refused to take his question seriously and enlighten him. . . . But besides that, he knew that his unfortunate discovery of the expiring Mr. Henry Stephens meant that he couldn't look forward to following his own trail much farther in the obscurity which he would have chosen. It looked like nothing but cogent common sense to do what he could with the brief anonymity he could look forward to.

Thus it happened that after a couple of grilled sandwiches in the hotel coffee shop he set out to stroll back down into the business district with the air of a tourist who had nowhere to go and all night to get there.

And thus his stroll brought him to the Ascot Hotel just a few blocks from the waterfront. The Ascot was strictly a business man's bunk-house, the kind of place where only the much-maligned couriers of commerce roost briefly on their missions of peculiar promotion.

Simon entered the small lobby and approached the desk. The plaque above the desk said, without cracking a smile: "Clerk on duty: MR. WIMBLETHORPE." Simon Templar, not to be outdone in facial restraint, said without smiling either: "Mr. Wimblethorpe. I'm looking for a Mr. Matson of St. Louis."

"Yes, sir," said the clerk. "Mr. Matson was staying here, but——"

"My name," said the Saint, "is Sebastian Tombs. I'm a mining engineer from west Texas, and I have just located the richest deposit of bubble gum in the state. I wanted to tell Mr. Matson about it."

"I was trying to tell you," said the clerk, "that Mr. Matson has checked out."

"Oh," said the Saint, a bit blankly. "Well, could you give me his forwarding address?"

The clerk shuffled through his card file.

"Mr. Matson didn't leave an address. A friend of his came in at five o'clock and paid his bill and took his luggage away for him."

Simon stared at him with an odd sort of frown that didn't even see the man in front of him. For the Saint happened to know that Mr. Matson was waiting for a passport from Washington, in order to take ship to foreign parts, and that the passport had not yet come through. Wherefore it seemed strange for Mr. Matson to have left no forwarding address—unless he had suddenly changed his mind about the attractions of foreign travel.

"Who was this friend?" Simon inquired.

"I don't know, Mr. Tombs. If you could stop by or call up in the morning you might be able to find out from Mr. Baker, the day clerk."

"Could you tell me where Mr. Baker lives? I might catch him at home to-night."

Mr. Wimblethorpe was a little hesitant, but he wrote his fellow employee's address on a slip of paper. While he was doing it, the Saint leaned on the desk and half turned to give the lobby a lazy but comprehensive reconnaissance. As he had more or less expected, he discovered a large man in baggy clothes taking inadequate cover behind a potted palm.

"Thank you, Mr. Wimblethorpe," he said as he took the slip. "And now there's just one thing. In another minute, a Mr. Yard of the police department will be yelling at you to tell him what I was talking to you about. Don't hesitate to confide in him. And if he seems worried about losing me, tell him he'll find me at Mr. Baker's."

He turned and sauntered leisurely away, leaving the bewildered man gaping after him.

He picked up a taxi at the next corner and gave the day clerk's address, and settled back with a cigarette without even bothering to look back and see how the pursuit was doing. There were too many more important things annoying him. A curious presentiment was trying to take shape behind his mind, and he wasn't going to like any part of it.

Mr. Baker happened to be at home, and recalled the incident without difficulty.

"He said that Mr. Matson had decided to move in with him, but he'd had a few too many, so his friend came to fetch his things for him."

"Didn't you think that was a bit funny?"

"Well, yes; but people are always doing funny things. We had a

snuff manufacturer once who insisted on filling his room with parrots because he said the old buccaneers always had parrots, and
Lafitte used to headquarter here. Then there was the music teacher
from Idaho who——"

"About Mr. Matson," Simon interrupted—"what was his friend's
name?"

"I'm not sure. I think it was something like Black, but I didn't
pay much attention. I knew it was all right, because I'd seen him
with Mr. Matson before."

"Can you describe him?"

"Yes. Tall and thin, with sort of grey-blond hair cut very
short——"

"And a military bearing and a sabre scar on the left cheek?"

"I didn't notice that," Baker said seriously. "Mr. Matson made a
lot of friends while he was at the hotel. He was always out for a
good time, wanting to find girls and drinking a lot. . . . I hope there
isn't any trouble, is there?"

"I hope not. But this guy Black didn't say where Matson was
going to move in with him?"

"No. He said Mr. Matson would probably stop in and leave his
next address when he sobered up." Baker looked at him anxiously.
"Do you have some business connection with Mr. Matson, Mr.
ah——"

"Titwillow," said the Saint. "Sullivan Titwillow. Yes, Mr. Matson and I are partners in an illicit diamond buying syndicate in
Rhodesia. I hope I haven't kept you up. . . . Oh, and by the way.
Don't jump into bed as soon as I go, because you'll have at least one
other caller to-night. His name is Yard, and he is the Law in Galveston. Please be nice to him, because I think his feet hurt."

He left the baffled day clerk on the front stoop and returned to
the cab which he had kept waiting.

He was whistling a little tune to himself as he got in, but his
gaiety was only in the performance. The presentiment in his mind
was growing more solid in spite of anything he could do. And he
knew that he was only trying to stave it off. He knew that whatever
happened, Fate had taken the play away from him.

"My name, if anybody should ask you," he said to his driver, "is
Sugarman Treacle. I am a Canadian in the lumber business. I have
sold myself on the job of investigating public vehicles with a view
to equipping them with soft pine blocks and coil springs as a sub-
stitute for rubber during the present tyre shortage. Please feel quite
free to discuss my project with any rival researchers who want to
talk it over with you."

"Okay, Colonel," said the cabby affably. "Where to now?"

And then the Saint's presentiment was much too firmly material-ised to be brushed off. It was something too outrageously coinci-dental to have been intelligently calculated, and at the same time so absurdly obvious that its only concealment had been that it had been too close to see.

The Saint said: "Do you know a joint called the Blue Goose?"

"Yeah," said the other briefly. "You wanna go there?"

"I think so."

"I can get you in. But after that you're on your own."

Simon raised one eybrow a millimetre, but he made no comment. He said: "Do you think you could shake off anybody who might be following us before we get there? My wife has been kind of inquisi-tive lately, and I'm not asking for trouble."

"I getcha, pal," said the driver sympathetically, and swung his wheel.

The Blue Goose had a sign outside and several cars parked in front; but the door was locked, and the chauffeur had to hammer on it to produce a scrap of face at a barred judas window. There was a line of muttered introduction, and then the door opened. It was all very reminiscent of Prohibition, and in fact it was much the same thing, for the state of Texas was still working on the package store system and hadn't legalised any open bars.

"There y' are, doc," said the cabby. "An' take it easy."

Simon paid his fare and added a generous tip, and went in.

It was apparent as soon as he was inside that at least the adjective in the name was justified. The decorator who had dreamed up the trimmings must have been hipped on Gershwin. Everything was done in a bluish motif—walls and tablecloths and glass and chairs. There was the inevitable from hunger orchestra, with too much brass and a blue tempo, and the inevitable tray-sized dance floor where the inevitable mixture of sailors, soldiers, salesmen, and stews were putting their work in with the inevitable assortment of wild kids who had drunk too much and wise women who hadn't drunk enough. Even the lighting scheme was dim and blue.

The only thing that wasn't clear from the entrance was whether the customer got goosed, or was merely a goose to be there.

Simon crossed to the bar and ordered a Scotch and water, saving himself the trouble of ordering Peter Dawson, which would have been no different anyway in spite of the label on the bottle. He got it with plenty of water in a shimmed glass, and saved his breath on that subject also.

He said to the bartender: "Throgmorton——"

"Call me Joe," said the bartender automatically.

He was a big blond man with big shoulders and a slight paunch, with a square face that smiled quickly and never looked as if the smile went very far inside.

"Joe," said the Saint, "do you know a gal here by the name of Olga Ivanovitch?"

The man paused only infinitesimally in his mopping.

At the Saint's side, a voice with strange intonations in it said: "My name is Olga Ivanovitch."

Simon turned and looked at her.

She sat alone, as certain other women did there, with a pale drink in front of her. He hadn't paid any attention to her when he chose his stool, but he did now. Because she had a real beauty that was the last thing he had expected there—in spite of the traditional requirements of a well-cast mystery.

Beauty of a stately kind that had no connection with the common charms of the other temptations there. A face as pale and aristocratic as that of a grand duchess, but with the more earthy touches of broad forehead and wide cheekbones that betrayed the Slav. Blonde hair as lustrous as frozen honey, braided severely around her head in a coiffure that would have been murder to any less classic bone structure. Green eyes that matched her deep-cut green gown. By her birth certificate she might have been any age; but by the calendars of a different chronology she had been old long ago—or ageless.

"Why were you looking for me?" she asked in that voice of unfamiliar harmonies.

The bartender had moved down the counter and was busy with other ministrations.

"I wanted to know," said the Saint steadily, "what you can tell me about a character called Henry Stephen Matson—possibly known to you as Henry Stephens."

III

HE had to admire the way she handled the mask of her face, even with the underlying configuration to help her.

"But why should you ask me?" she protested, with seductive bewilderment.

The Saint put one elbow on the bar and pillowed his chin on the hand attached to it.

"Darling," he said, with every kind of friendliness and good humour and amiable sophistication, "you are an exceedingly beautiful creature. You've probably been told that at least once before, if not ten times an evening. You are now hearing it again—but this time from a connoisseur. Nevertheless, ready as I am to swoon before you, the few fragments of sense that I have left will not let me go along with the gag of treating you as an *ingénue*."

She laughed; and it was something that he registered in her favour, if only because she was probably the only woman in the place who could have unravelled his phraseology enough to know whether to laugh or not.

She said: "Then I won't do?"

"You'll do perfectly," he assured her, "if you'll just take my word for it that I'm strictly in favour of women who are old enough to have had a little experience—and young enough to be interested in a little more. But they also have to be old enough to look at an old tired monument like me and know when I don't want to sit up all night arguing about storks."

It was a delight to watch the play of her shoulders and neckline.

"You're priceless. . . . Would you buy me a drink?"

"I'd love to. I expect to buy the whole joint, a small hunk at a time. If I have a drink too, it should be worth two tables and a dozen chairs."

He signalled the square-faced bartender.

"And a cigarette?" she said.

He took one out of his pack.

"You've got quite a sense of humour, Mr.——"

"Simon Templar," he said quietly, while the bartender was turning away to select a bottle.

Her perfectly pencilled eyebrows rose in perfectly controlled surprise.

"Simon Templar?" she repeated accurately. "Then you must be—— Here, let me show you."

She reached away to remove a newspaper from under the nose of a recuperating Rotarian on the other side of her. After a moment's search, she re-folded it at an inside page and spread it in front of the Saint.

Simon saw at a glance that it was the early morning edition of the *Times-Tribune*, and read the item with professional appraisal.

It was not by any means the kind of publicity that he was accustomed to, having been condensed into four paragraphs of a middle column that was overshadowed on one side by the latest pronunciamento of the latest union megaphone, and on the other by a woman in Des Moines who had given birth to triplets in a freight elevator. But it did state quite barrenly that an unidentified burned body had been found on the shore road east of Virginia Point by "Simon Temple, a travelling salesman from Chicago." The police, as usual, had several clues, and were expected to solve the mystery shortly.

That was all; and the Saint wondered why there was no mention of the name that the dying man had given him, or his gasped reference to the Blue Goose, and why Lieutenant Kinglake had been so loth to give out with any leads on the night life of Galveston. Perhaps Kinglake hadn't taken the Saint's question seriously at all. . . .

Simon turned his blue steel eyes back to Olga Ivanovitch again, and gave her a light for her cigarette. Once more he was aware of her statuesque perfection—and perfect untrustworthiness.

He lifted his newly delivered dilution of anonymous alcohol.

"Yes," he acknowledged modestly, "I am the travelling salesman. But you aren't the farmer's daughter."

"No," she answered without smiling. "My name is Ivanovitch."

"Which means, in Russian, exactly what 'Johnson' would mean here."

"But it's my name."

"And so is 'Templar' mine. But it says 'Temple' in the paper, and yet you placed me at once."

"For that matter," she said, "why did you ask me about—Henry?"

"Because, my sweet, if you'd like the item for your memoirs, your name was on dear Henry's lips just before he passed away."

She shuddered, and closed her eyes for a moment.

"It must have been a gruesome experience for you."

"How did you guess?" he inquired ironically, but she either didn't feel the irony or chose to ignore it.

"If he was still alive when you found him. . . . Did he say anything else?"

The Saint smiled with a soft edge of mockery.

"Yes, he said other things. But why should you be so interested?"

"But naturally, because I knew him. He was to have come to my house for cocktails this afternoon."

"Was he really?" said the Saint gently. "You know, I can think of one man in this town who'd be quite excited to hear that."

Her dark gaze was full of innocence.

"You mean Lieutenant Kinglake?" she said calmly. "But he has heard it. He's already talked to me to-night."

Simon took a gulp of his drink.

"And that's how you got my name right?"

"Of course. He asked me about you. But I couldn't tell him anything except what I've read in the papers."

Simon didn't take his eyes off her, although it called for a little effort to hold them there. His first reaction was to feel outstandingly foolish, and he hid it behind a coldly unflinching mask. He hadn't held anything back in his statement—he had no reason to—and so there was no reason why Kinglake shouldn't have been there before him. It was his own fault that he had made a slow start; but that was because he hadn't been receptive to a coincidence that was too pat to be plausible.

He couldn't tell whether her green eyes were laughing at him. He knew that he was laughing at himself, but in a way that had dark and unfunny undertones.

"Tovarich," he said frankly, "suppose we let our back hair down. Or are you too steeped in intrigue to play that way?"

"I could try, if I knew what you meant."

"I'm not one of Kinglake's stooges—in fact, the reverse. I just happened to find Henry. He mumbled a few things to me before he died, and naturally I repeated what I could remember. But on account of my evil reputation, which you know about, I end up by qualifying as a potential suspect. So I'd have to be interested, even if I wasn't just curious. Now it's your move."

Olga Ivanovitch eyed him for a long moment, studying his clean-cut devil-may-care face feature by feature.

She said at last: "Are you very tired of being told that you're a frighteningly handsome man?"

"Very," he said. "And so how well did you know Henry?"

She sipped her drink, and made patterns with the wet print of her glass on the bar.

"Not well at all. I work here as a hostess. I met him here like I meet many people. Like I met you to-night. It was only for a few days. We had a lot of drinks and danced sometimes."

"But he was coming to your house."

"Other people come to my house," she said, with a dispassionate directness that disclaimed innuendo and defied interrogation.

The Saint blew a careful smoke-ring to bridge another uncomfortable gap; but this time he bowed to a rare dignity that he had seldom met, and would never have looked for in the Blue Goose.

"Did Henry tell you anything about himself?"

"Nothing much that I can remember. Perhaps I didn't pay enough attention. But men tell you so many things, I think he said he'd been working in a defence plant somewhere—I think it was near St. Louis."

"Did he say anything about where he was going, or what his plans were?"

"He said he was going to work in another plant in Mexico. He said he was waiting for a ship to Tampico or Vera Cruz."

"What sort of people was he with?"

"All sorts of people. He drank a lot, and he was very generous. He was—what do you call it?—a Good Time Charlie."

"He had plenty of moula?"

"Please?"

"Dough. Cabbage. The blue chips."

"Yes, he seemed to have plenty of money. And he bought plenty of drinks, so of course he made many friends."

"Can you remember any particular guy with a name like Black?"

She wrinkled her brow.

"I don't think so."

"Tall and thin, with sort of grey-blond hair cut very short."

"How can I be sure?" she said helplessly. "I see so many people."

The Saint drew a long breath through his cigarette that was not audibly a sigh, but which did him as much good.

He was very humbly baffled. He knew that Olga Ivanovitch had told him almost as little as he had told her; he knew at the same time that she was holding back some of the things she knew, exactly as he was. He knew that she had probably told him precisely as much as she had told Kinglake. But there was nothing that he could do about it. And he guessed that there had been nothing that Kinglake had been able to do about it, either. She had a good straight story in its place, and you couldn't shake it. The only thing a police officer could have done about it was to obscure the issue with some synthetic charges about morals and the illegality of the

Blue Goose, which Kinglake probably wouldn't stoop to even if the political system would have let him.

And yet the Saint knew to his own satisfaction that Olga Ivanovitch was watching and measuring him just as he was watching and measuring her. And if he was tired of being told how fascinating he was, she was indubitably just as tired of hearing about her exotic harmonies of ivory skin and flaxen hair, and the undeniable allure that they connived at. He took stock of the plain pagan perfection of her lip modelling, and could have done without the illegitimate ideas it gave him.

"In that case," he said, "let's have some more coloured water and go on seeing each other."

The small hours of the morning were starting to grow up when he finally admitted that he was licked. By that time he must have bought several gallons of the beige fluid which was sold by the Blue Goose as Scotch, and it had made no more impression on Olga Ivanovitch than it had on himself. He decided that if the late Mr. Matson had cut a wide swathe there, he must have worked diligently over lubricating his mower before he went in. But Olga Ivanovitch had given out nothing more. She had been gay and she had been glowing, and with her poise and intelligence she had really been a lot of fun; but every time the Saint had tried to cast a line into the conversation she had met him with the same willing straightforward gaze and been so genuinely troubled because she could add nothing to what she had already told.

"So," said the Saint, "I'm going to get some sleep."

They were back at the bar, after some time sitting at a table through a floor show of special talent but questionable decorum. Simon called for his check, and decided that by that time he should own everything in the place except possibly the ceiling. But he paid it without argument and added a liberal percentage.

"I'm going to check out, too," Olga said. "Would you give me a lift?"

The square-faced bartender gave them his big quick skin-deep smile.

"Come again, folks," he said, and made it sound almost like a pressing invitation.

"Good night, Joe," said the Saint, and made it sound almost like a promise.

He took the girl out to a taxi that was providentially waiting outside. It was so providential that he was prepared to believe that some less altruistic agency had brought it there; but that detail didn't distress him. If the ungodly wanted to find out what they would have a chance to find out that night, it wouldn't be hard for them to find it out anyway. When he seriously wanted to exercise them, he would do a job on it.

After they had gone a short way, Olga Ivanovitch said very prosaically: "You owe me ten dollars for the evening."

In identically the same prosaic manner, he peeled a ten-dollar bill out of his pocket and handed it to her.

She put it away in her purse.

After a while she said: "I don't know what you're trying to find in Galveston, Saint, but don't find anything you don't want."

"Why should you care?" he inquired mildly.

He had his answer in something yielding and yearning that was suddenly all over him, holding his mouth with lips that fulfilled all the urgent indications that he had been doing his earnest best to ignore.

It was more or less like that until the cab stopped again on Seawall Boulevard.

"Won't you come in for a nightcap?" she said.

Her face was a white blur in the dark, framed in shadow and slashed with crimson.

"Thanks," he said, "but I have to think of my beauty. So do you."

"You won't have to spend any more."

"I'll see you again," he said.

"Are you sure?"

"Quite sure."

"You'll remember the address?"

"Yes."

He took the taxi back to the Alamo House, and found Detective Yard snoring in a leather armchair in the lobby. It grieved him sincerely to have to interrupt such a blissful orchestration; but these were circumstances in which he felt that noblesse obliged.

"Good evening, Brother Yard," he murmured. "Or, if you want to be literal, good morning. And don't tell me your first name is Scotland, because that would be more than I could bear at this moment. . . . I trust you have enjoyed your siesta."

The field representative of the Kinglake Escort Service had a chance to gather his wits together during the speech. He glared at the Saint with the overcooked malignance which was only to have been expected of a man who had been rudely awakened with such a greeting.

"What's your name, anyhow?" he growled indignantly. "Giving your name as Sebastian Tombs at the Ascot! Telling Baker

your name was Sullivan Titwillow! Telling that taxi driver you
was Sugarman Treacle!"

"Oh, you tracked him down, did you?" said the Saint interestedly.
"So by this time you know that I've been to the Blue Goose. Wait
till you check back there and find that I've been masquerading all
evening as Shirley Temple."

"What," demanded the detective cholerically, "is the idea of all
these names?"

Simon shook a disappointed head at him.

"Tut, Mr. Yard. In fact, a trio of tuts. How can a man with a
name like yours ask such kindergarten questions? Don't all suspicious characters use aliases? Isn't it an inviolable rule on page
thirty-six of the Detective Manual that a fugitive may change his
name but will always stick to his proper initials? I was merely
following the regulations to make things easy for you. I could just
as well have told any of these people that my name was Mont-
gomery Balmworth Wobblehouse, and loused the hell out of things.
The trouble is, you don't appreciate me."

Detective Yard explained in a few vivid phrases just how much
he appreciated Simon Templar.

"Thank you," said the Saint gratefully. "And now if you'd like
to rest for a while, you can go back to sleep. Or go home to your
wife, if she's attractive enough. I promise you that I'm going to bed
now and stay there for several hours. And if it'll help you at all,
I'll phone you before I go out again."

He stepped into the elevator and departed towards his floor with
the depressing conviction that he had added one more notch to his
record of failing to Win Friends and Influence Policemen. More
practically, he knew that his visit to the Blue Goose was now certain
to be misinterpreted.

He consulted the mirror in the elevator about wiping lipstick off
his mouth, and hoped that Detective Yard had had as much fun
out of noting it as he himself had had out of acquiring it.

IV

In spite of the lateness of his bedtime, the Saint was up reasonably early the next morning. He was expecting to be officially annoyed before noon, and he preferred to get some breakfast under his belt first.

Port Arthur Jones met him as he stepped out of the elevator. "Mawnin', Mistah Templah, sah. Ah been waitin' for you. One of them gennelmen you was askin' about is sittin' in the co'nah of the lobby."

"I know," said the Saint. "His name is Yard. He's worried about me."

The bell-boy's grin shrank in from between his ears so abruptly that Simon was sorry for him.

He said. "Never mind, Po't Arthur. Here's five dollars anyway. Keep up the counter-espionage."

The negro beamed again.

"Yassah, thank you, sah. And there was something else— ."

"What?"

"Another gennelman was nosin' around this mawnin', askin' questions about you. He didn't give no name, and Ah never saw him befo'."

"Was he tall and thin, with grey-blond hair cut very short?"

"Nawsah. He was kinda short and fat, and he had a red face and red hair and pale grey eyes. Ah dunno nothin' 'bout him, but he wasn't no Galveston policeman."

"Po't Arthur," said the Saint, "you have exceeded my fondest hopes. Here is another V for Victory. Carry on."

He went into the coffee shop and ordered tomato juice and ham and eggs. His mind revolved ineffectually while he fortified himself with them.

The late Mr. Matson had considerately bequeathed him three names, beside Olga Ivanovitch. Blatt, Weinbach, Maris. Blatt, who sounded like Black, was probably the tall grey-blond one who had been seen at the Ascot. The guy with the red face and red hair was one of the other two. So there was still one without any kind of identification. But even that made very little difference. There was no other detail in their pictures—no links, no attachments, no place to begin looking for them. Unless it was the Blue Goose. But unless they were very stupid or very well covered, they wouldn't be going back there.

He certainly had something on his hands, and all he could do was to wait for something to lead at him.

It did, while he was smoking a cigarette, and stretching out his coffee. It looked just like Detective Yard, in a different suit that needed pressing just as badly as the last one.

"If you've finished," Yard said heavily, standing over him, "Lieutenant Kinglake would like to see you at Headquarters."

"That's fine," said the Saint. "I was only waiting for you to issue the invitation, so I could get a ride in a police car or make you pay for the taxi."

They travelled together in an uncongenial aloofness which the Saint's efforts at light badinage did nothing to alleviate.

The atmosphere at Headquarters was very similar; but the Saint continued to hand it to Kinglake for a restraint which he hadn't anticipated from a man with that air of nervous impatience. The Lieutenant looked just as tough and irascible, but he didn't rant and roar.

He left the official authority behind him make the noise for him, and said with impeccable control: "I hear you were getting around quite a bit last night."

"I tried to," said the Saint amiably. "After all, you remember that survey I told you about. If the Blue Goose meant things to you, you should have tipped me off. You could have saved me a lot of dollars and a slight hangover."

"I didn't think it was any of your business," Kinglake said. "And I still want to know why it was."

"Just curiosity," said the Saint. "In spite of anything you may have read, it isn't every day that I pick up a lump of talking charcoal on the highway. So when it says things to me, I can't just forget them."

"And you didn't forget Ivanovitch, either."

"Of course not. She was mentioned too. I'm sure I told you."

"According to Yard, you came home last night with lipstick on you."

"Some people are born gossips. But I think he's just jealous."

Lieutenant Kinglake picked up a pencil from his desk and fondled it as if the idea of breaking it in half intrigued him. Perhaps as an act of symbolism. But he still didn't raise his voice.

"I'm told," he said, "that you asked a lot of questions about this Henry Stephens—only you knew that his name was Matson. And you were asking about him all over town under that name. Now you can explain that to me, or you can take your chance as a material witness."

Simon rounded a cigarette with his forefingers and thumbs.

"You want to ask me questions. Do you mind if I ask a couple? For my own satisfaction. Being as I am curious."

Kinglake's chilled gimlet eyes took another exploratory twist into him.

"What are they?"

"What did Quantry get out of his autopsy?"

"No traces of poison or violence—nothing that came through the fire, anyway. The guy burned to death."

"What about the newspapers and the matches?"

"Just a piece of a local paper, which anybody could have bought or picked up. No fingerprints."

"And where did you get the idea that I was a salesman?"

"I didn't give out anything about you. If some reporter got that idea, he got it. I'm not paid to be your press agent." Kinglake was at the full extension of his precarious control. "Now you answer my question before we go any further."

The Saint lighted his cigarette and used it to mark off a paragraph.

"The deceased's name," he said, "was Henry Stephen Matson. Until recently, he was a foreman at the Quenco plant near St. Louis. You may remember that Hobart Quennel got into a lot of trouble a while ago, on account of some fancy finagling with synthetic rubber—and mostly because of me. But that hasn't anything to do with it. The Quenco plants are now being run by the Government, and the one outside St. Louis is now making a lot of soups that go bang and annoy the enemy. Matson pulled out a while ago, and came here. He used his real name at the Ascot, because he'd applied for a passport to Mexico and he wanted to get it. But in his social life he called himself Henry Stephens, because he didn't want to die."

"How do you know all this?" Kinglake rapped at him. "And why didn't you——"

"I didn't tell you yesterday, because I didn't know," said the Saint tiredly. "The thing I found on the road said it was Henry Stephens, and it was all too obvious to bother me. So I was too smart to be sensible. It wasn't until I started hunting for Matson that it dawned on me that coincidences are still possible."

"Well, why were you hunting for Matson?"

The Saint pondered about that one.

"Because," he said, "a Kiwanis convention just picked him as

Mr. Atlantic Monthly of 1944. So in the interests of this survey of mine I wanted to get his reaction to the Galveston standards of strip-teasing. Now, the grade of G-string at the Blue Goose . . ."

There had to be a breaking-point to Detective Yard's self-control, and it was bound to be lower than Kinglake's. Besides, Mr. Yard's feet had endured more.

He leaned down weightily on the Saint's shoulder.

"Listen, funny man," he said unoriginally, "how would you like to get poked right in the kisser?"

"Pipe down," Kinglake snarled; and it was an order.

But he went on glaring at the Saint, and for the first time his nervous impatience seemed to be more nervous than impatient. Simon was irresistibly reminded of his own efforts to cover confusion with a poker pan, only the night before.

"Let me tell you something, Templar," Kinglake said dogmatically. "We've made our own investigations; and no matter what you think, our opinion is that Stephens, or Matson, committed suicide by pouring gasoline on himself and setting himself alight."

It took a great deal to shatter the Saint's composure, but that was great enough. Simon stared at the Lieutenant in a state of sheer incredulity that even took his mind off the crude conventional ponderance of Detective Yard.

"Let me get this straight," he said slowly. "Are you going to try and work off Henry as a suicide?"

Lieutenant Kinglake's hard face, if anything, grew harder.

"On all the evidence, that's what it looks like. And I'm not going to make a monkey out of myself to get you some headlines. I told you, I don't want any trouble in this town."

"So what're you gonna do about it?" demanded Detective Yard, with an aptness which he must have learned from the movies.

Simon didn't even notice him.

"Evidence, my back door," he said derisively. "So this guy who was so reckless with his gas ration was careful enough to swallow the flask he carried it in so it could eventually be recovered for the scrap drive."

"We just didn't happen to find the container yesterday. But if we search again, we may find it."

"Probably the coke bottle that Scotland Yard takes out with him to keep his brain watered."

"One more crack like that outa you," Yard said truculently, "an' I'll——"

"You might just tell me this, Kinglake," said the Saint bitingly. "Is this your idea of a brilliant trick to trap the killers, or are you just a hick cop, after all? The only thing you've left out is the standard suicide note. Or have you got that up your sleeve too?"

The Lieutenant's thin lips tightened, and his battleship jaw stuck out another half inch. He had all the chip-on-the-shoulder characteristics of a man in the wrong who wouldn't admit it while there was a punch left in him; yet he met the Saint's half jeering and half furious gaze so steadily as to almost stare Simon out of countenance.

"Get this, Templar," Kinglake said coldly. "We think Stephens committed suicide——"

"In the most painful way he could think of——"

"He must have been nuts. But I've met nuts before."

"And even while he was dying he tried to make up a story——"

"He was out of his mind. He must have been, after a burning like that. You haven't been burned yet, so you use your head. And if you want to keep your nose clean, you will forget the whole thing —or you may find yourself with your can in the can. Do I make myself clear?"

The Saint met his eyes lengthily.

"If you were rolled flat, you could rent yourself out as a window," he said. "Instead of which, you have the colossal crust to sit there and spew that pap at me even after I've told you that I know more about Matson than you did."

"Yes," was all Kinglake replied.

"You aren't even going to make an issue out of the Blue Goose and my going there."

"No," Kinglake said curtly.

For once in his life, Simon Templar was frankly flabbergasted. He searched the shreds of his brain for a better word, and couldn't find one. Theories whirled through his head; but they were too fast and fantastic to be co-ordinated while he had to think on his feet.

Which was where he was thinking, since Kinglake's impenetrable stonewall had brought him up there, shrugging off Detective Yard's clumsily physical obstruction as if it had been a feather which had accidentally drifted down on to him out of a cloud.

"I've met an astonishing variety of cops in my time," he remarked absorbently; "but you, chum, are an entirely new species. You don't even attempt to give me the guileless run-around or the genteel brushoff. . . . Have you said your last word on the subject?"

"Yes," snapped the Lieutenant. "Now will you kindly get the hell out of here and go on with the survey you were talking about?"

"I will," retorted the Saint. "And don't blame me if you find G-men in your G-string."

He stalked out of there with another unique feeling that was the precise antithesis of the sensation he had had when a certain leg moved on the shore road. His blood had run cold then. Now it was boiling.

He had had to cope with local politics and obstruction before, in different guises and for different reasons. But this game was something else. And in that swift invigorating anger, the Saint knew just what he was going to do about it.

Kinglake had taunted him about publicity. Well, the Saint didn't need to hire any press agents. . . . He had seen himself waiting and hoping for a lead; but he could always ask for one. He had used newspapers before, in sundry ways, when he wanted to lead with his chin and invite the ungodly to step up and introduce themselves while they looked at it.

Almost literally without looking to left or right, he followed Centre Street towards the waterfront on the north or channel side of the city. He walked into the building that housed the *Times-Tribune*, and worked his way doggedly through the trained interference until he stood in front of the city editor's desk.

"My name is Simon Templar," he said for about the fourteenth time. "If you spelt me right, I'd be the travelling salesman who found that blotched biscuit on the shore road yesterday. I want to cover that case for you; and all I want out of you is a by-line."

The editor scrutinised him quite clinically.

"Our police reporter must have messed up his spelling," he said. "It's funny—the name started to ring a bell when I read it. . . . So you're the Saint. But what are you selling?"

"I'm selling you your lead story for the afternoon edition," said the Saint. "I may be nuts, but I'm still news. Now shall we play gin rummy, or will you lend me a typewwriter and stop the press?"

V

IF only to be different in one more way from most typical men of action, Simon Templar was perfectly happy with words and paper. He could play just as fluently on the legitimate or L. C. Smith form of typewriter as he could on the well-known Thompson variety, and he handled both of them in much the same way. The keys rattled under his fingers like gunfire, and his choice of words had the impact of bullets. He worked at white heat, while his wrath still had all its initial impetus.

He told his own full story of the finding of "Henry Stephens," and every word that the dying man had said, together with a general summary of the other facts as he knew them, in a fusillade of hard-boiled sinewy prose that would have qualified him for a job on the toughest tabloid in the country. Then he squared off to a fresh sheet of paper and went into his second movement. He wrote:

It now grieves me to have to break it to all you nice people that these sensitive nostrils, which long ago became extraordinarily appreciative of certain characteristic smells, have caught wind of the grand inspiration that this guy committed suicide, which Lieutenant Kinglake was feeling out this morning.

Now I am in here with quite a different story, and it has got to be known that Bulldog Templar does not brush off that easy.

I am remembering a legend, true or not, that once when S. S. Van Dine happened to be close to the scene of another murder, it was suggested by some newspaper that he might co-operate with the gendarmerie and help run the villain to earth in the best Philo Vance manner; whereupon Mr. Van Dine placed himself in the centre of four wheels and trod on the loud pedal so rapidly that his shadow had to be sent after him by express.

We Templars are made of sterner stuff. Just give us a chance to stick our neck out, and a giraffe is not even in our league.

So we are going to sign our name to this invitation to all of you voting citizens to take a good long look at the suicidal Mr. Stephens.

He was, we observe, the stern and melancholy type which can get along without life anyway. He proved that by the way he spent his last days here, drinking all night in speakeasies and dancing with the girls. He didn't go much for fun of any kind, which is said to soften people up. He was strictly an ascetic; and when he knocked himself off he was still going to be tough. He wouldn't jump out of a window, or take an overdose of sleeping tablets, or put a gun in his ear and listen to see if it was loaded. He deliberately picked the most painful way that a man can die.

He figured he had some suffering coming to him. After all, he wasn't broke, for instance, which has been known to make some people so unhappy that they have let air into their tonsils with a sharp knife. He seems to have had plenty of spending money. So he was going to have his hard times on his deathbed instead of before.

He even went twenty miles out of town to do it, walking all the way, since the street cars don't go there, so that he'd have lots of time to look forward to it and enjoy the prospect.

He was a consistent guy, too. He didn't mean to be selfish about his suffering. He wanted somebody else to have some of it, too. So after he'd taken his gasoline shower, and before he struck the match, he carefully chewed up and ate the bottle he'd brought it in, so that Lieutenant Kinglake could have something to worry about. Not knowing, of course, that Lieutenant Kinglake wouldn't worry about a little thing like that at all.

It always gives us Templars a great respect for the benignness of Providence to observe how frequently a hard-pressed police department, facing a nervous breakdown before the task of breaking a really difficult case, has been saved in the nick of time by discovering that there never was a murder after all. It makes us feel pretty good to think that cops are practically people, and God takes care of them as well as Pearl White.

The Saint was beginning to enjoy himself by then. He lighted a cigarette and gazed at the ceiling for a while, balancing his ideas for the finale. Then he went on when he was ready.

But let's pretend that we don't have the clear and penetrating vision of Lieutenant Kinglake. Let's just pretend that we are too dumb to believe that a man in the dying agonies of third degree burns cooked up that wonderful story about three men who did it to him, just because he was too modest to want to take the credit. Let's pretend there might really have been three other men.

Men with names. Blatt, Weinbach, Maris. A nice trio of Herrenvolk.

Then we might go along with the gag and say, suppose Henry Stephen Matson was a traitor. Suppose he'd gotten into some sabotage organisation, and he'd been given a job to do in this explosives plant in Missouri. Suppose he'd even drawn payment in advance—

just to account for what he was using for dough in Galveston.

Then suppose he welshed on the job—either from an attack of cold feet or a relapse of patriotism. He knew that the heat was on. He couldn't stay in this country, because they might have turned him in to the F.B.I. If they didn't do anything worse. He took it on the lam for here, hoping to get a passport, and hoping he'd shaken off his pals. But they were too good for him. They tracked him down, struck up an acquaintance with him, and gave him what he had coming. In a very nasty way, just to discourage imitators.

That's my fairy-tale. And I like it.

Blatt, Weinbach, Maris. I have a description of two of those men, and I've got my own good ideas about the third. And I am hereby announcing that I shall now have to get them for you myself, since we must not disturb Lieutenant Kinglake in his august meditations.

The city editor read it all through without a change of expression. Then he tapped the last page with his forefinger and said: "It's an ingenious theory, but what's your basis for it?"

"Nothing but logic, which is all you can say for any theory. The facts are there. If you can do better with them, you can join Kinglake's club."

"This last statement of yours, about the three men—is that a fact?"

"Some of it. But the main point of it is that that's what you pay me with. If I can make them believe that I know more than I do, I may scare them into making some serious mistakes. That's why I'm making you a present of all the rest of that luscious literature."

The editor pulled at his under-lip. He was a pear-shaped man with a long forbidding face that never smiled even when his eyes twinkled.

"It's good copy, anyway, so I'll print it," he said. "But don't blame me if you're the next human torch. Or if Kinglake has you brought in again and beats hell out of you."

"On the contrary, you're my insurance against that," said the Saint. "Going my own way, I might have had a lot more trouble with Kinglake at any moment. Now, he won't dare to do anything funny, because it would look as if he was scared of me."

"Kinglake's a good officer. He wouldn't do a thing like this unless there was a lot of pressure on him."

Simon recalled the Lieutenant's tight-lipped curtness, his harried and almost defensive belligerence.

"Maybe there was," he said. "But whose was it?"

The editor put his fingertips together.

"Galveston," he said, "has what is now called the commission form of government. Commissioner Number One—what other cities would call the mayor—is coming up for re-election soon. He appoints the Chief of Police. The Chief controls such men as Lieutenant Kinglake. Nobody wants any blemish on the record of the police department at this time. I'm quite confident that neither the Commissioner nor the Chief of Police is mixed up in anything crooked. It's just best for everybody concerned to let sleeping dogs —in this case, dead dogs—lie."

"And that is perfectly jake with you."

"The *Times-Tribune*, Mr. Templar, unlike yourself, is not addicted to sticking its neck out. We are not a political organ; and if we did start a crusade, it would not be on the basis of this one sensational but insignificant killing. But we do try to print the whole truth, as you'll see by the fact that I'm ready to use your article."

"Then you still haven't told me where the pressure would come from."

The city editor's long equine face grew even more absorbed in the contemplation of his matched fingers.

"As a stranger in town, Mr. Templar, it may surprise you to know that some of our most influential citizens sometimes go to the Blue Goose for their—er—relaxation. The Blue Goose is one of the leads in this story as you have it. So while none of these people, from the Commissioner down, might want to be a party to hushing up a crime, you can see that they might not be keen on too comprehensive an investigation of the Blue Goose. So that the management of the Blue Goose, which naturally doesn't want the spot involved in a murder mystery, might find a lot of sympathetic ears if they were pointing out the advantages of forgetting the whole thing. I shall not allow you to print that in your next article, but it might help you personally."

"It might," said the Saint. "And thank you."

He spent several hours after that on a conscientious job of verifying his background material that would have amazed some people who thought of him as a sort of intuitive comet, blazing with pyrotechnic violence and brilliance to ends and solutions that were only indicated to him by a guardian angel with a lot of spare time and an incurable weakness for piloting irresponsible characters. His research involved visits to various public places, and ingenuous conversations with a large number of total strangers, each of them a cameo of personality projection that would have left Dale Carnegie egg-bound with awe. But the net yield was negatively and concisely nothing.

The Commissioner appeared to be a bona fide native of Galveston who had made his money in sulphur and still controlled an important business. There seemed to be no particularly musty bones in his family skeleton. He came of Texas stock from away back, and he was set solid with business and family ties.

The Sheriff of the county came out with the same sort of background and clean bill of health. Nobody seemed to know much about the type of deputies in his office, but there had never been any scandal about his administration. He was frankly a member of the same political machine as the Commissioner.

Nor were there any crevices in the armour of the Chief of Police. Kinglake was not too popular, very likely because of his personality; but his record was good. Quantry was negligible.

Which meant that the *Times-Tribune* editor's analysis stood unshaken, and there was no evidence to brand the official eagerness to turn a blind eye on a murder as anything but a local issue of political expediency.

Except for the one thin thread that curled into a question mark and asked who it was at the Blue Goose who had turned the heat on even a complaisant political machine.

Olga Ivanovitch?

The Saint knew she was beautiful, he thought she was clever, and he suspected that she was dangerous. But how clever and how dangerous? He could learn nothing about her that sounded at all important. If she had any political connections, they weren't common gossip. But he knew that she had a definite place in the picture.

He made another call at the Ascot Hotel; but Mr. Baker hadn't remembered any more overnight, and could add nothing to his information about Blatt or Black.

"But I'm sure, Mr. Titwillow, he wasn't a local man. I've been here so long that I think I know all the important people in Galveston by sight."

Blatt, Weinbach, Maris.

The names made no impression on anyone to whom he mentioned them. But he did find some representatives of their clans in the telephone directory, and studiously checked on each of them. Each of them had the kind of unimpeachable clearance that it would have been simply a waste of time to investigate any further.

It was a long and strenuous day, and dusk was creeping over the city as Simon headed back towards the Alamo House. He bought an evening paper and a bottle of Peter Dawson on the way.

The *Times-Tribune* carried his article on the front page, unabridged and unexpurgated, but with a box that gave a brief explanation of the Saint's background for the benefit of the ignorant, and stated that Mr. Templar's theories were his own and did not necessarily represent the editorial opinion of the *Times-Tribune*.

There was special justification for that in a short column which ran alongside his, which reported succinctly that at an inquest held that afternoon the coroner's jury had brought in a verdict of suicide.

Simon Templar crushed the newspaper in his hand with a grip that almost reverted it to its original pulp, and said several things which even our freedom of the Press will not allow us to print.

So Kinglake hadn't backed down. He had gone right out from their interview and helped to railroad that fantastic verdict through. Maybe he had a wife and children and just wanted to go on feeding them; but he had done it.

In his room at the Alamo House, Simon sent for ice and opened his bottle, and tried to simmer down again over a highball.

He only had one other clue to think about, and that was in another snatch of words that the dying man had managed to get out. He could hear them just as clearly now as when they had been dragged hoarsely through the charred, tortured lips.

"*Ostrich-skin—leather case—in gladstone lining . . . Get case—and send . . . send . . .*"

Send where?

And why?

And anyhow, Black or Blatt had the gladstone now.

One of three practical killers, probably strangers to Galveston themselves, possibly from Chicago (he remembered the 606 Club match booklet) who had trailed Matson on their mission of vengeance, carried out the assignment and vanished.

He had another drink, and didn't get any further on that one.

It was later still when the telephone rang.

He had an electric moment as he went to answer it. He knew that the call had to have some bearing on the case, since he had no personal friends in Galveston; but the exquisite suspense was in wondering—who? A soft-pedalling politician? A raging Kinglake? Or the first nibble at his bait?

It was a voice that he knew, even if he had not known it long—a deep musical voice with appealing foreign reflections.

"You aren't only handsome, but you have talent," she said. "Why didn't you tell me you were a writer too?"

"My union doesn't allow it."

"Am I going to see you again? I'd like to very much."

He reached for a cigarette.

"I'm flattered. But I've only just paid one instalment on the Blue Goose."

"I don't have to be there till ten. What are you doing for dinner?"

"Eating with you," he said with abrupt decision. "I'll meet you in the lobby here at eight o'clock."

He hung up, and still wondered which category that belonged in. But anything would be better than waiting in idleness.

He washed and freshened himself and changed his shirt, and went downstairs a little before eight. There was a note in his box when he turned in his key.

"It was delivered by hand just a few minutes ago," said the clerk.

Simon slit open the envelope. The letter inside was written in pencil on a cheap lined paper of an uncommon but typical pattern. There was no address; but Simon knew what that would be even without the clues in the context:

DEAR MR. TEMPLAR,

I just read your piece in the paper, and I can tell you you sure have got it over these dumb bums. I am getting a chap to take this out for me. I can tell you a lot more about this case and I will tell you if you can fix it to talk to me alone. You are right all the way and I can prove it, but I will not talk to anyone except you. After that you can do what you like with what I tell you but I will not give these dumb cops anything.

Yours truly,

NICK VASCHETTI.

Simon looked up from the note because someone was practically leaning on him and breathing in his face.

"Got a love-letter?" asked Detective Yard. "Or is it fan mail?"

Simon put the letter in his pocket.

The detective's face swelled as if he were being strangled.

"Listen, you," he got out. "One of these days——"

"You're going to forget your orders and be unkind to me," said the Saint. "So I'll be kind to you while I can. In a few minutes I'll be going out to dinner. I'll try to pick a restaurant where they'll let you in. And if I start to leave before you've finished, just yell and I'll wait for you."

Simon thought afterwards that it was criminal negligence on his part that he was so seduced by the frustration of Detective Yard that he didn't even notice the thin grey-blond man and the fat red-haired man who occupied chairs in the farther reaches of the lobby. But there was an excuse for him; because while he had heard their names and heard their sketchy descriptions, he had never before laid eyes on Johan Blatt and Fritzie Weinbach.

VI

He went back up to his room and phoned the city desk of the *Times-Tribune*.

"Could you work it for me to have a private chat with a prisoner in the City Gaol?"

"It might be done," said the editor cautiously, "if nobody knew it was you. Why—have you had a bite?"

"I hope so," said the Saint. "The guy's name is Nick Vaschetti." He spelt it out. "He says he won't talk to anybody but me; but maybe the gaol doesn't have to know me. See what you can do, and I'll call you back in about an hour."

He sat on the bed in thought for a minute or two, and then he picked up the telephone again and asked for Washington. He hardly had to wait at all, for although the hotel operator didn't know it the number he asked for was its own automatic priority through all long distance exchanges.

"Hamilton," said the phone. "I hear you're a newspaper man now."

"In self-defence," said the Saint. "If you don't like it, I can pack up. I never asked for this job, anyway."

"I only hope you're getting a good salary to credit against your expense account."

The Saint grinned.

"On the contrary, you'll probably be stuck for my union dues . . . Listen, Ham: I'd rather lay it in your lap, but I think I'd better bother you. These three men——"

"Blatt, Weinbach, and Maris?"

"Your carrier pigeons travel fast."

"They have to. Is there anything else on them?"

Simon gave him the two rough descriptions.

"There's a good chance," he said, "that they may have come on from Chicago. But that's almost a guess. Anyway, try it."

"You never want much, do you?"

"I don't like you to feel left out."

"You're not leaving out the beautiful swooning siren, of course."

"In this case, she's a blonde."

"You must like variety," Hamilton sighed. "How much longer are you expecting to take?"

"Depending on what you can dig up about the Three Neros, and

what breaks to-night," said the Saint, "maybe not long. Don't go
to bed too early, anyhow."

Which left him laughing inwardly at the breath-taking dimen-
sions of his own bravado. And yet it has already been recorded in
many of these chronicles that some of the Saint's tensest climaxes
had often been brewing when these almost prophetic undercurrents
of swashbuckling extravagance danced in his arteries. . . .

Olga Ivanovitch was waiting in the lobby when he came downstairs again.

"I'm sorry," he said. "There was a letter I had to answer."

"*Nitchevo*," she said in her low warm memorable voice. "I was
late myself, and we have plenty of time."

He admitted to himself after he saw her that he had had some
belated misgivings about the rendezvous. The lighting in the lobby
of the Alamo House was a different proposition from the blue dimness of the Blue Goose: she might have looked tired and coarsened,
or she might have been over dressed and over-painted into a cheap
travesty of charm. But she was none of those things. Her skin was
so clear and fresh that she actually looked younger than he remembered her. She wore a long dress; but the *décolletage* was chastely
pinned together, and she wore an inappropriate light camel-hair
polo coat over it that gave her a kind of carelessly apologetic swag-
ger. She looked like a woman that any grown man would be a little
excited to take anywhere.

"I've got a car," he said. "We can take it if you can direct me."

"Let me drive you, and I'll promise you a good dinner."

He let her drive, and sat beside her in alert relaxation. This could
have been the simplest kind of trap; but if it was, it was what he had
asked for, and he was ready for it. He had checked the gun in his
shoulder holster once more before he left his room, and the slim
two-edged knife in the sheath strapped to his right calf was almost
as deadly a weapon in his hands--and even less easy to detect. It
nested down under his sock with hardly a bulge, but it was accessible
from any sitting or reclining position by the most innocent motion
of hitching up his trouser cuff to scratch the side of his knee.

Simon Templar was even inclined to feel cheated when the drive
ended without incident.

She steered him into a darkened bistro near the Gulf shore with
bare wooden booths and marble-topped tables and sawdust on the
floor.

"You have eaten *bouillabaisse* in Marseilles," she said, "and perhaps in New Orleans. Now you will try this, and you will not be too
disappointed."

The place was bleakly bright inside, and it was busy with people who looked ordinary but sober and harmless. Simon decided that it was as safe as anything in his life ever could be to loosen up for the length of dinner.

"What made you call me?" he asked bluntly.

He had always felt her simple candour as the most cryptic of complexities.

"Why shouldn't I?" she returned. "I wanted to see you. And you turn out to be such an unusual kind of travelling salesman."

"There are so few things you can sell these days, a guy has to have a side line."

"You write very cleverly. I enjoyed your story. But when you were asking me questions, you weren't being honest with me."

"I told you everything I could."

"And I still told you everything I knew. Why do you think I was —what do you call it?—holding out on you?"

"I told you everything I knew, tovarich. Even if you did place me for a salesman."

"You didn't ask me about Blatt, Weinbach, and Maris."

"Only about Blatt."

He had to say that, but she could still make him feel wrong. Her air of straightforwardness was so unwavering that it turned the interrogator into the suspect. He had tried every device and approach in a rather fabulous repertoire the night before, and hadn't even scratched the surface of her. He knew exactly why even Lieutenant Kinglake might have left her alone, without any political pressure. Take her into court, and she could have made any public prosecutor feel that he was the prisoner who was being tried. It was the most flawlessly consistent stonewall act that Simon Templar had ever seen.

"You could have asked me about the others," she said. "If I could have told you anything, I would have. I'd like to help you."

"What could you have told me?"

"Nothing."

At least she had told him the truth about the *bouillabaisse*. He gave himself up to that consolation with fearful restraint.

It was half an hour later when he made one more attempt to drag the conversation back from the delightful flights of nothingness into which she was able to lead so adroitly.

"Aside from my beautiful profile and my great literary gifts," he said, "I'd still like to know what made you want to see me again."

"I wanted you to pay for my dinner," she said seriously. "And I do like you—very much."

He remembered the way she had kissed him at her door, and forced himself to consider that if he had gone for that he would probably have been going for something as calculated as her simplicity.

"It couldn't have been, by any chance, because you wanted to find out if I knew any more?"

"But why should I? I am not a detective. Do I keep asking you questions?" She was wide open and disarming. "No, I am just guilty of liking you. If you wanted to tell me things, I would listen. You see, my dear, I have that Russian feeling which you would think stupid or—corny: that a woman should be the slave of a man she admires. I am fascinated by you. So, I must be interested in what you are doing. That is all."

The Saint's teeth gripped together while he smiled.

"Then, sweetheart, you'll be interested to know that I'm going to make an important phone call, if you'll excuse me a minute."

He went to a coin phone at the rear of the restaurant and called the *Times-Tribune* again.

"It's all set," said the flat voice of the city editor. "Any time you want to pick me up."

"I'm just finishing dinner," said the Saint grimly. "If nothing happens on the way, I'll pick you up within thirty minutes."

He went back to the table, and found Olga placidly powdering her perfect nose.

"I hate to break this up," he said, "but I have a short call to make; and I have to deliver you back to the Blue Goose in time to catch the next influx of salesmen."

"Whatever you like," she replied. "I don't have to be exactly on time though, so you do whatever you want to do."

It was impossible to stir her even with virtual insult.

But he drove the Ford himself this time, knowing that it could have seemed a much better moment for ambush than before dinner. Yet even then nothing happened, in such a way that the mere failure of anything to happen was a subtle rebuke in exactly the same key as all her refusals to rise to his varied provocations.

His sleepless sense of direction enabled him to drive without a mistake to the offices of the *Times-Tribune*; and he arrived there with no more alarm than a slight stiffness in muscles which had been poised too long on an uncertain fuse. But then, the egregious efficiency of Detective Yard had still conspired to blind him to the shift of concealing newspapers which had punctuated his exit from the Alamo House.

"I have to complain to my editor about the size of my headlines," he said. "It's a union rule. Do you mind waiting a little while?"

"Of course not," she said with that sublime and demoralising pliability. "Waiting is an old Russian pastime."

Simon went up to the editorial floor, and this time he swept through the interceptor command without interference, powered by the certainty of his route and destination.

The city editor saw him, and took his feet off the desk and crammed a discoloured and shapeless panama on to the small end of his pear-shaped head.

"I'll have to go with you myself," he explained. "Not that I think you'd sell out to the U.P., but it's the only way I could fix it. Let me do the talking, and you can take over when we get your man."

"What's he in for?"

"Passing a rubber cheque at his hotel. I hope you have some idea what strings I had to pull to arrange this for you."

Simon handed him the note that had been delivered to the Alamo House. The editor read it while they waited for the elevator.

"Smuggled out, eh? . . . Well, it might come to something."

"Is there a back alleyway out of the building?"

"When I was a copy boy here, we used to know one. I haven't noticed the building being altered since." The city editor turned his shrewd sphinxlike face towards Simon with only the glitter of his eyes for a clue to his expression. "Are we still expecting something to happen?"

"I hope, yes and no," said the Saint tersely. "I left Olga in my car outside, for a front and a cover. I'm hoping she either fooled herself or she'll fool somebody else."

He knew that he had seldom been so vulnerable, but he never guessed how that flaw in his guard was so mature. He just felt sure that a prisoner in the City Gaol couldn't be the trigger of any of the potential traps that he was waiting to recognise. Provided he took the obvious precautions, like leaving Olga Ivanovitch in his car outside the newspaper building while he slipped out through a back alley . . .

The *Times-Tribune* man's dry bulbous presence was a key that by-passed tired clerks and opened clanging iron doors, and exacted obedience from soured disinterested gaolers, and led them eventually into a small barren and discouraging office room with barred windows where they waited through a short echoing silence until the door opened again to admit Mr. Vaschetti with a turnkey behind him.

The door closed again, leaving the turnkey outside; and Mr.

Vaschetti's darting black eyes switched over the city editor's somnolent self-effacement and made one of their touch landings on the Saint.

"You're Templar," he stated. "But I said this had to be private."

"This is Mr. Beetlespats of the *Times-Tribune*," said the Saint inventively. "He published the article you read, and he organised this meeting. But we can pretend he isn't here. Just tell me what you've got on your mind."

Vaschetti's eyes whirled around the room like small dark bugs exploring the intricacies of a candelabra.

"I can tell you," he said, "you were dead right about Matson. I've been a courier for the Bund for a long time. I took a letter to Matson in St. Louis, and I brought a letter to your Mr. Blatt and other people in Galveston, too."

VII

He was a rather small man, spare and wiry, with the heavy eyebrows and hollow cheeks which so often seem to go together. His hair needed combing and his chin needed scraping. His clothes were neither good nor bad, but they were rumpled and soiled as if they had been slept in, which they doubtless had.

The Saint gave him a cigarette and said: "I don't think there are any dictographs planted here, so just keep talking. What made you write to me?"

"Because I don't like cops. I see where you've made suckers out of the cops plenty of times, and I'd like to see you do it again. Especially to those sons of guns which threw me in here."

"You did pass a bum cheque, didn't you?" Simon mentioned.

"Yeah, but only because I had to, because Blatt didn't come through with my dough and I was broke. I wouldn't have squawked just for that, though. I've taken raps before. I've stood for a lot of things in my time, but I don't want any part of this." Vaschetti puffed at his cigarette shakily, and moved about the room with short jerky strides. "Not murder. No, sir. I don't want to sit in the hot seat, or dance on the end of a rope, or whatever they do to you in this state."

Simon kindled a cigarette for himself, and propped himself on the window sill.

"Why should anyone do things like that to you? Or were you one of the three fire-bugs?"

"No, sir. But that Kinglake might find out any time that I'd seen Blatt and been asking for him at the Blue Goose, and what chance would I have then? I don't want Blatt gunning for me either, and I guess he might be if he thought I might put the finger on him. I'd rather squeal first, and then if they know it's too late to shut my mouth maybe they won't bother with me."

"I see your point," said the Saint thoughtfully. "Suppose you sit down and tell me about your life as a courier."

Vaschetti attempted a laugh that didn't come off, licked his lips nervously, and sat down on a creaky chair.

"I met Fritz Kuhn when I was doing time in Dannemora. We got on pretty well, and he said if I wanted to make some money when I got out I should see him. Well, I did. I got this job carrying packages from place to place."

"How did that work?"

"Well, for instance, I'd have a package to deliver to Mr. Smith at the Station Hotel in Baltimore. I'd go there and ask for him. Maybe he'd be out of town. I'd hang around until he showed up— sometimes I'd have to wait for a week or more. Then I'd give Smith the package; and he'd pay me my dough and my expenses, and maybe give me another package to take to Mr. Robinson, at Mac- farland's Grill in Miami. Any time there wasn't anything more for me, I'd go back to Jersey and start again."

"These Smiths and Robinsons weren't anything to do with the joints you met them in?"

"Mostly not. I'd just ask a bartender if he knew Mr. Smith, and he'd point out Mr. Smith. Or sometimes I'd be hanging around and Mr. Robinson would come in and say he was Robinson and had anyone been asking for him."

"How much did you get for this?"

"Seventy-five a week and all my expenses."

"You got paid by the Smiths and Robinsons as you went along."

"Yeah."

"You knew that this was obviously connected with something illegal."

Vaschetti licked his lips again and nodded.

"Sure, sure. It had to be things they didn't want to send through the mail, or they didn't want to chance having opened by the wrong person."

"You knew it was more than that. You knew it was for the Bund, and so it was probably no good for this country."

"What the hell? I'm an Italian, and I got brothers in Italy. And I never did like the damn British. This was before the war got here. So what?"

"So you still went on after Pearl Harbour."

Vaschetti swallowed, and his eyes took another of those fluttering whirls around the room.

"Yeah, I went on. I was in it then, and it didn't seem to make much difference. Not at first. Besides, I still thought Roosevelt and the Jews were getting us in. I was scared, too. I was scared what the Axis people here might do to me if I tried to quit. But I got a lot more curious."

"So——?"

"So I started opening these packages. I was taking one to Schenec- tady at the time. I steamed it open, and inside there were four smaller envelopes addressed to people in Schenectady. But they had wax seals on them with swastikas and things, and I was afraid it might show if I tried to open them. So I put them back in the big envelope and delivered it like I was told to. Sometimes I had big parcels to carry, but I didn't dare monkey with them. I still had to eat, and I didn't want no trouble either. . . . But then I got more scared of the F.B.I. and what'd happen to me if I got caught. Now there's this murder, and I'm through. I been a crook all my life, but I don't want no federal raps and I don't want to go to the chair."

Simon's sapphire blue eyes studied him dispassionately through a slowly rising veil of smoke. There was nothing much to question or decipher about the psychology of Signor Vaschetti—or not about those facets which held any interest for the Saint. It was really nothing but a microcosmic outline of Signor Mussolini. He was just a small-time goon who had climbed on to a promising band-wagon, and now that the ride ahead looked bumpy he was anxious to climb off.

There could hardly be any doubt that he was telling the truth—he was too plainly preoccupied with the integrity of his own skin to have had much energy to spare on embroidery or invention.

"It's a fine story," said the Saint lackadaisically. "But where does it get us with Matson?"

"Like you wrote in the paper, he must have been paid to do some sabotage. He didn't do it, but he kept the money and took a powder. But you can't run out on that outfit. That's why I'm talking to you. They traced him here and gave him the business."

"That *is* about how I doped it out," Simon said with thistledown satire. "But what are you adding besides the applause?"

"I'm telling you, I took one of those letters to Matson in St. Louis. That proves he was being paid by the Germans, and that proves you're right and Kinglake is a horse's——"

"But you made this delivery in St. Louis. Why are you here in Galveston now?"

Vaschetti sucked on the stub of his cigarette, and dropped it on the floor and trod on it.

"That's on account of Blatt. I came here from El Paso two weeks ago with a package to give to Blatt at the Blue Goose. I didn't know Matson was coming here. I didn't know anything about Matson, except he told me he was working for Quenco. Blatt only paid me up to date and kept me hanging around waiting for some letters he said he'd be sending out. I ran up a pretty big bill at the hotel, and Blatt never came around and I couldn't reach him. That's why I flew the kite."

"Did you meet any of my other friends?"

"I met Weinbach. He's a fat kraut with a red face and red hair and the palest eyes you ever saw."

Simon placed the word-picture alongside the description that Port Arthur Jones had given him of the stranger who had been inquiring about him at the Alamo House, and it matched very well. So that was Weinbach.

And that left Maris, whom nobody seemed to have seen at all.

The Saint went on staring at the twitching representative of the Roman Empire.

"You could have told Kinglake this," he said.

"Yeah. And I'd be here as an accessory to murder, if that sour-pussed bum didn't try to make out I was all three murderers in one. No, sir. It's yours now. Gimme a break, and I'll write it down and sign it. I'm not going to give any of these dumb cops a free promotion. I'd rather you showed 'em up instead. Then I'll feel better about the spot I'm in."

Simon spun out his smoke in a few moments' motionless contemplation.

"If it was some time ago that you met Matson in St. Louis," he said, "how come you connected all this up?"

"I remembered." The other's eyes shifted craftily. "And I got notes. I didn't dare play with those inside envelopes, but I been writing down the names of people. And the places I went to in different cities. A fellow never knows when some things will come in handy. You can have that list, too, if you take care of me, and I don't care what you do with it. None of those bums tried to do anything for me when I got in this jam, so the hell with them."

The Saint barely showed polite interest; yet he felt so close to one of the real things that he had come to Galveston for that he was conscious of rationing his own breathing.

"It's only fair to tell you, Comrade," he said very carefully, "that if you give me any information that seems worth it, I shall have to turn it straight over to the F.B.I."

Vaschetti's face was pale in the clearings between his eyebrows and the stubble on his chin, yet in a foolish way he looked relieved.

"What you do after you've got it is your affair," he said. "Just gimme a couple hundred dollars and a chance to blow this town, and it's all yours."

Simon glanced at the city editor of the *Times-Tribune*, who was reclining in a junk-pile armchair in the corner with his shabby hat tilted over his eyes, who might have been passed over as asleep except that the eyes were visible and open under the stained straw brim. The eyes touched the Saint briefly and brightly, but nothing else in the composition looked alive. The Saint knew that he was still on his own, according to the agreement.

He said: "What hotel were you working on?"

"The Campeche."

"How much for?"

"Fifty bucks. And my bill."

"I'll take care of all that. You can probably be sprung in a couple of hours. Then I'll meet you at the Campeche and give you two hundred bucks for that statement and your list of names. Then I'll give you two hours to start travelling before I break the story. After that, you're on your own."

"You made a deal, mister. And as soon as I get that dough, I'll take my chance on getting out of here or I'll take what's coming to me. I don't want anything except to be all washed up with this."

His cathartic relief or else his blind faith in his ability to elude the seines of the F.B.I. was either way so pathetic that Simon didn't have the heart to freeze him down any more. He hitched himself out of the window frame and opened the office door to call back the gaoler.

The city editor rocked his antique panama back on his head and tried to keep step beside him as they left.

"I suppose," he said, "you want me to take care of everything and get the Campeche to withdraw the complaint."

"I suppose you can do it. You didn't say anything, so there it is."

"I can put a man on it. I'll have him out in a couple of hours, as you said. But don't ask what happens to me for conspiring to suppress evidence, because I don't know."

"We write up the story," said the Saint, "and we hand Kinglake a proof while the presses are rolling. He gets the complete dope, and we get the beat. What could be fairer?"

The city editor continued to look dyspeptic and unhappy with all of his face except his bright eyes.

"Call me at the Alamo House as soon as your stooge has Vaschetti under control," Simon told him. "I've got to take Olga to her treadmill, if she hasn't run out by this time."

But Olga Ivanovitch was still sitting in the Saint's car, to all appearances exactly as he had left her, with her hands folded in her lap and the radio turned on, listening happily to some aspiring and perspiring local comedy programme.

She was able to make him feel wrong again, even like that, because she was so naïvely and incontestably untroubled by any of the things that might have been expected to rasp the edges of deliberate self-control.

"I'm sorry I was so long," he said, with a brusequeness that burred into his voice out of his own bewilderment. "But they've started teaching editors two-syllable words lately, and that means it takes them twice as long to talk back to you."

"I've been enjoying myself," she said; and in her own Slavic and slavish way she was still laughing at him and with him, enjoying the tranquillity of her own uncomplaining acceptance of everything. "Tell me how you talk to editors."

He told her something absurd; and she sat close against him and laughed gaily aloud as he drove towards the Blue Goose. He was very disconcertingly conscious of the supple firmness of her body as she leaned innocently towards him, and the loveliness of her face against its plaque of yellow braided hair; and he had to make himself remember that she was not so young, and she had been around.

He stopped at the Blue Goose, and opened her door for her without leaving the wheel.

"Aren't you coming in?" she asked.

He was lighting a cigarette with the dashboard gadget, not looking at her.

"I'll try to get back before closing time," he said, "and have a nightcap with you. But I've got a small job to do first. I'm a working man—or did you forget?"

She moved, after an instant's silence and stillness; and then he felt his hand brushed away from his mouth with the cigarette still freshly lighted in it, and her mouth was there instead, and this was like the night before only more so. Her arms were locked around his neck, and her face was the ivory blur in front of him, and he remembered that she had been a surprising warm fragrance to him when she did that before, and this was like that again. He had a split second of thinking that this was it, and he had slipped after all, and he couldn't reach his gun or his knife with her kissing him; and his ears were awake for the deafening thunderbolts that always rang down the curtain on careers like his. But there was nothing except her kiss, and her low voice saying, docilely like she said everything: "Be careful, tovarich. Be careful."

"I will be," he said, and put the gears scrupulously together, and had driven quite a fair way before it co-ordinated itself to him that she was still the only named name of the ungodly whom he had met and spoken to, and that there was no reason for her to warn him to be careful unless she knew from the other side that he could be in danger.

He drove cautiously back to the Alamo House, collected his key from the desk, glanced around to make sure that Detective Yard had found a comfortable chair, and went up to his room in search of a refreshing pause beside a cool alcoholic drink.

Specifically, the one person he had most in mind was the venerable Mr. Peter Dawson, a tireless distiller of bagpipe broth who, as we recollect, should have been represented among the Saint's furniture by the best part of a bottle of one of his classic consommés. Simon Templar was definitely not expecting, as an added attraction, the body of Mr. Port Arthur Jones, trussed up and gagged with strips of adhesive tape, and anchored to his bed with hawsers of sash cord, and looking exactly like a new kind of Ethiopian mummy with large rolling eyes; which is precisely what he was.

VIII

SIMON untied him and stripped off the tape. The bell-hop at least was alive, and apparently not even slightly injured, to judge by the ready flow of words that came out of him when his mouth was unwrapped.

"Two men it was, Mistah Templah. One of 'em was that fat man with red hair that Ah done tole you about. Ah'd been off havin' mah supper, and when I come back, there he is in the lobby. He's with another tall thin man, like it might be the other gennelman you was askin' me about. So Ah was goin' to call your room so you could come down and have a look at them, but the clerk tole me you just went out. Then these men started to get in the elevator, and Ah knew there was somethin' wrong, Ah knew they wasn't stayin' here, and with you bein' out Ah just figured they was up to no good. So Ah ran up the stairs, and sho' 'nuff there they were just openin' your doah. So ah ask them what they was doin', and they tried to tell me they was friends of yours. 'You ain't no friends of Mistah Templah's,' Ah says, 'because Mistah Templah done tole me to keep mah eyes open for you.' Then the fat man pulled out a gun and they hustled me in here and tied me up, and then they started searchin' the room. Ah don't think they found what they was huntin' for, because they was awful mad when they went off. But they sho' made a mess of your things."

That statement was somewhat superfluous. Aside from the disorder of the furnishings, which looked as if a cyclone had paused among them, the Saint's suitcase had been emptied on to the floor and everything in it had been tossed around and even taken apart when there was any conceivable point to it.

"Don't let it get you down, Po't Arthur," Simon said cheerfully. "I know they didn't get what they wanted, because I didn't leave anything here that they could possibly want. Unless one of them coveted an electric razor, which it seems he didn't. Just give me a hand with straightening out the wreckage."

He began to repack his suitcase while Port Arthur Jones became efficient about replacing the carpet and rearranging the furniture.

He was puzzled about the entire performance, for he certainly had no precious goods or papers with him; and if he had had any he certainly wouldn't have left them in his room when he went out. The ransacking must have stemmed from his connection with the

Matson murder, but it seemed a long way for the ungodly to have
gone with the mere hope of picking up some incidental information
about him. The only reasonable explanation would be that they
suspected that Matson might have given him something, or told him
where to find something, before he died. But Matson had only muttered about an ostrich-skin case in a gladstone lining; and they had
the gladstone. If they had taken the trouble to collect the gladstone,
hadn't they looked in the lining? Or had they just picked it up
along with other things, in the broad hope of coming across what
they were searching for?

He said: "This happened just after I went out?"

"Yassah. The desk clerk said you hadn't been gone more 'n a few
minutes. He said you went out with a lady."

"What about that Detective Yard?"

"Ah didn't see him, sah. Ah guess most likely he went out when
you did."

It had been a nice job of contrivance anyhow. If the ungodly knew
or assumed that the police were watching Simon Templar, they
could also assume that the police would go out when Simon Templar
went out. So the coast would be relatively clear when they knew he
was going out.

He had been on his guard against uninvited shadows, when it
seemed like a good idea to watch out for uninvited shadows. He
hadn't bothered much about those who stayed behind, because he
hadn't been thinking about anything worth staying behind for. But
they had been.

The three faceless men. Blatt, Weinbach, and Maris. Two of
whom he had only heard described. And Maris, whom nobody
had heard of and nobody had even seen.

But Olga Ivanovitch must have known at least one of them. Or
even more positively, at least one of them must have known her.
They must have sat and looked at each other in the lobby while she
was waiting for him. One way or another, the Saint was being taken
out of the way for a safe period; and some of them had known it
and watched it when he went out. Quite probably, Olga.

Simon's lips hardened momentarily as he finished refolding the
last shirt and laid it on top of the stack in his bag. He turned back
from the job to watch Port Arthur Jones fastidiously fitting a chair
back into the scars which its standard position had printed on the
nap of the carpet. The room looked as tidy again as if nothing had
ever happened there.

"Thanks, chum," said the Saint. "Have we forgotten anything?"

The coloured man scratched his close-cropped head.

"Well, sah, Ah dunno. The Alamo House is a mighty respectable hotel——"

"Will you be in trouble on account of the time you've been shut up in here?"

"Nawsah, Ah can't say that. Ah goes off for mah supper, and then Ah comes back and just stays around as long as there's a chance of earnin' an honest tip. Ah don't clock out at no definite time. But with people breakin' into rooms and pullin' a gun on you and tyin' you up, it seems like the management or the police or somebody oughta know what's goin' on."

He was honestly confused and worried about the whole thing.

Simon took a ten-dollar bill out of his pocket and flattened it between his hands so that the numbers were plainly visible.

"Look," he said, as one man to another, "I don't want any trouble with the hotel. And I don't want any help from the cops. I'd rather take care of these guys myself if I ever catch up with them. Why can't we just pretend that you went home early, and none of this ever happened, except that you did spot two more of those people I asked you about and pointed them out to me; and I'll pay you off on that basis."

The scruples of Mr. Port Arthur Jones were probably no less sincere and confirmed than those of Mr. Henry Morgenthau; but he eyed the dangling sawbuck and was irresistibly swayed by its potentialities in his budget. You could see box cars rolling majestically over the murky tracks of his mind.

"Yassah," he said, beaming. "Ah don't wanna start no trouble. Ah'll just forget it if that's what you say, sah."

Simon watched him stow away the green consolation and close the door contentedly after him.

Then he poured himself the highball which he had come home for in the first place. He was glad that at least his guests hadn't been searching for something that might have been soluble in alcohol.

He was just getting acquainted with the drink when his telephone rang.

"I've taken care of your friend," said the *Times-Tribune*. "He should be back at the Campeche in just a little while. One of the boys is taking care of him."

"Good," said the Saint. "I'll be over there in just a little while too."

"I was able to fix it with the hotel and get to the judge," persisted the voice, rather mournfully. "At this time of night, that's not so easy."

"Congratulations," said the Saint. "You must be *persona* very *grata*."

There was a brief hiatus where the city editor silenced as if he was digging out a new lead.

"I liked the way you talked to that man, Vaschetti," he excavated at length, "and I think I ought to talk to you the same way. I'll hold everything while you bring in your story; but I have to live here, too. So whatever you bring in, I'll have to turn over to the police and the F.B.I."

"I'll give you a personal commendation for your fine public spirit," said the Saint.

He could see the pear-shaped figure with its feet on the desk and the battered hat tilted over the eyes that were the only sparkle in the dried poker face, as if it were sitting directly in front of him.

"You've said things that sounded as if you had a hell of a lot of inside dope on this case," said the city editor finally. "What are you doing in Galveston anyway, and why don't you give me the whole story and earn yourself some real dough?"

"I'll think about it," said the Saint, "after I've talked to Vaschetti again."

He dropped the phone, and tried to resume relations with his highball.

He had absorbed one good solid sip when the bell rang again.

This time it was Washington.

"Hamilton," said the line. "I hope this is an awkward moment."

Simon grinned for his own benefit, and said: "No."

"This is all I've got so far on those names. During Prohibition, there were two trigger men in Milwaukee named Johan Blatt and Fritzie Weinbach. They usually worked together. Racketeers. One or two charges—assault, carrying concealed weapons, and so on. Associated with un-American activities in Chicago just before the War. I can read you their full records, but they just sound like a couple of mercenary hoodlums."

"Don't bother," said the Saint. "What about Maris?"

"Nothing yet. A name doesn't mean anything. Hasn't anyone even seen the colour of his eyes?"

"Nobody ever sees Maris," said the Saint. "They don't notice anything about him at all. But I'll find him before you do. I'm still working. Have some more black coffee and wait up for me."

He pronged the transceiver again, and reached for his glass once more with indomitable determination.

Maris—the man nobody saw. The man who might be much more than the mere trick answer to a riddle that had been posed by the premature cremation of Henry Stephen Matson. The man who might materialise into one of those almost legendary spear-carriers who were primarily responsible for Simon Templar's excursions as a talent scout even to such outposts as Galveston. The man who might be more concerned than anyone about the contents of the ostrich-skin leather case which had consumed Matson's dying breath.

Or about the lists or memory of Nick Vaschetti, a glorified errand-boy with a bad case of fright or fluctuating conscience.

He crumpled out the stub of his cigarette and went downstairs.

Port Arthur Jones, shining like refurbished ebony, intercepted him as he left the elevator.

"Mistah Templah, sah, that Detective Yard just gone home. Another detective took over for him. His name's Mistah Callahan. He's sittin' half behind the second palm across the lobby. A stout gennelman with a bald head in a grey suit——"

Simon slipped another Lincoln label into the bell-boy's pink palm.

"If you keep on like this, Po't Arthur," he said, "you're going to end up a capitalist whether you want to or not."

It was a well indicated move which should have been taken before, to replace the too familiar Mr. Yard with somebody else whom the Saint might not recognise. Simon's only surprise was that it hadn't happened sooner. But presumably the whimsical antics of the Selective Service System had not excluded the Galveston Police Department from the scope of their ruthless raids upon personnel.

That wasn't the Saint's business. But for the most immediate future, at least until he had consummated the Vaschetti diversion, Simon Templar preferred to get along without the politically complicated protection of the Galveston gendarmerie.

Wherefore he shelved Mr. Callahan by the rather kindergarten expedient of climbing very deliberately into his parked car, switching on the lights, fiddling with the starter, and then just as leisurely stepping out of the other door, boarding a passing cab, and going away in it while Mr. Callahan was still glued to the bridge of his municipal sampan and waiting for the Saint's wagon to weigh anchor so that he could pursue it.

Which was an entirely elementary technique, but didn't even begin to tackle the major problem of the Law in Galveston.

What Simon wanted more than anything at that moment was Mr. Vaschetti's autographed statement, and the list of names and addresses which he had promised. Those things, as weapons, would be worth even more to him than the gun that still bulked under his left arm, or the knife which he could feel with every swing of his right leg.

The Campeche Hotel was down on Water Street, and it appeared to be a very popular bivouac, for there was such a large crowd of citizens clustered around the entrance that they obstructed the traffic, and the Saint left his taxi a few doors away and walked into the throng. As he edged his way through them he was conscious of the crunching of broken glass under his feet; but he didn't think much about it until he noticed some of the crowd glancing upwards, and he glanced upwards with them and saw the jagged gaping hole in the shattered marquee overhead. Then with the advantage of his height he looked over a few heads and shoulders and saw the thing that was the nucleus of the assembly. A rather shapeless lump of something in the centre of a clear circle of blood-spattered sidewalk, with one foot sticking out from under a blanket that covered its grosser deformations.

Even then, he knew; but he had to ask.

"What gives?" he said to the nearest bystander.

"Guy just got discouraged," was the laconic answer. "Walked outa his window on the eighth floor. I didn't see him jump, but I saw him light. He came through that marquee like a bomb."

Simon didn't even feel curious about getting the blanket moved for a glimpse of anything identifiable that might have been left as a face. He observed the uniformed patrolman standing rather smug guard over the remains, and said quite coldly: "How long ago did this happen?"

"Only about five minutes ago. They're still waitin' for the ambulance. I was just goin' by on the other side of the street, and I happened to look around——"

The Saint didn't weary his ears with the rest of the anecdote. He was too busy consuming the fact that one more character in that particular episode had elected to go voyaging into the Great Beyond in the middle of another of those unfinished revelations which only the most corny of scenario cookers would have tolerated for a moment. Either he had to take a very dim view of the writing talent in the books of Destiny, or else it would begin to seem that the abrupt transmigration of Nick Vaschetti was just another cog in a divine conspiracy to make life tantalising for Simon Templar.

IX

THE links went clicking through Simon's brain as if they were meshing over the teeth of a perfectly fitted sprocket.

The ungodly had ransacked his room at the Alamo House while they knew he would be out of the way, and had drawn a blank. But they would have had plenty of time to pick him up again, and it would have been childishly simple for them to do it, because they knew he was with Olga Ivanovitch, and the place where she was going to steer him for dinner had been decided in advance. The Saint had been alert for the kind of ambuscade that would have been orchestrated with explosions and flying lead, but not for ordinary trailing, because why should the ungodly trail him when one of them was already with him to note all his movements? He had left Olga Ivanovitch in his car outside the *Times-Tribune* building, as he said, for a front and a cover; it hadn't occurred to him that she might be a front and a cover for others of the ungodly. She sat there covering the front while they took the precaution of covering the other exits. When he came out of the back alley, they followed. When he went to the City Gaol, they remembered Vaschetti and knew that that must have been the man he had gone to see. Therefore one of them had waited for a chance to silence Vaschetti; and when Vaschetti was released and led back to the Campeche, the opportunity had been thrown into their laps. It had been as mechanically simple as that.

And Olga Ivanovitch had done a swell job all the way through. All those items went interlocking through his mind as he stood at the desk inside and faced an assistant manager who was trying somewhat flabbily to look as though he had everything under perfect control.

Simon flipped his lapel in a conventional gesture, but without showing anything, and said aggressively: "Police Department. What room was Vaschetti in?"

"Eight-twelve," said the assistant manager, in the accents of a harassed mortician. "The house detective is up there now. I assure you, we——"

"Who was with him when he jumped?"

"No one that I know of. He was brought in by one of the men from the *Times-Tribune*, who redeemed his cheque. Then the reporter left, and——"

"He didn't have any visitors after that?"

"No, nobody asked for him. I'm sure of that, because I was standing by the desk all the time. I'd just taken the money for his cheque, and told Mr. Vaschetti that we'd like to have his room in the morning, and I was chatting with a friend of mine——"

"Where are the elevators?"

"Over in that corner. I'll be glad to take you up, Mr.——"

"Thanks. I can still push my own buttons," said the Saint brusquely, and headed away in the direction indicated, leaving the assistant manager with only one more truncated sentence in his script.

He had very little time to spare, if any. It could be only a matter of seconds before the accredited constabulary would arrive on the scene, and he wanted to verify what he could before they were in his hair.

He went up and found 812, where the house detective could be seen through the open door, surveying the scene with his hands in his pockets and a dead piece of chewing cigar in the corner of his mouth.

Simon shouldered in with exactly the same authoritative technique and motion of a hand towards the flap of his buttonhole.

"What's the bad news?" he demanded breezily.

The house detective kept his hands in his pockets and made a speech with his shoulders and the protruding cud of his cigar that said as eloquently as anything: "You got eyes, ain'tcha?"

Simon fished out a pack of cigarettes and let his own eyes do the work.

It didn't take more than one wandering glance to rub in the certainty that he was still running behind schedule. Although not exactly a shambles, the room showed all the signs of a sound working over. The bed was torn apart, and the mattress had been slit open in several places, as had the upholstery of the single armchair. The closet door stood wide, and the few garments inside had been ripped to pieces and tossed on the floor. Every drawer of the dresser had been pulled out, and its contents dumped and pawed over on the carpet. The spectacle was reminiscent of the Saint's own room at the Alamo House—with trimmings. He wouldn't have wasted a second on any searching of his own. The search had already been made, by experts.

So someone already had Vaschetti's diary; or else no one was likely to come across it there.

The Saint scraped a match with his thumbnail and let the picture shroud itself in a blue haze.

"What about the men who were up here with Vaschetti?" he asked.

"I never saw anyone with him," responded the house dick promptly.

He had a broad beam and an advancing stomach, so that he had some of the air of a frog standing upright.

"I didn't get your name," he said. "Mine's Rowden."

"You didn't hear any commotion up here, Rowden?"

"I didn't hear a thing. Not until the crash Vaschetti made going through the marquee. I didn't even know he was back out of gaol until just now. Where's Kinglake? He usually comes out on death cases."

"He'll be along," Simon promised, with conviction.

There was one fascinating detail to consider, Simon observed as he narrowed down the broad outlines of the scene. In the middle of the strewn junk on the floor there was an almost new gladstone bag, empty and open, lying on its side. He moved to examine it more closely.

"Anybody else been up here?" he inquired.

"Nope. You're the first. Funny I don't know you. I thought I'd met all the plain-clothes men in Galveston."

"Maybe you have," said the Saint encouragingly.

Indubitably that was the gladstone which he had heard about. It even had the initials "H.S.M." gold-stamped beside the handle. But if there had ever been an ostrich-skin leather case in the lining, it wasn't there any more. The lining had been slashed to ribbons, and you could have found a long-lost pin in it.

It was a picturesque mystery-museum piece, but that was all. The current questions were, how had it come to rest there, and why? Johan Blatt had removed it from the Ascot; and by no stretch of imagination could his description have been confused with that of the latest failure in the field of empirical levitation. Vaschetti and Blatt were even more different than chalk and cheese: they didn't even begin with the same letter.

Simon Templar pondered that intensely for a time, while the house detective teetered batrachianly on his heels and gnawed on his bowsprit of cigar. The house detective, Simon thought, would surely have been a great help in detecting a house. Aside from that, he was evidently content to let nature and the Police Department take their course. He would have made Dick Tracey break out in a rectangular rash.

They remained in that sterile atmosphere until the sound of voices and footsteps in the corridor, swelling rapidly louder, presaged the advent of Lieutenant Kinglake and his cohorts.

"Ah," said Detective Yard wisely, as he sighted the Saint.

Kinglake didn't even take time out to show surprise. He turned savagely on the frog-shaped house detective.

"How in hell did this bird get in here?"

"I came in under my own power," Simon intervened. "I was thinking of moving, and I wanted to see what the rooms were like. Don't blame Rowden. He was trying to tell me about the wooden mattresses. If you look again, you'll see where he was even ripping them open to show me the teak linings."

The Lieutenant was not amused. He had never looked like a man who was amused very often, and this was manifestly not one of his nights to relax in a bubble bath of wit and badinage.

He glared at the Saint balefully and said: "All right, Templar. You asked for it. I told you what was going to happen to you if you didn't keep your nose clean in this town. Well, this is it. I'm holding you as a material witness in the death of Nick Vaschetti."

The arch of the Saint's brows was angelic.

"As a witness of what, Comrade? The guy bumped himself off, didn't he? He stepped out of a window and left off his parachute. He'd heard about the Galveston Police, and he knew that the most precious legacy he could bequeath them was an absolutely watertight suicide. What makes you leave your ever-loving wife warming her own nightie so you can come here and improve your blood pressure?"

Kinglake's mouth became a thin slit in his face, and his neck reddened up to his ears; but he kept his temper miraculously. The blood stayed out of his slate-grey stare.

"Why don't you save the wisecracks for your column?" he said nastily. "You've been mixed up in too many fishy things since you've been here——"

"What makes you assume that I was mixed up in this?"

"You talked to Vaschetti in the City Gaol this evening. You arranged for him to be sprung, and you arranged to meet him here. I call that being mixed up in it."

"You must be psychic," Simon remarked. "I know I got rid of your Mr. Callahan. Or who told you?"

"I did," said the voice of the *Times-Tribune*.

He stood in the doorway with a vestige of apology on his mild stolid face. Simon turned and saw him, and went on looking at him with acid bitterness.

"Thanks, pal. Did you bring out a special edition and tell the rest of the world, too?"

"I did not," said the city editor primly. "I acted according to the agreement I made with you, as soon as I heard what had happened to Vaschetti."

"How did you hear?"

"The reporter who was supposed to be taking care of him and waiting for you arrived back at the office. I asked him what he thought he was doing, and he said he'd been given a message that I wanted him back at once. Since I hadn't sent any such message, I guessed something was going on. I wasn't any too happy about my own position, so I thought I'd better come over and look into it myself. I met Lieutenant Kinglake downstairs, and I told him what I knew."

"And so we come up here," Kinglake said comfortably, "and catch the Saint just like this."

The repetition of names ultimately made its impression on the comatose house detective.

"Gosh," he exalted, with a burst of awed excitement, "he's the Saint!" He looked disappointed when nobody seemed impressed by his great discovery, and retired again behind his cigar. He said sullenly: "He told me he was the police."

"He told the assistant manager the same thing," Kinglake said with some satisfaction. "A charge of impersonating an officer will hold him till we get something better."

Simon studied the Lieutenant's leathery face seriously for a moment.

"You know," he said, "something tells me you really mean to be difficult about this."

"You're damn right I do," Kinglake said without spite.

At that point there was a sudden sharp exclamation from Detective Yard, who had been quartering the room with the same plodding method that he had used out on the flats where the late Henry Stephen Matson had become his own funeral pyre.

"Hey, Lieutenant, look what we got here."

He brought over the shredded gladstone, pointing to the initials stamped on it.

"H.S.M.," he spelt out proudly. "Henry Stephen Matson. This could of belonged to that guy we found yesterday!"

Lieutenant Kinglake examined the bag minutely; but the Saint wasn't watching him.

Simon Templar had become profoundly interested in something else. He had still been fidgeting over that bag in the back of his mind even while he had to make more immediate conversation, and it seemed to be sorting itself out. He was scanning the hodge-podge of stuff on the floor rather vacantly while Yard burgeoned into the bowers of Theory.

"Lieutenant, maybe this Vaschetti was the guy who called himself Blatt an' got away with Matson's luggage. So after they throw him out the window, they tear that bag apart while they're rippin' up everything else."

"Brother," said the Saint in hushed veneration, "I visualise you as the next Chief of Police. You can see that whole slabs of that lining have been torn right out; but in all this mess I bet you can't find one square inch of lining. I've been looking to see if the un-godly had been smart enough to think of that, but I don't think they were. Therefore that bag wasn't chopped up in here. There-fore it was planted just for the benefit of some genius like you."

"What else for?" Kinglake demanded curtly.

"To throw in a nice note of confusion. And most likely, in the hope that the confusion might take some of the heat off Blatt."

"If there ever was a Blatt before you thought of him."

"There was a Blatt," the city editor intervened scrupulously. "I think I told you. Vaschetti spoke about him and described him."

The Lieutenant handed the gladstone back to his assistant, and kept his stony eyes on the Saint.

"That doesn't make any difference," he stated coldly. "All I care about is that whatever went on here was done inside the city limits of Galveston. There's no question about my jurisdiction this time. And I'm tired of having you in my hair, Templar. You wanted Vaschetti out of the calaboose. You arranged to meet him here. And I find you in his room in the middle of a mess that makes it look as if he could have been pushed out of that window instead of jumped. You've been much too prominent in every bit of this— from finding Matson's body to going around with Olga Ivanovitch. So I'm just going to put you where I'll know what you're doing all the time."

"Has there been a political upheaval in the last half-hour," Simon inquired with sword-edged mockery, "or do you happen to be kidding yourself that if you bring me into court on any charge I won't manage to tie this job in with the Matson barbecue and raise holy hell with all the plans for a nice peaceful election?"

Kinglake's jaw hardened out like a cliff, but the harried expres-sion that Simon had noticed before crept in around his eyes.

"We'll worry about that when the time comes. Right now, you're going to do all your hell-raising in a nice quiet cell."

Simon sighed faintly, with real regret. It would have been so much more fun playing it the old way, but he couldn't take any more chances with that now. This game mattered so much more than the old games that he had played for fun.

"I hate to disappoint you," he said, "but I can't let you interfere with me to-night."

He said it with such translucent simplicity that it produced the kind of stunned silence that might exist at the very core of an exploding bomb.

Detective Yard, the least sensitive character, was the first to recover.

"Now, ain't that just too bad!" he jeered, advancing on the Saint, and hauling out a pair of handcuffs as he came, but moving warily because of his own affronted confidence.

Simon didn't even spare him a glance. He was facing Kinglake and nobody else, and all the banter and levity had dropped away from his bearing. It was like a prize-fighter in the ring shrugging off his gay and soft silk robe.

"I want five minutes with you alone," he said. "And I mean alone. It'll save you a lot of trouble and grief."

Lieutenant Kinglake was no fool. The hard note of command that had slid into the Saint's voice was pitched in a subtle key that blended with his own harmonics.

He eyed Simon for a long moment, and then he said: "Okay. The rest of you wait outside. Please."

In spite of which, he pulled out his Police Positive and sat down and held it loosely on his knee as the other members of the congregation filed out with their individual expressions of astonishment, disappointment and disgust.

There was perplexity even on Kinglake's rugged bony face after the door had closed, but he overcame it with his bludgeon bluff of harsh peremptory speech.

"Well," he said unrelentingly. "Now we're alone, let's have it. But if you were thinking you could pull a fast one if you had me to yourself—just forget it, and save the City a hospital bill."

"I want you to pick up that phone and make a call to Washington," said the Saint, without rancour. "The number is Imperative five, five hundred. Extension five. If you don't know what that means, your local F.B.I. gent will tell you. You'll talk to a voice called Hamilton. After that you're on your own."

Even Kinglake looked as briefly startled as his seamed face could.

"And if I let you talk me into making this call, what good will it do you?"

"I think," said the Saint, "that Hamilton will laugh his head off; but I'm afraid he'll tell you to save that nice quiet cell for somebody else."

The Lieutenant gazed at him fixedly for four or five seconds.

Then he reached for the telephone.

Simon Templar germinated another cigarette, and folded into the remnants of an armchair. He hardly paid any attention to the conversation that went on, much less to the revolver that rested for a few more minutes on the detective's lap. That phase of the affair was finished, so far as he was concerned; and he had something else to think about.

He had to make a definite movement to bring himself back to that shabby and dissected room when the receiver clonked back on its bracket, and Kinglake said, with the nearest approach to humanity that Simon had yet heard in his gravel voice: "That's fine. And now what in hell am I going to tell those mugs outside?"

X

The Saint could string words into barbed wire, but he also knew when and how to be merciful. He smiled at the Lieutenant without the slightest trace of malice or gloating. He was purely practical.

"Tell 'em I spilled my guts. Tell 'em I gave you the whole story, which you can't repeat because it's temporarily a war secret and the F.B.I. is taking over anyhow; but, of course, you knew all about it all the time. Tell 'em I'm just an ambitious amateur trying to butt into something that's too big for him: you scared the daylights out of me, which is all you really wanted to do. Tell 'em I folded up like a flower when I tried to sell you my line and you really got tough. So I quit; and you were big-hearted and let me hightail out of here. Make me into any kind of a jerk that suits you, because I don't want the other kind of publicity and you can get credit for the pinch anyway."

"Why didn't you tell me this in the first place?" Kinglake wanted to know, rather petulantly.

"Because I didn't know anything about you, or your political problems. Which were somewhat involved, as it turns out." The Saint was very calmly candid. "After that, I knew even less about your team. I mean guys like Yard and Callahan. This is a small town, as big towns go, and it wouldn't take long for one man's secret to become everybody's rumour. You know how it is. I might not have gotten very far that way."

Kinglake dragged another of his foul stogies out of his vest pocket, glared at it pessimistically, and finally bit off the end as if he had nerved himself to take a bite of a rotten apple. His concluding expression conveyed the notion that he had.

"And I always knew you for a crook," he said disconsolately.

The Saint's smile was almost nostalgically dreamy.

"I always was, in a technical sort of way," he said softly. "And I may be again. But there's a war on; and some odd people can find a use for even odder people. . . . For that matter, there was a time when I thought you might be a crooked cop, which can be worse."

"I guess you know how that is, too," Kinglake said, sourly but sufficiently. "You sounded as if you did."

"I think that's all been said," Simon replied temperately. "We're just playing a new set of rules. For that matter, if I'd been playing some of my old rules, I think I could have found a way to pull a fast one on you, with or without the audience, and taken that heater away from you, and made time out of here no matter what you were threatening. I've done it before. I just thought this was the best way to-night."

The Lieutenant glanced guiltily at his half-forgotten gun, and stuffed it back into his hip holster.

"Well?" He repeated the word without any of the aggressive implications that he had thrown into it the last time. "Can you feed me any of this story that I'm supposed to have known all along, or should I just go on clamming up because I don't know?"

Simon deliberately reduced his cigarette by the length of two measured inhalations. In between them, he measured the crestfallen Lieutenant once more for luck. After that he had no more hesitation.

If he hadn't been able to judge men down to the last things that made them tick, he wouldn't have been what he was or where he was at that instant. He could be wrong often and anywhere, incidentally, but not in the fundamentals of situation and character.

He said quite casually then, as it seemed to him after his decision was made: "It's just one of those stories . . ."

He swung a leg over the arm of his chair, pillowed his chin on his knee, and went on through a drift of smoke when he was ready.

"I've got to admit that the theory I set up in the *Times-Tribune* didn't just spill out of my deductive genius. It was almost ancient history to me. That's what brought me to Galveston and into your hair. The only coincidence I wasn't expecting, and which I didn't even get on to for some time afterwards, was that the body I nearly ran over out there in the marshes would turn out to be Henry Stephen Matson—the guy I came here to find."

"What did you want him for?"

"Because he was a saboteur. He worked in two or three war plants where acts of sabotage occurred, although he was never suspected. No gigantic jobs, but good serious sabotage just the same. The F.B.I. found that out when they checked back on him. But the way they got on to him was frankly one of those weird accidents that are always waiting to trip up the most careful villains. He had a bad habit of going out and leaving the lights on in his room. About the umpteenth time his landlady had gone up and turned them out, she thought of leaving a note for him about it. But she didn't have a pencil with her, and she didn't see one lying around. So she rummaged about a bit, and found an Eversharp in one of his drawers. She started to write, and then the lead broke. She tried to produce another one, and nothing happened. So she started fiddling with it and unscrewing things, and suddenly the pencil came apart and a lot of stuff fell out of it that certainly couldn't have been the inner workings of an Eversharp. She was a bright woman. She managed to put it together again, without blowing herself up, and put it back where she found it and went out and told the F.B.I.—of course, she knew that Matson was working for a defence plant. But it's a strictly incredible story, and exactly the sort of thing that's always happening."

"One of these days it'll probably happen to you," Kinglake said; but his stern features relaxed in the nearest approximation to a smile that they were capable of.

The Saint grinned.

"It has," he said. . . . "Anyway, Matson had an F.B.I. man working next to him from then on, so he never had a chance to pull anything."

"Why wasn't he arrested?"

"Because if he'd done other jobs in other places, there was a good chance that he had contacts with a general sabotage organisation, and that's what we've been trying to get on to for a long time. That's why I went to St. Louis. But before I arrived there, he'd scrammed. I don't think he knew he was being watched. But Quenco was much tougher than anything he'd tackled before. You don't have any minor sabotage in an explosive factory. You just have a loud noise and a large hole in the ground. I think Matson got cold feet and called it a day. But he wasn't a very clever fugitive. I'm not surprised that the mob caught up with him so quickly. He left a trail that a wooden Indian could have followed. I traced him to Baton Rouge in double time, and when I was there I heard from Washington that he'd applied for a passport and given his address as the Ascot Hotel in Galveston. He was afraid that his goose was cooked. It was, too—to a crisp."

"You were figuring on getting into his confidence and finding out what he knew."

"Maybe something like that. If I could have done it. If not, I'd have tried whatever I had to—even to the extent of roasting him myself. Only I'd have done it more slowly. I thought he might have some informative notes written down. A guy like that would be liable to do that sort of thing, just for insurance. Like Vaschetti. . . . I want that ostrich-skin case that was in his gladstone lining; and I want Vaschetti's diary of his trips and meetings. With those two items, we may be able to clean up practically the whole sabotage system from coast to coast."

"What do you mean by 'we'?" Kinglake asked curiously. "I've heard of this Imperative number; but is it a branch of the F.B.I.?"

Simon shook his head.

"It's something much bigger. But don't ask me, and don't ask anyone else. And don't remember that I ever mentioned it."

Kinglake looked at the chewed end of his stogie.

"I just want you to know," he said, "that I had Matson figured as an ordinary gang killing, and that's why I would have let it ride. If I'd known it was anything like this, nobody could have made me lay off."

The Saint nodded.

"I guessed that. That's why I've talked to you. Now we've spent enough time for you to be able to put over your story; and I've got to be moving."

"You know where you're going?"

"Yes." Simon stood up and crushed out his cigarette. "You may hear from me again to-night."

The Lieutenant held out his hand and said: "Good luck."

"Thanks," said the Saint, and went out.

Rowden and Yard and the *Times-Tribune*, standing in a little huddle down the corridor, turned and fanned out to stare at him as he strolled towards them. Then the Lieutenant's voice came from the doorway behind him.

"Mr. Templar is leaving. Now you can all come back here."

"You know," Simon said earnestly to Detective Yard, "I do wish your first name was Scotland."

He sauntered on, leaving his favourite plain-clothes man gawping after him like a punch-drunk St. Bernard whose succoured victim has refused to take a drink out of its keg.

Kinglake's trephining eyes reamed the blank questioning faces of his returned entr'acteurs. He clamped his teeth defiantly into his stogie, and drew a deep breath. In that breath, every wisp of the convenient alibi that Simon Templar had suggested was swept away, and he was standing stolidly on a decision of his own.

"If you want to know what we were talking about," he clipped out, "Templar was giving me a stall, and I pretended to fall for it. Now I'm going to see where he takes me. Yard, you can take charge here. I'm going to follow the Saint myself, and I'm going to bust this whole case if it takes me till Christmas."

"But, Lieutenant," protested the dumbfounded Yard, "what about the Chief? What about? . . ."

"The Chief," Kinglake said shortly, "and the Commissioner, and the Sheriff, and everybody behind them can——"

He did not say that they could jump in the lake, or go climb a tree, or perform any of the more conventional immolations. It is indeed highly doubtful whether they could have done what the Lieutenant said they could do. But Kinglake was not very concerned just then with literal accuracy. He had an objective of his own which mattered a lot more to him, and he left his extraordinary statement fluttering forgotten in the air behind him as he stalked out.

Simon Templar was also dominated by one single idea. The murder of Matson had been unfortunate, but he could exonerate himself from it. The murder of Vaschetti had been still more unfortunate, but the excuses he could make for himself for that were flimsy gauze before his own ruthless criticism. But his reaction to that had already reversed itself into a positive driving force that would go on until the skies fell apart—or he did. For the ungodly to have murdered two men almost under his nose and within split seconds of giving him the precious information that he had to get was an insolence and an effrontery that he was going to make them wish they had never achieved. The Saint was angry now in a reckless, cold savage way, not as he had been when he first went from Police Headquarters to the offices of the *Times-Tribune*, but in a way that could only be soothed out in blood.

And now he thought he knew where he was going to find the blood that night.

A taxi took him to the Blue Goose; but this time he didn't need the driver to vouch for him. The door-keeper remembered him, and let him in at once. He walked through the blue melodious dimness towards the bar, loose-limbed and altogether at his ease; yet there were filaments stirring through all the length of him that kept no touch at all with that lazily debonair demeanour. He caught sight of Olga Ivanovitch sitting at a table with another girl and two obvious wholesale bottle-cap salesmen, but he only gave her a casual wave and went on to find a stool at the bar. He knew she would join him, and he waited good-humouredly while the brawny blond bartender worked over complicated mixtures for a complicated quartet at the other end of the counter.

Then she was beside him; and he knew it by the perfume she used and the cool satin of her hand before he looked at her.

"I'm glad you got here," she said. "Did you get your job done?"

She was exactly the same, lovely and docile, as if she was only glad of him and wanting to be glad for him; as if death had never struck near her or walked with the men she knew.

Simon made a movement of his head that seemed to answer the question, unless one stopped to wonder whether it meant yes or no. He went on before that could happen: "I nearly didn't come here.

What I'd really hoped to do was curl up at home with a good book from the circulating library."

"What was the book?"

"Just a piece of some guy's autobiography. However, when I went to pick it up, it was gone. A man named Nick Vaschetti had it earlier in the evening. He hadn't finished with it—but he has now. I suppose you wouldn't know where it is?"

Her eyes were still pools of emerald in the mask of her face.

"Why do you say that?" She seemed to have difficulty in articulating.

"Lots of people read. It occurred to me——"

"I mean that this—this Vaschetti—hadn't finished with the book —but he has now?"

"He's given up reading," explained the Saint carelessly. "He was so upset about having the book taken away from him that he stepped out of an eighth-floor window—with the help of a couple of your pals."

He watched the warm ivory of her face fade and freeze into alabaster.

"He's—dead?"

"Well," said the Saint, "it was a long drop to the sidewalk, and on account of the rubber shortage he didn't bounce so well."

The bartender was standing over them expectantly. Simon said: "Dawson for me; and I guess you know what the lady's drinking." He became absorbed in the way the man worked with his big deft hands.

And then suddenly he knew all about everything, and it was like waking up under an ice-cold shower.

He took his breath back gradually, and said without a change in his voice except that the smile was no longer there: "You don't know Brother Blatt and his playmates very well, do you, Olga? Especially Maris. But if I'd only been a little brighter I'd have just stayed here and found Maris."

She was staring at him rigidly, with wide tragical eyes. It was a good act, he thought cynically.

The bartender stirred their drinks and set them up, fastidiously wiping spots of moisture from the bar around them. Simon appealed to him.

"I should have asked you in the first place, shouldn't I, Joe? You could have shown me Maris."

The man's big square face began to crinkle in its ready accommodating smile.

And the Saint knew he was right—even though the conclusion

had come to him in one lightning-flash of revelation, and the steps towards it still had to be retraced.

Maris, the man nobody knew. Maris, the man nobody had ever heard of. The truly invisible man. The man whom the assistant manager of the Ascot might have been referring to, and have forgotten, even, when he said that he had been chatting with a friend when Nick Vaschetti came home to die. The man nobody ever saw, or ever would see; because they never looked.

Simon lifted his glass and took a sip from it.

"You could have told me, couldn't you?" he said, with his eyes like splinters of blue steel magnetised to the man's face. "Because everybody calls you Joe, but they don't give a damn about your last name. And I don't suppose you'd tell them it's Maris, anyway."

It was strange that everything could be so clear up to that instant, and then he blotted out in an explosion of blackness that sprang from somewhere behind his right ear and dissolved the universe into a timeless midnight.

XI

'THERE were bells tolling in the distance.

Enormous sluggish bells that paused in interminable suspense between each titanic *bong!* of their clappers.

Simon Templar was floating through stygian space towards them, so that the clanging became louder and sharper and the tempo became more rapid as he sped towards it.

He was hauling on the bell cords himself. It seemed vaguely ridiculous to be ringing peals for your own funeral, but that was what he was doing.

His arms ached from the toil. They felt as though they were being pulled out of their sockets. And the knell was blending into pain and sinking under it. A pain that swelled and receded like a leaden tide . . . like a pulse beat . . .

His mind came back gradually out of the dark, awakening to the realisation that the carillon was being played inside his own cranium, and the pain was synchronised with the beating of his own heart.

He became aware that he was in a windowless chamber with some sort of plastered rock walls. A naked light bulb shone in the middle of the low ceiling. It was a cellar. There were collections and scatterings of the kind of junk that accumulates in cellars. There was an ugly iron furnace; and lines of criss-crosses of pipe hung high under the ceiling, wandering from point to point on undivinable errands, like metal worms in exposed transit from one hole to another.

He was close to one of the walls, sagging downward and outward, his whole weight hanging from his outstretched arms. He had been tied by the wrists to two of the overhead pipes, about six feet from the floor and the same distance apart. That accounted for the ache in his arms. Otherwise, he was unconfined.

He found the floor with his feet and straightened his knees. That eased the racking strain on his joints and ligaments, and reduced the pain of the ropes biting into his wrists, and might eventually give the throbbing of his strangled circulation a chance to die down. But it was the only constructive movement he could make.

Then he saw Olga Ivanovitch.

She was against the wall at right angles to his, tied to the pipes in exactly the same manner; but she was quite conscious and standing upright. She didn't look trim and sleek as he had last seen her.

One of the braids of her coiled hair had broken loose and fallen over her shoulder like a drooping wing, and the demure dark dress she had been wearing was dishevelled and torn away from one creamy shoulder and the lift of a breast. She was watching the Saint's recovery with eyes like scorched holes in the desperate pallor of her beauty.

It was the shock of recognition as much as anything which helped to clear the rest of the fuzzy cobwebs from his brain. His headache was more bearable now, but he had an idea that he wouldn't want anyone to lay a heavy hand on the place behind his right ear where it seemed to come from.

"To digress a moment from what we were saying," he managed to remark aloud in a thick voice that grew clearer and stronger with each passing breath, "what the hell did Joe hit me with—a boomerang? I only took a sip of that drink, and it wasn't any worse than the stuff they served me before."

"Blatt hit you from behind," she said. "He came up behind you while you were talking. I tried to warn you with my eyes. He was very quick, and nobody would have seen it. Then he caught you, and they said you were drunk and passed out. They took you into a back room and that was the end of it."

Simon glanced at his surroundings again. They were depressingly reminiscent of many similar surroundings that he had been in before. He seemed to have spent a great deal of his life being knocked on the head and tied up in cellars.

"And so, by one easy transfer," he observed, "we arrive in the bomb-proof doghouse."

"This is the cellar of my house. There is a back way out of the Blue Goose. They took you out and brought you here."

"Well, well, well. We certainly do lead a hectic life. Never a dull moment."

Her gaze was wondering.

"You jest in the face of certain death. Are you a fatalist, or are you only a fool?"

"I've certainly acted like a fool," Simon admitted ruefully. "But as for this death business—that shouldn't lose you any sleep. You didn't have any nightmares over Matson, did you?"

"I have seen too much to have nightmares," she said wearily. "But I give you my word that I have never had a hand in any murder. I didn't know they were going to kill Matson. I knew nothing about him, except that he was one of their men, and I was told to amuse him. But after he had been killed—what could I do? I couldn't bring him back to life, or even prove that they did it.

And Vaschetti. I thought Vaschetti was safe in gaol when I . . ."

"When you what?"

"When I went to his room this afternoon to see if I could find—anything."

The Saint wondered if the blow on his head had done something to him. He looked at her through a film of unreality.

He said: "Such as a diary of names and places?"

"Anything. Anything I could find. I thought he might have kept something, and I wanted it."

"What for—blackmail?"

"To turn over to the F.B.I., when I had enough."

He had learned before that he couldn't needle her, but it was a discovery that she could astound him.

"You mean you were planning to sell your own gang down the river?"

"Of course."

Maybe it was better to occupy his twinging head with material things. On due consideration he admired the basic ingenuity of the way he was tied up. It was so simple and practical and economical of rope, and yet it completely eliminated all the standard tricks of escape. There was no chance of reaching a knot with the finger-tips or the teeth, or cleverly breaking a watch-glass and sawing the cords on a sharp fragment, or employing any of the other devices which have become so popular in these situations. It was one of the most effective systems the Saint had encountered in an exceptionally privileged experience, and he made a mental note to use it on his next prisoner.

Meanwhile he said, without much subtlety: "But would that have been cricket, tovarich? Do you want me to believe that anyone so beautiful could sink so low?"

For an instant he thought that he actually struck a flash from her green eyes.

"Why do you think I'm here now—tovarich?"

"I had wondered about that," he said. "But I decided you might have a fetish about being crucified."

"I'm here because they don't trust me any more. I helped to bring you here. I wanted them to believe I was still helping them. I couldn't do anything else. . . . And I was only waiting for a chance to help you. . . . They tied you up. I helped them. And then, sud-denly, they took hold of me and tied me up, too. I fought them, but it was no use."

"You have such a sweet honest face—why shouldn't they trust you?"

"That was because of what you said in the Blue Goose," she told him without resentment. "You asked me if I had Vaschetti's book. Before that, they thought it was you who had been there first. But when Maris heard you accuse me he was suspicious. They knew that I liked you, and I had seen you. And for Maris, a little suspicion is enough."

Simon decided that there was not so much profit in standing upright as he had hoped. If he rested his arms, the cords gnawed at his wrists again; if he favoured his wrists, the strain of fatigue on his shoulders tautened slowly into exquisite torture. He had had no sensation in his hands and no control of his fingers for some time.

"And you really expect me to swallow that without water?" he asked scornfully.

"It doesn't matter much what you believe now," she replied tiredly. "It's too late. We shall both be dead in a little while. We cannot escape; and Siegfried is pitiless."

"Pardon me if I get a bit confused among all these people, but who is Siegfried?"

"Siegfried Maris. You call him Joe. I think he is the head of the Nazi sabotage organisation in the United States."

The Saint thought so, too. He had had that all worked out before Blatt hit him on the head. It explained why Matson had ever gone to the Blue Goose at all. It explained why Vaschetti had touched there in his travels. It explained why the Blue Goose played such a part in the whole incident—why it was the local focus of infection, and why it could send its tendrils of corruption into honest local political dishonesty, squeezing and pressing cunningly here and there, using the human failings of the American scene to undermine America. A parasitic vine that used the unassuming and unconscious flaws in its host to destroy the tree. . . . It was not incredible that the prime root of the growth should turn out to be Siegfried Maris, whom everyone knew as Joe. Simon had always had it in his mind that the man he was hunting for would turn out to be someone that everybody called Joe. And this was the man. The man who could have anything around and not be part of it; who could always say, whatever happened, that he just happened to be legitimately there. The man nobody saw, in the place nobody thought of . . .

"Comrade Maris," said the Saint, "has been offstage far too much. It's not fair to the readers. What is he doing now?"

"I expect he's upstairs, with the others. Searching my house."

"He must like the place. How long have we been here?"

"Not very long. Not long at all."

"What's he searching for?"

"The book," she said. "Vaschetti's little book."

"Why here?"

"Because I did find it. Because it has half the code names and meeting places in this country listed in it. But Maris will find it. I couldn't hide it very well."

Simon was able to shrug his left shoulder tentatively. No weight dragged on it. They would have found and taken the gun in his spring holster, of course. It wouldn't have been much use to him if they hadn't. However ...

"So it was you who tore Vaschetti's room at the Ascot apart," he said. "But your mob thought it was me. That's why my room was gone over this evening while we were out together, and a coloured friend of mine nearly had coloured kittens. You aren't overlooking any bets, are you? And since Vaschetti's indiscreet memoirs are still missing—not to mention Brother Matson's notes and papers——"

"They have those," she said listlessly. "They were in the gladstone bag."

He was shaken as if he had been jolted in the ribs; but he went on.

"So anyway, we now have a well-staged scene in the old torture chamber, where you trick me into revealing where I have hidden all these priceless documents. You're doing a great show, Olga. If I could get my hands together I would applaud. You must be a full-fledged member of this lodge of Aryan cut-throats."

"Think what you please," she said indifferently. "It makes no difference."

She could always make him feel wrong. Like now, when she was not angry, but wounded in everything but dignity. Because that devastating ingenuousness of hers was real; because the bridges she walked on were firm and tried, and she had built them herself, and she was as sure of them and her way as he was sure of his own. There could be no facile puncturing of a foundation like that, with a skilled flick of the wrist.

She said, without any emotion: "You think of me as a mercenary adventuress. I don't deny it. I have worked for Maris—and other men—only for money. But that was before the Nazis invaded Russia. You will not believe that a greedy adventuress could have a heart, or a conscience. But it made all the difference to me. . . . I pretended that it didn't. I went on working for them—taking their money, doing what they told me, trying to keep their trust. But I was only waiting and working for the time when I could send all of them to the hell where they belong. . . . Yet, I had my own sins to redeem. I had done wrong things, too. That's why I thought that if I could bring something with me, something big enough to prove that all my heart had changed—then perhaps your F.B.I. would understand and forgive me, and let me begin again here. . . . I could swear all this to you; but what is swearing without faith?"

The Saint's head was much clearer now. He saw her again through the ruthless screen of his disbelief. And still she wasn't trying to sell him from behind the counter of any phoney job of tying-up. Her wrists were lashed as cruelly tight as his own. He could see the livid ridges in her skin where the ropes cut. Her face was damp like his from strain and pain.

"Damn it, tovarich," he said musingly, "you could act anyone in Hollywood off the screen. You've almost convinced me that you're on the level. You couldn't possibly be, but you sound just like it."

Her eyes were unwavering against his, and they looked very old. But that was from the patience of a great sadness.

"I only wish you could have believed me before the end. It would have been nicer. But it will not be long now. Siegfried Maris is one of the most important men that Hitler has in this country. He won't take any chances with us."

"At least," said the Saint, "we should feel flattered about getting the personal attention of the big shot himself."

He had crossed his left leg over his right now, but it was not with the idea of striking an elegant and insouciant pose. He was pressing the outsides of his legs together, feeling for something. He had been searched and disarmed, he knew; but there was his own special armoury which the ungodly didn't always . . .

"If we could have caught Maris," Olga was saying, out of that passionless and regretful resignation, "it would have meant as much as winning a battle at the front. I would have liked to do that very much. Then we could have been quite happy about this."

It was too good to be true; but it was true. He could feel the solid flat hardness of the haft and blade between the movements of his legs. And with that, he had a fantastic inspiration that might grow into a fantastic escape. But he had seen fantasy come real too often to discard it for nothing but its name.

The glint in his eyes was like sunlight on cut sapphires.

"Maybe we can still be happy, Olga," he said; and there was a lilt of exultant vitality in his voice. "We'll try to repeat a significant scrap of United Nations history. You, like some other Russians, were petting the wrong dog. Until you saw the error of your ways. And it bit you. Now I shall try to come through with the lend-lease material."

XII

OLGA IVANOVITCH stared at him as though she was certain now that he was out of his mind.

"No, darling, I'm not," he said, before she could put her own words to it. "I was just remembering a movie serial that I saw as a boy, which starred the greatest of all escape artists—Harry Houdini."

"How interesting," she said blankly.

It was lucky, he thought, that he liked his shoes loose and comfortable. Otherwise, getting them off might have been quite a problem. As it was, he was able to tread on one heel with the opposite instep and force one shoe off with only a moderate amount of violence. The other shoe presented a little more difficulty, without a hard welt to scrape against, but he went on working at it.

"Now don't go all Russian on me and relapse into brooding despair," he pleaded. "You ought to be interested in the late Mr. Houdini. He was a real maestro at getting out of situations like this. I was thinking of one instalment in which he was tied to some sort of Oriental torture wheel, in very much the same way as we're tied up now. He managed to worry his shoes and socks off, and neatly unfastened the knots on his wrists with his toes."

He had the other shoe off at last. The socks were easier. He only had to tread on a bit of slack at each toe in turn and pull his feet out.

"So what?" Olga said sceptically. "Can you even reach your wrists with your toes?"

"Now you're coming to life," Simon approved. "I used to be a fairly agile guy before I started drinking myself to death, and I think I can manage that." He twisted his body and balanced himself on one foot, and swung his other leg lithely up to kick his hand. "There. I always knew all those years I spent in the Follies chorus would come in handy some day," he said contentedly.

"But the knots," she said in the same tone as before; yet it was already being contradicted by the curiosity kindling in her eyes.

"I'm afraid I'm not quite that good," he confessed. "However, I have an alternative solution for them which Harry might not have considered entirely ethical."

He was already working up his right trouser leg with his naked left foot. Under the amazed eyes of the girl, the upper end of the sheath and the haft of his knife came into view. He grasped the haft with his toes and drew the blade gently out of the scabbard and laid it on the floor.

"When I was swinging through the trees in my last incarnation," he said, "this would have been duck soup for me. But I'm a bit out of practice these days."

He was concentrating singly on the knife, manœuvring it between his two feet, getting the firmest possible grip on the handle betwen his big toe and the one next to it, adjusting and testing it before he made a decisive move. There was no sound in the room but the faint scuff of his efforts. His wrists hurt like hell; but he had forgotten about them. The sweat was standing out on his forehead by the time he was satisfied.

"Now we get to the really fancy part of the trick," he said. "Like the man on the flying trapeze without a net, I won't be able to go back and start over if I muff it."

He poised himself in the same way as he had done for his preliminary experiment, but much more carefully, gauged his distances, and drew a deep breath and held it.

Then he swung his leg, aiming the razor edge of the blade at the link of rope between his left wrist and the pipe.

Once, twice, three times he repeated the same pendulum movement, trying to strike the same spot on the rope each time, feeling the keen blade bite the fibres at every stroke.

Then the knife twisted between his toes; but he managed to keep a precarious hold on it. He brought it gingerly down to the floor and adjusted it again, with the aid of his left foot, in an intolerable hush of intense patience and concentration.

He swung his leg again.

Once more.

Twice more.

The knife span out of his hold and clattered to the floor.

It was beyond his reach, and beyond hers.

He heard the girl's pent-up breath break out of her lungs in a long throaty sob, and saw tears swimming in her eyes.

He saw then, at last, without thinking about it any more, that she had told him the truth. He had been unsure. He had taken a chance on it, because he was forced to, but wondering all the time if this would end up as the supreme sadism of tantalisation— if after he had revealed his secret weapon, and freed himself, if he could free himself, she would only call out, and Maris would walk in with a gun, and all the hope and struggle would have been for nothing. Now he knew. She couldn't have gasped and wept like that, otherwise; wouldn't have needed to, no matter how well she was playing a part.

It was worth something to be sure of that.

The Saint smiled grimly as he inspected the section of rope that he had been working on. He had done a good job, in spite of everything. It wasn't anything like the rope it had been before.

"I forgot to mention," he murmured, "that when I was in the circus I also used to break chains and tow tanks around with one hand."

Then with an abrupt and feral outburst of titanic effort he threw all his weight and strength together against the partly severed cords, dropping his weight on them with a plunging jerk, and simultaneously thrusting himself away from the wall with his feet and contracting his arms together with all the power of his torso. The veins swelled in his back, and the muscles rippled over his body in quivering waves. For an instant it felt as if his wrists were being bitten off. . . .

And then, with a suddenness that was physically sickening, the frayed and slashed portion of rope parted with a snap that flung him whirling outward and around.

He heard the girl sob again; but this time it was with a note of almost hysterical laughter.

He regained his balance without a waste motion, and fell to attacking the knots that bound his right hand.

"I must be slipping," he said. "I used to do things like that just to warm up."

The knots weren't so easy. His hands were numb, and he had to drive deliberate commands through for every movement of his fingers. He worked as fast as he could through that nightmarish impediment.

At last he was free. His wrists were chafed and bleeding a little. But that was nothing. The sense of freedom, of triumph, was like an intoxicating wind blowing through the reviving spaces of his soul.

He scooped up his knife, a little awkwardly because of the cramp in his hands, and cut Olga loose. She almost fell against him, and he had to hold her up for a moment. Until her clinging grew up from the weakness of reaction into something else.

Then he steadied her on her feet and left her standing while he went back to put on his shoes and socks. The return of circulation was filling his hands with pins and needles; but gradually, with the relentless exertion, his fingers began to feel less like swollen frozen sausages.

"There is a way out of here without going through the house," she was saying breathlessly. "We can slip out without them ever knowing that we've gone."

"Slip out?" He glanced up at her. "Darling, that would be a hell of an anti-climax. I'm going upstairs now and get Matson's notes and Vaschetti's diary away from dear old Joe!"

"But how can you?" she cried. "He'll shoot you like a dog. They took your gun. I saw them. We can call the police——"

Simon straightened up, and looked down in silent reckless laughter at her desperate imploring face.

"I've got my knife," he said; "but I haven't got any guarantee that the police would get here in time. And meanwhile Maris and Co. might find out that we'd got away, and decide to take the brakes off themselves. We don't want to risk that now. And besides, we've got to deliver you as a certified heroine. Remember?" Her soft scarlet lips were only a few inches away, turned up to him below the liquid pool of her eyes; and once again he was aware of their distracting provocation. He said: "Thanks just the same for being so concerned about me. It ought to be worth at least . . ."

Then she was in his arms, her breath warm against his cheek, and all of her aching for him; and then he was bruising her moist mouth with his own, and it would never be like that again, but there was no time for that now and perhaps there never had been. It was like so many things in his life: they were always too late, and there was never any time.

He disengaged himself very gently.

"Now," he said, "we will have the last word with Joe."

The door on the other side of the cellar was not locked. Simon went up the crude wooden stairs, very quietly, and was conscious of Olga Ivanovitch following him. But he didn't look back. He came out through another unlatched door into the hall of the house. There was no guard there either. Obviously, Maris and his crew had great faith in the durability of manila hemp and the efficacy of their trussing system.

Which was reasonable enough; just as the Saint's faith in his knife was reasonable. He knew what it could do, and what he could do with it. He knew how it could transform itself into a streak of living quick-silver, swift as the flash of light from its polished blade, true as a rifle, deadly as any bullet that was ever launched by erupting chemicals.

He held it delicately in his re-sensitised fingers, frail and strong as a bird, only waiting for him to release it into life.

He was outside another door then, listening, when the voice

came firmly through it to his ears. Just a voice: the voice of Sieg-fried Maris, generally known as Joe. But coming with a clear sud-denness that was like travelling back in time and never having heard a talking picture, and suddenly hearing a screen speak.

It said: "Keep your hands well up, Lieutenant. Please don't try anything stupid. It wouldn't do you any good."

And then Kinglake's savage growl: "You son of a gun—how did you get out of the Blue Goose?"

The Saint's mouth opened and closed again in a noiseless gasp, and a ripple of irresistible laughter rose up through him like a stream of bubbles to break soundlessly at his lips. Even at a moment like that he had to enjoy the perfection of that finishing touch.

"We have our own way out," Maris replied calmly. "It's very useful, as you see. But if you didn't know about it, how did you follow us here?"

"I didn't. When I didn't find Templar at the Blue Goose, I thought he might have come here with Ivanovitch."

"An excellent deduction, Lieutenant. And quite correct. He did come here with Ivanovitch. But that wasn't his choice. . . . It's very fortunate that you're a detective and not a burglar, isn't it? If you'd been a burglar you wouldn't have made such a clumsy entrance, and it mightn't have been half so easy to catch you."

Simon settled his fingers on the door knob as if it had been a wafer-shelled egg. He began to turn it with micrometric gentleness.

"You bums," Kinglake said. "What have you done with them?"

"You'll see for yourself, when you join them in just a few minutes."

"So you're Maris, are you? I should have known it."

"A pardonable oversight, Lieutenant. But you may still call me Joe, if it will make you feel more comfortable."

Simon waited through an infinitesimal pause, with the door handle fully turned.

Kinglake said: "I guess you can have oversights, too. You aren't getting away with anything, Joe. I've got men outside——"

The low hard chuckle of Maris came through the door.

"An old bluff, Lieutenant, but always worth trying. I know that you came alone. Fritzie was watching you outside, and we made sure of that before we let you break in. Now if you'll be very careful about holding your arms while Blatt takes your gun——"

That was the pleasantly dramatic moment when it seemed right to the Saint to throw the door wide open.

It was a nice composition that framed itself through the opening, a perfect instant of arrested motion, artistic and satisfactory. There was Lieutenant Kinglake standing with his hands up and his jaw tensed and a stubborn snarl around his eyes, with Johan Blatt advancing towards him. Fritzie Weinbach stood a little off to the right, with a big snub-nosed automatic levelled at the detective's sternum. Simon could identify them both without ever having seen them before—the tall blond man and the fat red man with the cold bleached eyes.

He saw Siegfried Maris, too, for the first time as the man he was instead of the forgotten bartender called Joe. It was amazing what a difference there was. He sat behind a desk, without the disguise of the white coat and the quick obsequious serving movements, wearing an ordinary dark business suit, and obviously the dominant personality of the group. For ultimate proof, he even had a flat light tan case and a shabby pocket memorandum book among some papers on the blotter in front of him. Simon knew even from where he stood that they must be the notes of Henry Stephen Matson and the diary of Nick Vaschetti. It was all there.

And Maris was there, with his square powerful face that hadn't a natural smile in any line of it; and he was turning towards the interruption with his eyes widening and one of his strong swift hands already starting to move; and the Saint knew without any further study, without a second's hesitation, that this was the one man he had to get and be sure of, no matter what else happened afterwards.

The knife sped from his hand like a glitter of leaping silver, flying like a splinter of living light straight for the newly retired bartender's throat.

Then Lieutenant Kinglake had taken advantage of the diversion to make a grab for his gun, and the room was full of thunder and the dry stinging tang of cordite.

XIII

SIMON TEMPLAR didn't carve notches in the handle of his knife, because they would eventually have affected the balance, and he was used to it and he hoped it would last for a long time. He did worry about rust and the way it could dull a blade. He wiped the blade very carefully on Maris's shirt before he put the knife back in its sheath.

"Let's face it," he said: "he did pour some of the lousiest drinks I ever paid for."

Kinglake was reloading his Police Positive with the unconscious detachment of prehistorically rooted habit.

He said, almost awkwardly for him: "I just wanted to be in at the death."

"You were," Simon assured him, somewhat unnecessarily.

"Are there any more of 'em?"

"Quite a lot—I hope. But not around here. And we don't have to bother about them. Just turn that stuff on the desk over to the F.B.I. The rest will be their routine."

"I'd sure like to know what happened to you."

The Saint told him.

Kinglake scratched his head.

"I've seen plenty in my time, believe it or not," he said. "But you've topped all of it." He ended with an admission. "I'll have to think of a new story now, though; because I messed up the one you gave me."

"It doesn't matter," said the Saint. "Whatever you said, you can tell 'em you only said it for a stall, because you couldn't give out what you really knew. The true story is your story now. Only leaving me out. There's plenty of evidence on that desk. Go on and grab yourself some glory."

"But these are the three guys you named in the *Times-Tribune*."

"So what? So I happened to know too much, and I was too smart for anybody's good. You knew just as much if not more, but you were playing a cagey game. You say that by shooting my mouth off like that I told Maris and Co. that they were hot, and nearly ruined all your well-laid plans. That's why you were so hopping mad about me. In fact, you had to perform superhuman feats to salvage the situation after I balled it up. Say anything you like. I won't contradict you. It suits me better that way. And there's nobody else left who can call you a liar."

The Lieutenant's steely eyes flickered over the room. The truth of that last theorem was rather gruesomely irrefutable.

Then his glance went to Olga Ivanovitch.

She stood very quietly beside the Saint, her pale face composed and expressionless, her green eyes passing unemotionally over the raw stains and ungainly attitudes of violent death. You could tell nothing about what she thought or expected, if she expected anything. She waited, in an incurious calm that suddenly struck Simon as almost regal; she hadn't asked anything or said anything.

"What about her?" Kinglake asked.

Simon's pockets had been emptied completely. He bent over one of the bodies and relieved it of a packet of cigarettes that it wouldn't be needing any more.

"I'm afraid I was holding out on you about her," he answered deliberately. "She's one of our people. Why the hell do you think she was tied up in the cellar with me? But I couldn't tell you before."

He was so easy and matter-of-fact with it that the Lieutenant only tried to look unstartled.

"But what story am I supposed to give out?"

"Like me—the less you say about her the better," Simon told him. "She was just one of the hostesses at the Blue Goose, and Maris was making use of her through his rôle of bartender. He set her up in this house, so he had a key. But she wasn't here to-night. When the set-up began to look too sticky, she scrammed. You don't think she's worth fussing about."

Simon hadn't looked at the girl until then. He did now.

"By the way," he said casually, "you'd better get a move on with this scramming act. Kinglake is going to have to call Headquarters in a few minutes. You can scram in my car—it won't take me more than ten minutes to check out of the Alamo House. Go and put some things in a bag."

"Yes," she said impassively and obediently; and went out of the room.

Simon smoked his inherited cigarette with unalloyed enjoyment.

Kinglake gathered the papers on the desk together and frowned over them wisely.

The Saint made another search of the unlamented ungodly, and found his own automatic in Weinbach's pocket. He nested it affectionately back in his clip holster.

The Lieutenant gazed yearningly at the telephone, tightened a

spartan stopper on a re-awakening ebullience of questions, and got
out another of his miasmic cigars.

Olga Ivanovitch came in again.

She had changed into a simple grey suit with plain white trimmings. Her honey-coloured hair was all in place again, and her face
was cool and freshly sweetened. She looked younger than Simon
had ever remembered her. She carried a pair of suitcases. Kinglake
really looked at her.

Simon hitched himself off the corner of the desk where he had
perched.

"Well," he said, "let's be on our way."

He shook hands with Kinglake for the last time, and picked up
Olga's bags and went out with her. They went down the crushed
coral walk through a rambling profusion of poinsettias and bougain-
villea that were only dark clusters under the moon. The Gulf waters
rolled against the beach beyond the seawall with a hushed friendly
roar. Simon Templar thought about Jean Lafitte again, and decided
that in the line of piracy he could still look the old boy in the eye
on his home ground.

They left the gate; and the girl's step faltered beside him. He
slowed with her, turning; and she stopped and faced him.

"*Spassibo*," she said, with an odd husky break in her voice.
"Thank you, thank you, tovarich. . . . I don't think it's any use, but
thank you."

"What do you mean, you don't think it's any use?"

Light seeping from a window of the house behind them like a
timid thief in a dim-out touched her pale halo of hair and glistened
on her wide steady eyes.

"Where can I go now?"

The Saint laughed.

"My God, you Russians! Look, darling. You played along with
Maris for quite a while. Several of the ungodly must know it. But
they'll never know that Maris ever changed his mind about you.
They'll only know that you got out of Galveston one jump ahead
of the barrage. So you're all set to move in again somewhere else.
That's what you wanted, isn't it? Well, I wasn't kidding either.
That's what you're going to do. Only next time you'll do it legitimately—for the F.B.I. or something like that. I'm taking you to
Washington with me so you can meet a guy named Hamilton. I
have to see him anyway. . . . Besides," he added constructively, "it's
a dull trip, and we might make fun on the way."

THE LAST WORD

And so, my friends, dear bookworms, most noble fellow drinkers, frustrated burglars, affronted policemen, upright citizens with furled umbrellas and secret buccaneering dreams—that seems to be very nearly all for now. It has been nice having you with us, and we hope you will come again, not once, but many times.

Only because of our great love for you, we would like to take this parting opportunity of mentioning one small matter which we have very much at heart.

For that loyal and exclusive company who wanted a little closer contact with us than they could get by merely reading, Simon Templar and I founded, about fifteen years ago, THE SAINT CLUB. It is a pretty elastic organisation, and the rules are very much what you want to interpret them to be. The only one which we ruthlessly insist on is the annual minimum subscription of 5s. a year for readers over 16 years; 2s. 6d. a year for the under-16's. They are due on 1st August each year. We have to do this, because these funds assist the Arbour Youth Club in a blitzed East End area of London, a very charitable job in one of London's neediest and most neglected areas. If you would like to add your help, please write to the Hon. Secretary, THE SAINT CLUB, East Arbour Street, Stepney, London, E.1. A stamped addressed envelope for reply would be appreciated from U.K. readers.

Which leaves me, I think, with only one more of those standard questions to forestall. You need not go on writing to ask me whether there are going to be more Saint Stories. The standing answer, now and as for as long as the pair of us can keep it up, is—

WATCH FOR THE SIGN OF THE SAINT

HE WILL BE BACK